PUSH
COMES
TO
SHOVE

To Regge and Kyoko:
   who are well traveled in
the journeys of the mind and
heart.

Love,
Wesley
07/08/09

OTHER NOVELS BY WESLEY BROWN

Tragic Magic
Darktown Strutters

PLAYS

Boogie Woogie and Booker T
Life During Wartime
A Prophet Among Them

ANTHOLOGIES

Imagining America (co-editor)
Visions of America (co-editor)

Push Comes to Shove

A NOVEL BY

WESLEY BROWN

CONCORD
FREE
PRESS

Published by Concord Free Press
152 Commonwealth Avenue
Concord, Massachusetts 01742
www.concordfreepress.com

ISBN 978-0-9817824-1-6

Designed by Alphabetica Design
www.alphabeticadesign.com

Printed in the United States by Recycled Paper Printing
www.recycledpaper.com
First edition limited to 2,000 numbered copies

*In memory of Arverna Adams, Fatisha Hutson,
June Jordan, John Leonard and Robert Tishler*

Saints like revolutionaries, walk headlong into a cool, dry wind, are always serving a hidden fire, are terrifying because of what they do not need. The saint asks, what will you die for? The revolutionary adds, for what would you kill? Either way, sacrifice is an ugly business, as ugly as history itself. Choose between these terrible things, history often says. We are only commentators until, for us, it comes to that choice.

–Stephen Dunn

Whosoever would undertake some atrocious enterprise should act as if it were already accomplished, should impose upon himself a future as irrevocable as the past.

–Jorge Luis Borges

MURIEL

1969

LIKE THE REBELLIOUS OF EVERY GENERATION, I was horny with idealism and foolishly believed that throwing my body in the path of injustice was enough to stop it. Of course, that didn't happen. But protesting alongside black people from Georgia, Arkansas, Mississippi and Alabama, we discovered who we were. And we began to create the kind of world we wanted to live in.

What I didn't know at the time was that we are often most vulnerable when we're about to get what we want. Many of us were worn out by the effort to protect our beloved community from daily assaults in the South and indifference everywhere else. And in the summer of 1965, I discovered that fatigue is a hothouse for fear.

There were massive demonstrations in Jackson, Mississippi around an issue I can't remember. There were several hundred arrests. And because of overcrowding at the city jail, most of us were imprisoned temporarily in a huge fieldhouse used for rock concerts. We were separated by race and told not to cross a chalk line that divided the building in half. White policemen positioned themselves around the fieldhouse and stiff-armed their nightsticks.

There had been a time when nothing could have prevented us

from crossing that line. We believed that no matter how often we were threatened, jailed, beaten or even killed, we could still summon up whatever was necessary to get us through an ordeal. And if a few of us didn't have the strength to make it through on our own, someone was always there to help. But this time, none of us moved. Friends whose spines were usually straight as cornstalks started slouching. The muscles in my back clenched with reluctance. I had faced physical danger before. But when I reached for the strength to push me across that chalk line, my will power hung by a frail nerve. I had always been willing to put my body at risk. My inability or refusal to do it at that moment frightened me more than the police ever had.

I took refuge in the fact that my weakness was in good company. But that didn't give me much comfort. Every time I looked across that chalk line at the whites, with whom I had often faced down danger, it seemed like we were no longer as eager to resist efforts to keep us apart. The cops used their nightsticks to flex themselves into various poses of power. A few in our group began to shout that we were too white or not black enough, that we weren't woman or man enough for our own good.

And then blacks and whites on both sides of the chalk began taunting the police. They crossed the line and the rest of us followed. The police, who only moments before seemed pleased that we were arguing among ourselves, moved on us with a vengeance, using tear gas and whaling away with their clubs to let us know what they thought of our solidarity. It felt so good, in the thick of all that fear and hurt, to be in the company of people who'd been there with me so many times before. But I wondered if our delayed response would redeem our faith in each other. Or had some irreparable damage been done?

After five days, I was released with tear gas still burning my eyes and throat. When I left the South a few months later, I went back to New York and got involved in a group called Push Comes to Shove. It was led by Theodore Sutherland, whose normal behavior resembled James Brown in concert. He had a passing-lane mind, his thoughts rarely able to stay under the speed limit. Theo's body was him just as Theo bumped him from the front.

"You did that on purpose!" the landlord shouted.

"Since you understand body language so well," Theo said, "we're speeding up the language of the court order...and giving you only twenty-four hours to repair that boiler."

"What is this?" The landlord turned around to find the rest of us blocking his path.

"We're reconvening court out here on the street," Theo continued. "And if that boiler ain't fixed by tomorrow, you're gonna find the long arm of our law around your neck!"

"Are you threatening me?"

"No-o-o, you got me all wrong. I'm promising you!"

"Get out of my way!"

His words struck the air like bottles shattering on concrete.

Theo's eyes darted from the man, to us, and back again. And for an instant, I saw a flickering of indecision.

"Since you don't hear so good, maybe you'd be better suited for lip reading."

Theo smiled and opened his arms as though he was about to embrace the landlord. Then he clapped his hands against the man's ears in one quick, brutal motion. I heard the gasp from my own mouth at the same time pain wrecked the man's face and the horrible scream tore open his mouth. He covered his ears and crumpled to the ground. Theo stooped down, held the man's head gently between his hands and moved closer until their faces almost touched.

"Can...you...hear...me...now?" he whispered.

The man stopped screaming and slowly nodded his head, recognizing something far more terrifying than pain—he was deaf forever. Theo got to his feet. He took hold of my hands with the same tenderness that he held the man's head, then pulled them slowly away from my ears. Theo's brutality and kindness were only seconds apart. But his violence made me wonder if making change was no longer about what I could do for people who had the least, but what I could do to people who had the most.

•••••

A man stared at me at a street rally held soon after the incident near the courthouse. I wanted to get a better look at him, so I stood in a spot where he wouldn't lose sight of me. Even though I had my back to him, I knew where he was all the time. I wasn't at all surprised when someone touched me on the arm. His expression wasn't lecherous but more inquisitive, like a child's.

"Excuse me, but aren't you one of the people who were busting up bricks on that school building that doesn't have any windows?"

"What makes you think that?"

"Because I was there."

"That doesn't prove I was."

"Maybe not. But it does prove that if we keep seeing each other, one of us is going to have to do something about your memory."

It had been a while since anyone had come on to me in that way. When men hit on me, it was fueled by the latest headlines and the dim view they had of the world. I thought I preferred men who were very good at explaining what was wrong with the world. So I was surprised to find myself attracted to someone with what seemed like an undernourished political consciousness. His skin was as smooth as a seal's and free of the tension that raked through the faces of most of the people I knew. It made me wonder how he ever made it to the corner in a city like New York.

What eventually won me over was that Walter didn't try to impress me. He was more impressed by me! Of course, that didn't make him as magnetic as Theo. But it did make him a lot of fun. We took long walks in the park and went to see old movies. Walter also got me to laugh at myself, something I seemed to have forgotten how to do.

Some months after we met, Walter moved in with me. He didn't become as active in Push Comes to Shove as I was. But his regular job gave me the freedom to spend more time watching the neighborhood police. I wrote down the shield numbers of brutal cops, printed them on leaflets and handed them out at street rallies.

•••••

One night an explosion woke me. I was alone, since Walter often worked nights. I ran to the window, pushed it up and heard blasts from fire trucks. Word soon passed from streets to windowsills that the local police precinct had been firebombed. The next day, the newspapers reported that no one had been seriously injured. While there were no leads, one high-ranking police official was quoted saying that groups like Push Comes to Shove had created a climate that encouraged violence.

Over the next few days, I noticed that Theo was uncharacteristically subdued, offering no opinion on the bombing or how we might use it to our advantage. Just as unexpected was Walter confronting me one evening without his usual playfulness.

"You think anyone in Push Comes to Shove did it?" he asked.

"I don't know."

"How far do you think Theo's prepared to go?"

"As far as it takes to become a serious threat."

"How much of a threat do you want to be?" he asked.

"Enough to threaten you."

"Come on, Muriel. I'm serious."

I gave him a cold stare. "It's about time."

"You know, you're beginning to frighten me."

"I wish I could say the same for you," I said.

"Why's that so important?"

"Because fear's the only thing anyone respects anymore."

"I don't believe that," he said.

"You don't believe in anything."

"I believe in what happens to us."

"That leaves out a lot," I said.

"Like what?"

"Everything that's wrong with the world."

"Sometimes you need to take a break from all that. You won't miss anything. The world will still be as fucked up as it was when you left."

I laughed. "You're a lot of fun, Walter. But you don't break enough of a sweat. That's what I like to see—some anger."

His anger caved into fear. "I would have thought that you had your fill of anger when you left the South."

•••••

We lay in bed. I was trying to get up the nerve to apologize but didn't want to admit that my feelings for Walter had grown stronger. Walter had his back to me. I couldn't tell whether he was asleep or not. I pulled at the elastic of his jockey shorts and started tickling him.

"Stop!" he said, just as a thunderous blast shook the house.

Walter shoved me out of the bed. I thought about the gun I kept in the drawer of the nightstand. The bedroom door jumped away from the frame and crashed to the floor. Splintered pieces of wood stuck to the hinges. Men who looked like baseball umpires burst into the room with shotguns. Walter took a deep breath as if to keep as much life in him as possible. Two shotgun blasts jerked him up and back against the headboard. I thought he was grinning until I saw his face slip away from his head.

I couldn't move or feel anything. Someone led me out of the house and into a car. I smelled the foul breath from a man's voice as he spoke to me.

"Push sure has come to shove tonight, you fuckin' cunt!"

They had finally come to kill us. We had been right all along! And for days afterwards, my stomach heaved with self-loathing and rage, and the smell of Walter was still in every breath I took.

•••••

Several of us, including Theo, lived in the house. For whatever reason, Theo had not been there at the time of the police attack and no one could find him. What proved even more bizarre were the accounts in the newspapers. The police were answering a complaint from someone in the neighborhood and were fired upon when they tried to gain entry into the house. A gun battle ensued in which one person was killed.

Everything holding my life up had been pulled out from under me. I wondered why I wasn't killed along with Walter. Because of all the publicity the case received, a lawyer offered to represent me for a fraction of her usual fee. The first time I met her was at the Women's House of Detention. She stepped into the visiting room and sat down behind the bulletproof partition. I studied her carefully. I couldn't place her type, other than her being white. Her hair caressed her neck just below her stunning jaw. She had a fleshy mouth and worry marked the skin beneath her eyes.

"I'm Naomi Golden. With Kazin, Loomis and Bogan."

"That's fine," I said, "but who *are* you?"

"I'm someone who wants to represent you and believes she can get you off." She raised her arms, rested her elbows on the counter and intertwined the fingers of her hands. "Now, why don't you tell me about you," she said.

"Don't you read the newspapers?"

"What I want to know isn't in the papers."

"Oh? And what's that?" I asked.

"I want to know if you want to beat this thing. Or do you want to have a jury do to you like the police have already done?"

"What do you think?"

"Then I assume you've made your decision?"

"Which is?"

"To retain me as your attorney. Am I wrong?"

"I hope not, for my sake," I said.

•••••

A week after entering my plea of *not guilty* and having bail posted by some wealthy friends of Naomi's firm, she came to see me again.

"The Assistant D.A. wants to talk to us!"

"What about?"

"Maybe to make a deal."

"What do I have to trade?"

"He doesn't have a case on the attempted murder charge. He

may want you to cop to illegal possession of a firearm so he can come away with something."

•••••

Naomi and I met with Michael Aronson in his office. He sat in a leather-upholstered throne behind a bed-sized desk. His expression was cutting and lethal.

"Miss Golden, my office is prepared to offer your client a deal."

"If you're making me an offer, then talk to me," I said.

His thin mouth turned up slightly. "We'll drop all the charges, if you agree to help us locate Theodore Sutherland."

"I don't know where he is."

"Then we'll give you whatever assistance you need to find him."

"I'm sorry. Can't help you."

"Miss Pointer, I hope you realize you're not walking on any of these charges unless you cooperate."

"Look, Aronson," Naomi said, "either you make a real offer or we go to trial."

He leaned back in his chair, staring at both of us.

"Okay," he said finally, "we'll drop the attempted murder charge if she cops to illegal possession of a firearm."

"I don't like your arithmetic," Naomi said.

"And I don't like people who have a reckless disregard for the law but want to be protected by it!"

"That's democracy for you. It benefits even those who take advantage of it," Naomi said.

"Is that an admission of guilt?"

"No, just a philosophical aside. But getting back to my client. What if she accepts your offer?"

"I think I can get her five years probation."

"You *think!*"

"I can't give you any guarantees, but I'll do the best I can."

"I'd like to talk to my client alone for a moment."

"All right," he said, getting up. "But if I were you, I'd keep in mind the old jailhouse saying: *Study long, study wrong.*"

"That's very folksy," Naomi said.

"I believe in taking the lessons of life wherever I find them."

We sat without speaking as I looked at all the law books smothering the walls, documenting the legal existence of America. These books were the cancelled checks for whatever was done within or outside the law. I had aligned myself with those who didn't make the law, but took it out of books, put it in their mouths and wrote the Bill of Rights with their bodies.

"The only thing they can get you on is illegal weapons possession," Naomi said. "My advice is take the deal and consider yourself lucky."

I agreed. I was still shaky from Walter's murder and wanted to avoid a trial.

"I hope you reached the right decision," Aronson said, when he returned. "Because this offer won't be made again."

"It won't have to be," I said. "I'll take it."

"A wise decision, Miss Pointer."

•••••

"What are you thinking about?" Naomi asked, after we left the building.

"This strange feeling of gratitude toward Aronson. It bothers me."

"It shouldn't."

"But none of us in the house shot at any of those cops."

"Come on, Muriel. We're not talking lawyer to client now. You may not have shot at them, but you're not innocent of making threats against the police. Even if you didn't believe them yourself, the police obviously did."

"That's not what's really bothering me. It's just that I have this disgusting feeling that I accepted Aronson's offer, not just because it would get me off but because he wanted me to."

"Don't worry about it. It's the nature of authority. It repels and attracts."

"Is everything always so clear to you?"

"Not really," she said. "Look Muriel, I was as intimidated by Aronson as you were. He's a man. He's white. He has power. And he's not bad looking."

I was in danger of liking her more than I wanted to.

"You know, I think we should get together soon to celebrate," she said.

"What do you have in mind?"

"There's this place in the East Village called the Far Out. It's a café, sort of. I think you'd like it."

•••••

Naomi lived on the West Side in the 90s. When the apartment door opened, a bearded black man with paint ingrained in his jeans and work shirt stood in the doorway. He smiled at my surprise.

"How are you? You must be Muriel. I'm Gerald, Naomi's husband."

"Nice to meet you." I held out my hand.

"Excuse me if I don't shake your hand. Been painting all day and my hands are a mess."

I followed him into the living room, filled with paintings and sculpture. One painting in particular caught my attention.

"It's my version of the Hindu God, Kirtimukha," Gerald said, noticing my gaze. "He ate his own head in order to survive his own hunger. Sort of what I think we're doing to ourselves in this country. Have a seat. Naomi will be right out."

"Thank you," I said, not able to take my eyes completely away from the painting.

"You must be relieved to be out of jail."

"At this point, relief is about all I can feel."

"Hi Muriel!" Naomi walked in.

"Gerald's been showing me some of his work." I let my eyes drift back to the self-devouring god in Gerald's painting.

•••••

"Gerald was quite a surprise," I said, as Naomi drove down the West Side Highway.

"I just felt unless it came up naturally beforehand, meeting him was probably the best way for you to find out."

"I see."

"And what, exactly, is that?"

"Well, with me as a client and Gerald as your husband—seems like you can't get enough of us black folks."

Her hands gripped the steering wheel. "If you think that, I can drop you off right here. Then you won't have to wonder if I've gotten enough of you!"

"Sorry," I said.

"Muriel. What's wrong?"

"I don't know."

"Maybe we should forget about going to the Far Out?"

"No. Let's go. It couldn't be any further out than I am already."

•••••

Inside the Far Out, we were greeted by sirens and flashing lights hanging from the ceiling, spinning like beacons on top of police cars. The bouncer was dressed in a bear suit and wore a forest ranger hat that reminded me of Smokey the Bear. But the name tag on the chest of this furry forest cop of my childhood did not say Smokey, but Reefer. A poster on the wall near the entrance showed a drawing of Reefer the Bear, beckoning all campers away from the forest and toward the city with words in a cartoon bubble near its head—*Let's Roll the Forest Into Joints!*

A waiter dressed in U.S. Army fatigues led Naomi and me to our table. We took a seat. All the staff had faces smeared with grease-paint and wore giant feather headresses that hung down to their waists. Seats from commercial jets circled each cable spool table. Several jeeps welded together served as the bar, while the jukebox glowed inside the bubble-shaped cockpit of a helicopter. We ordered drinks, which came with fortune cookies with cosmic forecasts that ranged from grim to catastrophic. I scanned the club and paused at the stage, which had its very own diving platform.

"When did this place land?" I asked.

"About two years ago," said Naomi. "I represent the owner, Frank Livolsi."

"I'm surprised he got a license."

"Can you imagine how all this would manifest itself if there were no outlet for it?"

"I see what you mean. What else goes on here?"

"Well, there's a house band called Excess that plays on weekends. During the week people come in and perform within the theme of evil, which is *live* spelled backwards. As you see, it can get bizarre. By the way, did you know there's a man at the bar who's been staring at you?"

I looked over and saw him leaning against the bar. He was still looking in my direction but a baseball cap made it hard for me to see his face.

"How you doing, Naomi?"

I turned my head back to our table and saw a man standing with jet black hair, combed fastback style.

"Hi Frank. I'd like you to meet a friend of mine, Muriel Pointer."

I spoke and heard something come out of his mouth that I took to be a greeting.

"Oh, right!" he said. "You're from Push Comes to Shove."

"I hear she represents you too."

"Yeah, she's one smart lady. But I don't need to tell you that."

"Where did you get all this stuff you have in here?" I asked.

"America is a junk culture. Anything that's outlived its usefulness is a potential market for new consumers."

"What are you selling?"

"The destructive impulses of our age."

"Who's buying?"

"Voyeurs of all types, especially those who think evil is something they don't want any part of."

"Not sure I follow you."

Frank leaned closer. "After what you've been through, you should have a special appreciation for what I'm talking about. We're giving expression to what Push Comes to Shove was trying to do. The problem with your group was that you couldn't make up your mind whether you wanted your response to police violence to be theatrical or actual. You were right to be provocative. But when you threatened the State, you weren't able to get them to suspend their belief."

"Belief in what?"

"That you were serious."

"How'd you get the State of New York to suspend belief in this place?" I asked.

"By accepting the better things that hell has to offer."

"What's that supposed to mean?"

"As I understand it, that's the only way you stayed out of jail. Which is why I'm still in business and you're out of business."

"Francis!" It was the man at the bar, wearing the baseball cap.

"I hope you haven't been taking up this woman's time talking about this macabre circus you call a café."

"As a matter of fact, I was enlightening her on the harsh realities of show business, which makes it possible for unfulfilled university types like you to get a reprieve from being the walking stiffs you were educated to become."

I was amused.

"Name's Raymond," he said. Sparse whiskers gathered on both cheeks.

"Damn Raymond!" Frank said. "You look like you just ate dessert."

Raymond pointed to the New York Mets insignia on his cap.

"What about it?" Frank asked.

"Not it! Them! While you've been preoccupied with the evil that lurks in the hearts of men, the Mets were beating the Baltimore Orioles in the World Series!"

"You ought to read William Blake, Raymond. If you did, you'd realize that excess leads to the palace of wisdom."

"You know, Francis, you're so hooked on the diabolical that you can't understand the significance of the Mets' victory."

"Time is running out on such meaningless diversions," Frank said.

"Not hardly. It's the only game that takes people to a place where time doesn't matter."

"Have you read William Blake?" Frank asked, looking at me.

"No, I haven't."

"Well, your group of troublemakers reminds me of what Blake was saying in *The Marriage of Heaven and Hell*."

"Enough, Frank!" Naomi said.

He looked at her. "You know, the thing about coming back to the World was that people who never had any use for me personally wanted in on what I'd been through. It's like I was this walking obscenity who'd give them a piece of 'Nam like a tab of acid so they could get off. That's what gave me the idea for the café. Sorry if I was kinda rough on you. I hope you like the show. Talk to you later, Naomi. You too, Raymond." Frank wandered out of the café.

"Do you want to stay?" Naomi asked.

"You couldn't drag me away from here."

"I feel the same way," Raymond said. "Could it be that the attraction is mutual?"

"You're something else," I said.

"I know. That's what happens when you can't be what you want to be. When I realized I wasn't going to make history, I had to be content with teaching it."

"You don't really believe that, do you?" Naomi asked.

"Believe what?"

"About not being able to make history."

"Absolutely! I have the passion but I lack the instincts," he said. "Changing the course of events requires making the right dramatic choices. When the moment of truth arrives, it's not a matter of planning but instinct!"

"I don't agree," Naomi said. "Planning will affect the outcome of whatever you do. That holds true inside or outside the courtroom."

"I'm not disagreeing," Raymond said. "I'm just saying no amount of preparation can help at those moments when what we do or don't do can change our lives."

"Let me ask you this," I said. "Is fucking up a matter of planning or instinct?"

Before Raymond could answer, the whirling red and white lights overhead began to dim except for the swirling strawberry ribbons of light above the stage. Frank and several other people came onstage with sound equipment and instrument cases. They plugged guitars the shape of automatic weapons into amplifiers. They positioned huge door-size speakers at specific intervals. And they brought out several oil drums. Frank lined up two rows of magnesium flares from the audience to the back of the stage. He turned to us and pointed toward the flares.

"This is the warning at the beginning of an accident in progress," he shouted into a microphone. "We are called Excess and are committed to going to extremes in order to discover when we have gone far enough. We ask you to join us in turning the sounds of destruction into our own flesh!"

Frank stood behind the oil drums. He picked up two mallets from the floor and began pounding the inside of the drums. The bellowing gongs from the drums were followed by electric guitars, making the rapid sputtering sounds of helicopters and the deafening roar of planes taking off. Projected on the wall at the back of the stage were stills and film of the killing in Vietnam and the violence in America. As the mix of image and sound became more frantic, Frank turned one of the oil drums upside down. Lifting it over his head, he brought it down over his body.

One of the musicians picked up the mallets and began beating on the outside of the drum. The other members of Excess continued playing at an earsplitting volume, aiming their guitars like guns and sliding them between their legs. People from the audience got up from their flight chairs to join the band onstage. They jerked and hurled themselves around in a grotesque mimicry of being shot or beaten.

As the magnesium flares blazed, I glanced over at Naomi and Raymond. Like me, they hadn't joined the band in transforming from *live* to *evil*. Maybe Frank was right to assume I was one of those who preferred to get off on what other people went through. And why not? A day hadn't passed since Walter was killed without the taste of his blood in my throat or his smell in my sweat. The present had become a frightening place to live. I didn't want to risk anything in myself if I could help it. If my hold on what to do after Walter's murder was shaky, there was only one direction for me to go. And that was back to where my life started.

•••••

When I was five, my parents were killed in an automobile accident. They were in a line of cars waiting to pay the toll on the New York State Thruway, when a trailer truck whose driver had fallen asleep rammed them from behind. The car exploded and they were killed instantly. I was too young to be told what had actually happened. When I asked what it meant to die, I was told—you stopped living. When I thought about what it would be like to stop living, the first thing that came to mind was not being able to jump double-dutch. It followed that dying meant doing things that were no fun, like cleaning my room. This view of life and death has never left me. But it didn't prepare me for having to watch the mess Walter's murder made of my life. Although no one asked me, I felt it was my job to clean it up.

My parents came from families where they were the only children, and what blood relatives they had were either dead or too old to take care of me. Perceval and Matilda Satterwhite were apparently the only people in the village of Yorktown who were willing or able to take me in. I can't remember either of them ever raising their voices in anger at me or one another. They lived a life together that was just this side of a whisper. If I misbehaved, they would reprimand me or take away my privileges. My upset over being punished was as close as I got to the feeling of having my parents taken away from me. And I resented my stepparents for never allowing me to make them angry enough so I could feel their fury coming back at me with the force of the trailer truck ramming my parents' car. As for affection, it was like our meals: well balanced and served promptly without a big fuss made about it. Needless to say, the 1960s couldn't have come at a better time.

I talked with Miss Mattie and Mister Percy by phone after the police raided the house. I told them not to visit me in jail and was angry at how readily they complied. I hadn't seen them very often in the years after I graduated from college. And as I drove up to Yorktown, I was disoriented by the interconnecting expressways, loops and meandering entrances and exits that now complicated the way to their house.

Miss Mattie and Mister Percy lived on a tree-lined block of two-story brick and shingle houses. Their dusty gray 1958 Buick waited in the driveway when I pulled up. Some houses give you a distinct sense of something going on inside. But I could get no feel for their house in that way. And I was surprised when the door actually opened.

"How're you, Mister Percy?"

The corner of my mouth and the side of my face rubbed against his and I felt the unshaven stubble and smell of lemon-scented soap. Hugging him reminded me how frail he was. But Mister Percy's hands were huge, with knuckles the size of stones. We looked at each other for a few seconds without speaking before Miss Mattie walked into the sun porch.

"How've you been, Miss Mattie?"

"Better now that I know you're out of trouble."

"I'm not so sure about that. But at least I'm out of jail."

I moved to greet her and she offered me her cheek but not her arms. She was fleshier than Mister Percy, the bones underneath not as pronounced.

"I wish you would've let us come and see you," she said.

"You could've come anyway."

"But you said you didn't want us to," Mister Percy said.

"I'm not sure I knew what I wanted."

"You full grown now, Muriel. We figured you knew your own mind," Miss Mattie said.

"You hungry?" Mister Percy asked.

"Not right now, thank you," I said, irritated. Like always, they weren't interested in probing too deeply into anything. "So what're you doing with yourselves?" I asked.

"Not much since we retired," Miss Mattie said. "We work off the books now and then. But mostly, we take it easy."

"I can't remember a time when you didn't," I said.

"One day at a time, right Percy?"

"Half a day, sounds more like it." They smiled, savoring the humor of his remark. I wondered if they'd ever been genuinely surprised by anything.

"Miss Mattie? What were you like when you were my age?"

"Pretty much the way I am now," she said.

"But how was that?"

"I can't say as I've ever given myself that much thought. You Percy?" He shook his head.

"Not ever?" I asked.

"Not in the way you mean," she said. "I never wanted to do anything about my life the way you seem to."

"So you're satisfied with everything that's ever happened to you?"

"No. But I wasn't looking for anything in particular."

"You never dreamed?"

"If you mean wanting something I didn't have? Of course! You're living proof of that. Here was Percy and me, two people past forty, hearing about your parents being killed and you left alone. But I don't recall us ever talking that much about what we ended up doing."

"We didn't," Mister Percy said, then turned to me. "We knew your parents well enough to speak to them but not much more than that. We went to the wake to pay our respects and heard you hadn't been provided for. We looked into the matter and before we knew it, we were filling out adoption papers."

"What's bothering you, child?" Miss Mattie asked.

"I'm just not sure of anything anymore."

"Like what?"

"Like myself."

"With what you've been through, I would think you wouldn't be worrying yourself about such things."

"You know, I can count the times in all the years we lived together that either of you ever talked to me the way we are now."

"We raised you." Miss Mattie said.

"You don't understand!"

"I understand that I don't expect you to answer to me for your life. And I don't feel I have to answer to you for mine. There's nothing Percy and me can do about who you are now or what was done or not done in the past. If you want to do something about it, that's your job—not ours."

On the drive back to New York, anger coiled into a knot in the back of my head.

And I wasn't sure why.

RAYMOND

1969

NOTHING IN THE WORLD COMPARES with what I saw as a child looking out the window of my family's sixth floor apartment on Saint Nicholas Avenue in Harlem. From my front row balcony seat, I watched the cavalcade of characters who gave performances that were always cut from the prime parts of life: like a woman hustling a man into a hammerlock and placing him in the protective custody he thoroughly enjoys, or a woman holding a cigarette between two fingers and using it like an extra index finger to pave the way for whatever point she is trying to make, or a man going into a lean with his head in the opposite direction of the lamp post he knows will be there when he puts his hand out to catch his fall. Unless they were shouting, I could rarely make out what was being said. But that didn't matter because I usually figured out what went on in the streets almost entirely from the way people moved.

During the summer there were card games played on the sidewalk, all up and down the avenue. The one I watched began in the afternoon and continued long after I went to bed. The players changed but the spindly-legged card table and the four kitchen chairs, with the guts spilling out from punctures in the cushions, remained the same.

Uncle Aubrey showed up to play on Saturday afternoons when he got off from his job as a chauffeur. He would park the limousine in front of our building and showboat for his cronies before returning it to the garage. There was a funeral parlor on the first floor, so limousines were always around. But what impressed me most about my uncle was that he was the only person I knew driving one of those whale-on-wheels machines whose tour of duty was not limited to the graveyard but included trips to nightclubs and mansions. On the few occasions when he took me for a ride, it was like sitting in a moving living room while I inhaled the wonderful tobacco aroma coming from his cigar.

When my uncle joined the card game, he would leave his black chauffeur's jacket and cap in our apartment. He returned to the street tie-less and open-collared with his sleeves rolled up and his suspenders making tracks up his back and over his shoulders to the buttons hitching them to his pants. I could usually tell how well he was doing by the length of the trails of sweat on the back of his shirt and under his arms.

One particular night, my parents gave me a little more leeway in staying up since they were entertaining some friends in the kitchen.

Uncle Aubrey's white shirt clung to him like skin; and as he sat directly under the globe of a street lamp, his every move was washed in light. He cradled the cards to his chest, doting on them like newborn infants. Then he snatched each card between his thumb and forefinger, dangled them tantalizingly above his head for an instant before slamming them down one by one on the table. At other times, he placed the cards down gently, spreading them out with his fingers like someone playing the keys of a piano.

I knew all my uncle's moves, anticipating almost everything he did before it happened. But that night his concentration shifted from the game to a man standing in partial darkness, just outside the area of the card table, which was illuminated by the street lamp. He seemed a little tipsy and said something I couldn't hear. Uncle Aubrey laughed and said:

"So what! You're a cop!"

The man was much bigger than my uncle and grabbed him by the back of his shirt collar, lifting him out of his chair with the ease of a ventriloquist handling his dummy. I screamed and started to cry as the sound of my own voice frightened me. My mother and father rushed into the living room just as the man reached under his shirt as though seized by an uncontrollable itch.

"He's got a gun!" someone yelled.

My mother pulled me away from the window at the same instant I heard a sound like a truck backfiring in the street. I heard screams and the stairwell echoed with the pounding of feet as my parents rushed to get outside. I ran back to the window but couldn't see Uncle Aubrey. A crowd had gathered, everyone straining to get a better look at something on the ground. The man who had grabbed my uncle receded into the shadowed portion of the street with a dark object in his right hand.

"I'm a cop!" he shouted. "I told you I'm a cop!"

My parents ran from our building and when they finally broke through the crowd, my mother clapped both hands over her mouth. My father held her as she wailed like a banshee, flailing her arms about blindly and grabbing at the air. The police arrived and cleared a path for the ambulance. Heads turned in the direction of the siren, as though waiting for a float in a parade.

•••••

Uncle Aubrey was in the hospital for a week before he died. When I saw him again, he was dressed in a suit very much like the one he wore to work. After the funeral, he was put in a hearse and finally went for a ride to the cemetery without having to drive. But I was much more upset by my uncle's absence than the details of his death. I found myself expecting him to show up at our house to take me for a ride in his limousine. Or I would wait at the windowsill for him to arrive for his weekly card game. Uncle Aubrey was dead but I couldn't fill the space he occupied in my life. My parents never talked about him. The spot where he played cards was never used again. Even the raspberry splotch of my uncle's dried blood was scrubbed away. If people missed him, I never knew it. They went about their business as though death had removed every trace of his ever having lived.

The black man who killed my uncle was a cop who was off duty at the time of the shooting. I took that to mean that people were more likely to hurt each other after they got off from work. I wondered, if that was why cabdrivers never picked up anyone after they turned on their off duty signs. So the cop without an off duty sign was tried and convicted of manslaughter. My father told me that manslaughter meant killing someone without planning to do it ahead of time. None of this made any sense to me. Because if the cop didn't know he was going to kill Uncle Aubrey, how did he do it, even though he wasn't thinking about it when it happened?

•••••

Whenever confusion twisted up in my head like a pretzel, I walked up Edgecombe Avenue to the park overlooking the Polo Grounds where the New York Giants played. It was the color of dingy pistachio, rising like sheet rock out of the valley below near Eighth Avenue. Rows of exit stairways zigzagged down the side of the stadium like surgical stitches. I went to the highest point in the park where a portion of the outfield was visible and let my eyes feast on the well-groomed grass. If there was a game going on, I'd sit on a park bench and let the sighs, cheers and gasps carry me on a roller coaster ride of lead changes, errors, spectacular plays, failed rallies and bottom of the ninth heroics—which turned the world back into a place that made sense.

RAYMOND

October, 1969

I RECOGNIZED MURIEL as soon as I spotted her at the Far Out. Her picture had been in all the newspapers and I saved the articles about the case along with all the political events of the 1960s. I catalogued them in sequence, creating the illusion of chronology in a world where order didn't exist.

A few weeks later we had dinner. While we ate, I watched her eyes follow my reaction to everything she said.

"What's the matter?" she asked.

"I feel like you're watching every move I make."

"Yeah. Well, it's the only way for me to spot trouble even if I can't avoid it. But you've been doing the same thing."

"That's the historian in me," I said. "But most of my watching isn't done at the moment something happens."

"What do you do when distance doesn't help you see things more clearly?" she asked.

"I go to a ball game or watch one on TV."

"Suppose you can't?"

"Then I spend some time where the Polo Grounds used to be."

"Doing what?"

"Remembering all the amazing things that happened there."

"If I could find a place like that for myself," she said, "maybe I could get over some things."

"Like what?" I asked.

"Seeing the worst in people."

"What did you expect to happen when the police busted into your bedroom?"

"I didn't expect to be shocked," she said.

"So?"

"You don't get it! We talked about it all the time. How the cops would come after us, just like they did to the Panthers."

"You're being too hard on yourself. If you hadn't reacted, it would've been like saying what those cops did was okay."

"But when the police attacked us in the South, I was afraid but never shocked."

"I think you're going to need more time to sort that out," I said.

"Time? Is that what I need?"

"It's all we've got—unless, of course, you consider..."

"Yeah, I know," she said, "the great American pastime."

Muriel looked at me and seemed to be enjoying whatever she was thinking. "I'm going to play something on the jukebox," she said, getting up.

When she returned to the table, she didn't sit down but waited to hear her selection. Aretha Franklin sang: *I re-mem-ber. You've forgotten to re-mem-ber. I wonder why.*

"Dance with me," she said.

I hesitated, wondering what the waitresses would say.

"It's all right. I've been here before. The management doesn't mind."

I got up slowly from my chair and moved to put my arms around her. But she kept me at arm's length, squeezing my forearms as though trying to remember what touching someone was like. Muriel seemed on the verge of tears. I started to speak, but she shook her head and pulled me against her. She trembled in my arms and I could feel myself wanting to pull away.

When we left the restaurant, I told Muriel I wanted to make a stop before taking her home. There was a strong breeze coming off the Harlem River onto Edgecombe Avenue. It was the end of October and the air was breathing the last warmth before the first bite of frost set in. From the park, I looked down at the high-rise apartment buildings with scattered squares of light coming from windows on various floors.

"Did you know that's where the Polo Grounds used to be?" I asked.

"No I didn't."

"You ever go to a game?"

"No."

"Did you ever see Willie Mays play?"

"Only on television," she said.

"I was at the Polo Grounds when Mays made his famous catch against the Cleveland Indians in the 1954 World Series. All the films show him making the catch with his back to home plate; but I was lucky enough to be in the centerfield bleachers as he ran in the direction where I was sitting...There were men on first and second when Vic Wertz hit a drive to dead center field...Mays runs toward the bleachers with his head up like he's marveling at the flight of the ball rather than chasing it. I think the ball is going to travel forever but gradually it starts to fall. Mays is like a gazelle, running without any strain. He runs out from underneath his cap and is close enough for me to see the letters on his jersey, spelling G-I-A-N-T-S, bobbing up and down on his chest like they were floating in a pool of water. With every stride he takes, I see his thigh muscles clench inside his pant legs. His arms stop pumping and he brings his glove and bare hand together in a bouquet just in time to catch the ball over his left shoulder, then whirl and throw before going down on one knee to watch the effect of what he's done on the runners rounding the bases..."

Muriel said nothing, so I kept talking.

"This happens so quickly that the roars of approval and disbelief don't come until seconds after Mays has made the throw...Later, when I saw it on television, I was struck by the expression on his face after he made the throw to second base. He looked sad as though the moment of real joy had passed. It was like he was watching what he'd done begin to vanish and he was trying to hold the pieces of what had happened in his head before it was lost in the deafening noise of the crowd..."

Muriel smiled.

"Of course, years later, I realized that our memory of an event isn't the same as living it. Maybe that's why Mays was probably the most unaffected person in the Polo Grounds when he picked up his cap and walked back to take his position. In his prime, he was the most complete embodiment of instinct and boyish exuberance I ever saw...I've never been very good at knowing what I feel about anything while it's happening. My instincts are all wrong."

"Your instincts seem all right to me," she said.

"I think I need remedial help."

"You're sweating!"

Muriel touched my forehead and rubbed the perspiration between her fingers as though it were some precious oil. Before I could ask what she meant, she put her fingers to my mouth.

"I'll explain it to you sometime."

December 31, 1969

Frank Livolsi suggested that Muriel and Raymond spend the last night of the Sixties at the Jimi Hendrix concert at the Fillmore East. Naomi and Gerald, Raymond and Muriel took a cab to Frank's apartment in the East Village that he shared with a woman named Crystal. They arrived a few hours before the concert and sat around talking in the cramped living room, made even smaller by the overcrowded bookshelves lining the walls. The room was lit by two light bulbs in a ceiling fixture jutting from the tail rotor blade of a helicopter.

While everyone sprawled on blintz-shaped pillows, Frank spread a piece of newspaper on the floor and began rolling joints. His fingers worked with speed and skill. As Frank licked the paper to seal the first joint, he noticed Raymond taking some papers out of an envelope.

"What you got there, professor? Final exams?"

"You could say that. Every year I make a list of all the important events that've happened. Since we're going to bring in the New Year together, I made some copies so everybody could take a look at it."

Raymond passed the list around and waited for everyone to read it.

1969

Jan. 1:   U.S. troop strength in Vietnam reaches 542,000.

Mar. 10:   James Earl Ray pleads guilty to the murder of
         Martin Luther King, Jr.

Apr. 2:   21 Black Panthers charged with conspiracy to bomb various
         sites in New York City and the Tri-State area.

Apr. 19: Black students leave the occupied student union building at Cornell University carrying guns.

Apr. 21: Jack Kerouac dies of abdominal hemorrhaging at his mother's home in St. Petersburg, Florida while watching "The Galloping Gourmet" on TV.

May 15: Squatters are forcibly evicted from People's Park in Berkeley.

Jun. 27: New York City police raid the Stonewall Inn, a gay bar on Christopher Street in Greenwich Village.

Jul. 3: Brian Jones of the Rolling Stones drowns in his swimming pool in England.

Jul. 14: Premiere of "Easy Rider," starring Dennis Hopper, Peter Fonda and Jack Nicholson.

Jul. 20: Neil Armstrong and Buzz Aldrin become first humans to walk on the surface of the moon.

Aug. 9: The Sharon Tate/LaBianca murders in Los Angeles.

Aug. 15-17: Woodstock Music Festival held in White Lake, New York.

Sep. 3: New York City police raid the home of members of Push Comes To Shove and one of their members, Walter Armstead, is murdered.

Sep. 24: Chicago Eight Conspiracy trial begins. Defendants include Bobby Seale, Jerry Rubin, Abbie Hoffman and Tom Hayden.

Oct. 8-11: Four "Days of Rage" by Weatherman faction of SDS takes place in Chicago.

Oct. 15 Vietnam Moratorium Day

Oct. 16: The New York Mets beat the Baltimore Orioles 5-3 in New York to win the World Series in five games.

Nov. 12: Lieutenant William Calley is charged with the multiple murders of civilians at Song My, Vietnam.

Dec. 1: The first draft lottery of the decade is held.

Dec. 4:   Police murder Black Panthers Fred Hampton and Mark Clark in a Chicago apartment.

Dec. 6:   Gun-wielding black man is stabbed to death by Hell's Angels at the Rolling Stones concert at Altamont Speedway outside San Francisco.

Dec. 31:   Jimi Hendrix and the Band of Gypsies play at the Fillmore East in New York City.

•••••

Everyone was still looking over the document as Frank lit two joints and passed them around. Crystal pulled strands of her salmon-colored hair behind both ears and drew the smoke from the burning weed into her mouth. She noticed Gerald staring at her before passing the joint to Muriel. Crystal had met him at a recent opening of an exhibition of his paintings. She remembered feeling overwhelmed by them and unable to speak.

Gerald averted his eyes when Crystal looked in his direction. He had been admiring the way her back stretched so straight out of her hips. He wondered if she might be interested in posing for him.

"You want some?" Muriel asked.

Startled, Gerald jerked his head around toward her.

"What?" he asked.

"This," she said, passing him the joint.

Gerald took it without saying anything; he knew Muriel's remark had nothing to do with reefer. He hadn't forgotten her reaction to him the night she came by the apartment to pick up Naomi.

"So what does this all mean?" Frank asked, holding up Raymond's end-of-the-year summary.

"You're the master of excess and surprise," Raymond said. "I was hoping you could tell the rest of us."

"I still don't see why you think what some baseball team did is so important."

"The Mets were underdogs. And they beat the favorite in a year when the underdog hasn't fared too well."

"So?"

"Well, it only goes to show that anything can happen in a short series."

"That's the trouble with this fuckin' country," Frank said. "Whether it was fighting the war or poverty, everybody thought it wasn't gonna take very long!"

"That's why we need baseball! If more of us had an appreciation for the game, we'd be less likely to turn our lives into one."

"What do you think, Muriel?" Frank asked, passing her a new joint.

"About what?"

"Was Push Comes to Shove playing games?"

"I don't know."

"What about the war? Do you know anything about that? Or are all the anti-war protests just another game everybody's playing?"

"That's not fair, Frank," Naomi said.

"Fuck fair! I wanna know why so many of you can be so sure about the shit that's going down in Vietnam when you ain't been in it!"

"Oh, I see," Raymond said. "Unless you've been there, you're not entitled to have an opinion?"

"You got it, professor!" Frank said, lifting his chin up and flicking his fingertips against it.

"I hope you communicated that to the government you used to work for."

"Every chance I got!"

"Frank? What you just did?" Crystal asked. "What's that mean?"

"It's something the people in my tribe do," Frank said, "when they want someone to go on an exotic trip by putting their head up their ass."

Everyone but Crystal, who looked puzzled, burst into laughter. Muriel had laughed out loud with the rest, but what she really liked was the lightness beneath Frank and Raymond's argument.

"You know," Gerald said, after everyone had caught their breath, "I've been thinking a lot about Hendrix. I remember seeing him at a concert, bashing his guitar up against these huge amps. And then another time, he poured lighter fluid on it and set it on fire. The sound of the guitar broadcasting its own destruction through the amps was something I never could've imagined him doing...That's what Altamont was all about. It was the first rock concert where a human sacrifice was offered up to exorcise the demons let loose by the Stones. And it was obscenely fitting that a black man would be the one sacrificed. What better candidate to die for America's sins!"

"I can't wait to see what Hendrix is gonna do tonight," Frank said.

"Maybe we should go," Crystal said, "so we can hear what Hendrix has to say for himself."

•••••

Second Avenue turned loud and wild as people rummaged through the streets for anything to commemorate the final hours of the decade. Raymond and Frank walked ahead of the others, continuing their debate about games. Crystal and Gerald were behind them, Naomi and Muriel followed.

"How're things?" Naomi asked.

"Not bad."

"So I noticed." Naomi pointed ahead at Raymond.

Muriel poked Naomi gently in the ribs.

"How was your visit with your parents?" Naomi asked.

"Just the way they like it. Uneventful."

"Don't you think you're being a little hard on them?"

"No harder than Raymond and Frank were on each other a little while ago."

"But anyone can see they're very close," Naomi said.

"Oh, I know. They were having a great time."

"That's because they had us for an audience."

"It had nothing to do with us. They were doing it for themselves," Muriel said.

"So you don't think men fight because they know women are watching?"

"No. I think it's purely a male thing. And women like to watch men fight for their own reasons."

"Which are?" Naomi asked.

"I haven't quite figured that out. But maybe you can help me?"

"How?"

"I want to find Theo."

"Why can't you let it go, Muriel? It's over."

"Maybe it is. But I'm not."

•••••

Crystal and Gerald walked for a while without speaking and she could sense his uneasiness.

"What you said about Hendrix was far out," she said. "I mean, like, I never really thought that much about what Hendrix was doing. But the way you explained it really blew my mind."

Gerald looked at Crystal and for the first time realized how young she was.

"I heard him in the Village before he made it big," he said. "I've always wanted to do in painting what he does with sound."

"That would be the ultimate for me too."

"In what way?"

"I've studied ballet since I was three. But at some point, I realized that all those years of training weren't going to help me do the things I wanted to do with my body. Frank's been trying to get me to perform with his group at the café. But I haven't gotten it together yet."

"What are you doing in the meantime?" Gerald asked.

"I make pots."

"Is there a connection?"

"Do you think there might be?"

It occurred to Gerald that her answer was typical of many young people he talked to. There was no chain of circumstances that accounted for events. Shit just happened.

•••••

A huge crowd gathered in front of the Fillmore East. The freezing temperature caused the breath to rush from their mouths like steam from a radiator valve. But no one seemed bothered by the cold. A swaying movement caught hold of everyone, bringing them together in a kind of preparatory exercise before a ritual. And then, as if drawn by a lunar pull, the crowd surged forward into the theater. Four long streamers cut in the shape of 1969 hung from the rafters above the stage. A light show projected on the wall at the back of the stage looked like flames about to engulf what was left of the year.

"Here they are!" a voice said over the public address system. "A Band of Gypsies!"

The audience quieted and offstage a long groan from a guitar was followed by an amplified sound like a strummed rubber band. Two men walked out on stage. One carried an electric bass and wore a derby with a bright red ribbon around it. The other was stocky with a sculptured bush of hair on his head. He sat down behind a set of drums with microphones hovering crane-like around the various percussion instruments. The bass player plucked out a sound from the heavy bottom of the rhythm; the drummer's foot thudded against the bass drum, probing the vital life signs of the audience.

Jimi Hendrix walked onto the stage and was washed in flames of light. He was twig and branch thin. But his unmistakable lion's head and fingers, extending from his wrists, made him loom taller than his actual height. Hendrix's voice was summoned up from a cavernous space. Tunneling deep in his throat it see-sawed between a growl and a wail. With his gigantic, spatula-shaped guitar, Hendrix dug, shoveled, hip-banged, and scrambled out sounds both human and animal.

As midnight approached, the audience had sweated itself high from the moonshine kick of the music. Hendrix hollered out for more from the drummer who answered with yodeling that spun itself into a rooster's wake-up call. The Fillmore rocked in full giddy-up and Hendrix came on like pots and pans, sounding the call to come and get it. He finished up by unleashing a kennel of high amp dog barks, ravaging what was left of the song.

After leaving the stage to the ecstatic uproar from the crowd, The Band of Gypsies returned for an encore. Hendrix approached the microphone stand.

"We want to dedicate this one to all the soldiers fighting in Chicago, Milwaukee, New York and Vietnam..."

The bass player opened up with a startling burst of notes, followed by the drummer machine-gunning a rat-tat-tat on his snare.

Caught in the crossfire, Hendrix's guitar moaned as though

wounded. He began singing, giving trombone voicings to the lyrics.

> "Evil man make me kill you
> Evil man make me kill you
> Evil man make me kill you
> Even though we're only families apart...
> Same way you shoot me down, baby
> You'll be going just the same with three times the pain
> And yourself to blame."

The drummer crept up on Hendrix and whistled doom and delight in the voice of a loon. Hendrix aired out his guitar until all that was left was the sound of the world dragging its feet, exhausted by its power to destroy. The drummer's bass pedal had the last word, uttering the final p-o-o-f that dissolved with a shimmering high hat into sand, dust and a hiss.

Before anyone could shake themselves free from silence, Hendrix led the drums and bass on a marching band strut; then he put the pedal to the tempo until their revved up fanfare collided with the pandemonium throughout the building, which all but drowned out the drummer's final refrain:

> "We got to live together
> We got to live to...
> We got to live...
> We got to..."

People filed out of the Fillmore with a death rattle in their teeth, not sure exactly what had been laid to rest. The streets were buzzing with the sound of kazoos, welcoming 1970. A block away from the throng in front of the theatre, the nasal sound of a guitar bobbed in the air, accompanied by the tingle of tambourines, the soft chatter of drums and a throaty voice:

> "This is the end,
> My only friend, the end
> Of our elaborate plans, the end

No safety or surprise, the end
I'll never look into your eyes again."

A group of revelers stopped to stare at a man looking into a trash can who seemed to be near the source of the music. He was shaggy-haired with a bald spot in the back of his head. He put the lid back on the can, looked up toward the rooftops of tenement buildings and bent down to search underneath parked cars. He stood up, turned to face the group and a clash of symbols erupted from his chest, followed by the words:

"This is the end."

A cassette recorder was attached to the left side of the man's Navy peacoat like a vital organ. His eyes were rimmed with red.

"What're you looking for?" someone asked.

"The Sixties!" the man said, moving past them with the floating sound of voices, guitars and drums encircling him.

MURIEL

1970

I HADN'T SEEN GENEVA SINCE OUR ARREST. Naomi offered to represent her but she chose to act as her own attorney. Geneva was presented with the same deal the assistant district attorney gave me but she turned it down. Surprisingly, the D.A. didn't pursue the indictment and dropped the charges. She was somewhat distant when we talked but agreed to get together.

When I reached the landing of Geneva's apartment, she was standing in the doorway. We made an attempt at being glad to see each other but neither of us was very convincing.

"Would you like some tea?" she asked.

"Yes."

"Sit with me in the kitchen while I make it."

I sat in one of the high chairs in front of the counter.

"My name is Khadijah now," she said.

"Why'd you change it?"

"Khadijah was the wife of Mohammed. I've always had a

weakness for prophets, so I figured why not be connected to one who was already dead. Also after the case was dropped, it made me feel like I had some say over my life."

"But you did. It took a lot of courage to refuse to cooperate with the D.A."

"How do you know what it took?"

"Because I was frightened just by the thought of doing what you did."

"What makes you think I didn't act out of fear?" she asked.

"Fear of what?"

Khadijah let my question hang in the air and leaned over to smell the tea brewing in the kettle.

"The fear of acting out of weakness," she said, smiling. "But that's what I get for being attracted to men who put themselves in danger when they're afraid."

"What do you think happened to Theo?" I asked.

"Unlike the rest of us, he knew not to be in the right place at the wrong time."

"How come we didn't know that?"

"Cause we left it up to Theo. And unfortunately, he neglected to tell us."

"Do you miss him?" I asked.

"Not if I can help it."

"Were you in love with him?"

"Only the idea of him."

"You know...Khadijah," I said, pausing to let the sound of her name pass through my mouth. "What keeps coming back to me is the instant before Walter was shot, I felt closer to him then than at any other time. I ask myself how I could be closer to the violence that killed him than to our life together."

Khadijah moved over and put her arms around me. Tears ran into my mouth. As she wiped them away, I smelled hibiscus on her fingers.

"Don't be so hard on yourself, Muriel. Violence has a way of getting our attention in ways that tenderness never does."

"You remember when Theo took my hands away from my ears

after he shattered that man's eardrums?" I asked.

"Yeah."

"I haven't been able to get any of that out of my mind either."

"If I were you, I'd try."

"I want to find Theo," I said.

"What for?" she asked, loosening her hold on me.

"I need to find out what I believe all over again."

"What's that got to do with Theo?"

"He's part of it. Just like you are."

"Good luck," she said.

"Can you help me?"

"In case you hadn't noticed, Theo and I haven't exactly been in touch."

"You know what I mean."

"The lines of communication to the radical underground run wide and deep. It'll take a while and there's no guarantee he'll want to see you even if I could find him."

"He may not want to see me, but I've never known Theo to pass up an opportunity to have a forum for his ideas."

"What forum?" she asked.

"*Out In Left Field* has asked me to become a regular contributor. My first piece is on Push Comes To Shove and the police raid. I suggested doing another piece on Theo and they seemed very interested."

"You don't waste much time, do you?"

"Not since I almost ran out of it."

"Speaking of time, what else have you been doing with yours?" she asked.

"What do you mean?"

"Come on, Muriel! Don't make this into a quiz show. Just tell me who you're seeing."

"His name is Raymond. He's into history and baseball."

"Is he into you?"

"He's getting there."

"And where are you getting to?"

"I'm getting nostalgic about the future."

"We never learn, do we?"

"So who are you learning your lessons from these days?" I asked.

"No one. But I did meet this guy named Lucius. He's a Vietnam vet and is involved in this group called the Grunt Collective. You may have read about them in papers last year. They got benefits for black veterans being stonewalled by the bureaucracy."

"Where'd you meet him?"

"I'm not involved with him!" she said.

"That's not what I asked you."

"In a cab."

"On your way in or out?"

"He drives a cab and he picked me up downtown after I'd been waiting in the cold for over half an hour. When I got in, it was like stepping into an army barracks. He had all kinds of military gear on the dashboard and his dog tags were hanging from the rearview mirror. We talked and he told me about the Collective. About a week later, I ran into him on the street. He and some other vets had taken over an abandoned building in the neighborhood and had started renovating it themselves."

"What about your weakness for men who are looking for trouble?" I asked.

"After Vietnam, he's not looking for trouble."

"What about you?" I asked.

"I was looking for answers. But he had more questions than I knew what to do with."

·····

I wanted to raise these hard questions in the first piece I wrote for *Out In Left Field*. But I was disappointed by my failure to capture what I felt at the moment when the police shot Walter. I was used to the words and actions of the powerful obstructing my vision. But I wasn't prepared to have my own words undermine my credibility as a witness for what I thought was the truth. When the article appeared in the paper, except for a few letters to the editor, there was no groundswell of empathy for—or opposition to—what I had written.

I'd been given a tiny cubicle in the offices of *Out In Left Field* where I could work if I wanted to. The receptionist called to tell me that there was a police detective who wanted to see me. I walked out to the reception area and saw a black man who was looking with obvious amusement at the clutter around him.

"You wanted to see me?" I asked.

"Yes. I'm Detective Garrett. I'd like to talk to you for a few minutes, if I may."

"What about?"

"Theodore Sutherland."

"I already told the police I don't know where he is."

"I know. This won't take very long."

"Can I see some I.D.?"

"Of course," he said, smiling and produced a badge that covered the palm of his hand.

I led him back to my cubicle. When he settled into a chair, I was struck by the dresser-wide physical mass of his body.

"So when was the last time you saw Sutherland?"

"It was the same day your fellow officers busted into my bedroom and killed Walter Armstead."

Anger flashed briefly in Garrett's eyes.

"Well, if you do hear from him," he said, handing me a card, "I'd appreciate you telling him to give me call."

"That would be difficult for me to do since my dealings with the police have convinced me that talking isn't what you really want to do."

"Yeah, I know. I read your article."

"What did you think?" I asked.

"It's interesting. But since I haven't read the police account of what happened, I can't say much more than that."

"You can't or you won't."

"Well, I could say you're just some pampered little black girl who thinks the world is an amusement park where she can play shoot-em-up!"

"That's not true!"

"But you're insinuating that I want to entrap Sutherland, right?"

"I wasn't accusing you personally."

"Miss Pointer, you might be surprised to know how many police officers there are who would agree with you about rogue cops on the force. Don't write us all off. All I want Sutherland to do is establish his whereabouts on the evening the 33rd Precinct was firebombed."

He rose from the chair and waved me off when I started to get up.

"I'll find my way out," he said. "By the way, what's your next piece going to be about?"

"Charismatic leaders."

"You ought to do a story about police officers from the inside. We may not be charismatic. But most of us are decent human beings trying to do the job we're paid to do."

I didn't know quite what to make of him. In a way, I felt hustled. All that talk about the unsung decency of the majority of cops seemed like a diversion to get what he was really after. What that was exactly, I didn't know.

I called Naomi and told her I needed to talk about something but couldn't discuss it over the phone. We agreed to meet for lunch. I'd grown to like her bluntness and her way of acting puzzled when she made me laugh. I'd come to trust her enough to show my anger. I could enjoy her company without concealing my distrust of white people.

As I told Naomi about my meeting with Detective Garrett, she sat motionless, moving only to take a sip of wine.

"So what do you think?" I asked.

"You're right about him not expecting you to tell him anything about Theo. He really wanted to know more about you."

"Like what?"

"How you felt about Theo leaving. And whether you were sleeping with him."

"Why would that be important?"

"It would tell him whether you felt betrayed politically, romantically or both."

"What about Khadijah? She was the one involved with Theo. But from what she told me, the police haven't questioned her."

"Your situation is more complicated than hers. Your loss was greater and you have more to be bitter about. They're hoping to turn that into information about Theo."

"Why should I be bitter about Theo disappearing?"

"My guess is it was Theo and not Walter they were after that night."

"Oh, come on! How could they mistake Walter for..." I stopped myself, realizing how foolish it was to be surprised that one black man might be mistaken for another.

"What makes them think Theo would risk getting in touch with me?" I asked.

"Theo probably read your piece and the police are counting on the same thing you're counting on."

"Which is?"

"That his craving for public attention is stronger than his fear of capture."

"What about Garrett wanting me to write something about the police?" I asked.

"He was probably playing on your ambivalence."

"What ambivalence?"

"So you're not interested in writing about cops?"

"Not that interested."

"I would be."

"Why?"

"Because most of the people I represent are not particularly likable. But there's always something about them that attracts me."

"I don't understand that."

"I think you do."

"Don't play lawyer with me, Naomi. I'm not in the mood."

"Are you afraid you'll find out that not all cops are killers?"

"No! Just that not ENOUGH aren't! And I don't want to be used."

"Maybe you have to decide how much you're willing to be used to get what you want."

I didn't know what to do with that, so I changed the subject. "I've been meaning to thank you for hiring Khadijah. How's she working out?"

"I haven't heard any complaints from any of the other lawyers," Naomi said with a detached cool.

"What about the lawyer sitting across the table from me?"

"I think she's fine. If anything, her performance is too good. She never lets her guard down and only gives up what is required to do the job."

"Isn't that what she was hired to do?"

"Of course. But working with someone like that every day can be very taxing."

"It seems like it would be even more taxing working with someone who was charming but incompetent."

"You're right. I was just making an observation."

"You don't like her, do you?"

"That has nothing to do with it!"

"Obviously, it has everything to do with it. You got Khadijah the job and she's not grateful enough. And it's the ultimate indignity for a black woman who's been messed over by white people to show ingratitude to someone white, who's gone out of their way to help. Right?"

"Muriel! You take everything to extremes! I don't think it's unreasonable to expect Khadijah to be a little more friendly and not act as though she's doing the firm a favor by working for us."

"She probably feels she was hired because she was qualified to do the job. Obviously, she didn't consider that her job description included being your friend."

"To be frank about it, Muriel, Khadijah was hired because you're my friend. And she should realize there's a trade-off in everything, even if it's as simple as being civil to people who've helped you."

"Naomi," I said, reaching over and placing my hand over hers, "isn't it enough that you have Gerald's and my love? Do you want *all* black people to love you too?"

She snatched her hand away. But I could tell she wasn't really angry.

•••••

One of the local television stations had picked up a story about a group of black Vietnam vets who took over an abandoned building in Central Harlem and began doing renovations. I watched a newscaster on the eleven o'clock news interview the spokesman of the group, Lucius Braxton. It was the same man Khadijah had told me about. He had these gorgeous eyes with more lid showing than eyeball. There was defiance in his thick, woolly hair, but as Braxton spoke to the reporter, I was impressed by the absence of any swagger.

"What's the point of taking over an abandoned building?" the reporter asked.

"Abandoned is how a lot of us feel who've come back from Vietnam. So we can identify with a building that nobody wants. It's a natural alliance. While we rehabilitate this building, it gives us hope and something useful to do. Two things that've been in short supply since we got back."

"What about the fact that what you're doing is illegal?"

"Right now, we're more concerned that what we're doing is legitimate!"

"Does that justify breaking the law?" the reporter fired back.

"In Vietnam an M16 justified everything."

"You're not in Vietnam anymore."

"No. But we brought it back with us."

The interview broke off at that point with the image on the screen cutting back to the television studio, where the reporter spoke about her unsuccessful attempts to find out the status of the seized building. She ended by saying that she would continue to follow the developments in the occupation of the building by the Grunt Collective.

I called Khadijah the next morning and said I wanted to write a piece on the Collective and asked if she would put me in touch with them. She got back to me and said Lucius would agree to an interview on the condition that we meet informally first and talk off the record. We arranged to get together a few days later at Khadijah's apartment for dinner.

I arrived early in order to have some time to visit with Khadijah alone. The aroma of coconut incense filled the apartment.

"How're things working out at the law office?" I asked.

Khadijah frowned, "What's Naomi been telling you?

"Nothing. I just wanted to know how you're making out."

"Come on, Muriel! I'm a secretary! That should tell you how I'm making out!"

"What are you getting upset about? All I asked was a question."

"I should've never taken this job," she said. "These bleeding-ulcer white liberals are a pain in the ass! Why can't they be like your run-of-the-mill white folks, who don't want to be friends but just want you to do your job?"

"It wouldn't hurt to be a little more sociable," I said.

"Are you talking about me or yourself?"

"Okay. Maybe we should just talk about the two people here in this room."

"Fine with me," she said. "You seem to have found a home at *Out In Left Field*."

"I like the work I'm doing. Have you thought about what you really want to do?"

"Yeah. But I haven't settled on anything yet. When I do, I want it to do for me what writing does for you."

"Is Lucius doing anything for you?" I asked.

"I haven't known him that long, which may be a compliment to both of us. You know me with men. No sooner than I find one, I'm trying to figure him out. And once I do that, I'm about ready to forget him."

Khadijah and I laughed. We looked around for something to munch on while we waited for Lucius.

I don't know." She reached into a bag of tortilla chips before handing it to me. "I just want to be more than a cheerleader for somebody else. Although I wouldn't be surprised if there were things Lucius could do for me that I'd find impossible not to cheer about!"

"You ought to stop!" I said, as the doorbell rang.

When Khadijah opened the door, I noticed they didn't touch each other. We were introduced and Khadijah left the room to see about dinner.

"I read your piece about what the police did," Lucius said. "Must've been difficult trying to write all that."

"It was even more difficult trying not to write it."

"I hear that...Khadijah tells me you're writing something about people like King and Malcolm."

"Yeah, but it's really about me trying to understand more about myself," I said.

"Like what?"

"Like how I can hear two people say the same thing, but how it's said will determine which one I'll listen to."

"Does that mean you'll go for bullshit depending on how it's served up?" he asked.

I smiled. "That's a question I haven't answered yet. But my guess is that we can all be had."

"So what has all this to do with me?"

"You're someone that people listen to."

"That's just the way it worked out."

"For whatever the reason, you've become more than just one man's voice. You're giving a voice to all black Vietnam vets. That's a quality few people have. King had it. Malcolm had it. Theodore Sutherland had it before he disappeared. And I have a feeling you have it too."

Lucius frowned and shifted slightly in his chair.

"All I'm doing is pointing out what I see in front of me, which was the same thing I did when I was point man for my platoon."

"They're not many men who would've done that."

"Maybe not. But being in the 'Nam taught me that it was always better to know trouble was coming ahead of time."

"Well," Khadijah broke in, "you two are going to be in serious trouble with me unless you sit down at the dinner table before this food gets cold."

•••••

Lucius agreed to be included in my story only if I talked to other vets and wrote about their collective efforts to reclaim abandoned buildings. A few days later, I visited the building they had taken over after the city refused to sell it to them. Crisscrossing clothes-lines stretched throughout the bottom floor. Light bulbs in wire encasements hung from the lines of rope, creating the sensation of being in a tunnel. Several black men were plastering the walls. When they took a break for lunch, a huge piece of plywood was placed on two wooden sawhorses for a table. They took very little notice of me while they ate.

"Had any of you met before you became involved in the collective?" I asked.

One of the men looked up at me after taking a bite of a sandwich.

"We'd met. We just didn't know it. It took Lucius to bring it to our attention."

"How'd he do that?"

"He organized a meeting at the Harlem Y.M.C.A., so we all could come together. I remember him saying at the first meeting that as hard as Charlie was to find in the 'Nam, it was even more difficult to find himself once he got back in the world. That's when I recognized him as someone I knew." He paused for a second. "It's like he spoke a language I didn't know was mine until I heard him speak."

The other men nodded, and I envied them for having found—and kept alive among themselves—what I'd lost and was still looking for.

•••••

The week after my story appeared in *Out In Left Field*, I got a message that the City had called off negotiations with the Grunt Collective and ordered them to leave the building or be arrested. I took a cab uptown. When I got there, I saw a surging crowd held back by police barricades. I flashed my press pass and was let through. The police were in the street and on rooftops, wearing bulletproof vests and heavily armed. As I pushed my way closer to the brownstone I saw members of the collective peering out of the windows. I also caught sight of Lucius engaged in conversation with what looked like city marshals. Reporters thrust their microphones between them to catch as much of what was said as possible.

"You must vacate the building at once," one of the marshals said.

"This looks more like an invasion than an evacuation," Lucius said, gesturing toward all the police.

"The police are here only as a precautionary measure."

"As a precaution against what?"

"Resistance."

"We have no intention of resisting if you allow us to leave."

"Then there shouldn't be any problems."

"Is it all right if I go in and tell my people that?"

"Okay. But don't take too long!"

Lucius turned away from the crush of people, walked slowly up the steps of the house and went inside.

"You're the last person I expected to see in this crowd," someone said.

I turned around to see Detective Garrett, looking quite pleased.

"Why wouldn't I be here? I just finished a piece on the Grunt Collective."

"I know that. I'm just surprised you would allow yourself to be surrounded by the police."

"I don't mind as long as they're in plain sight."

"I'll try to remember that," he said.

"Isn't this a little out of your territory?"

"Not really. I'm a kind of roving detective."

One of the marshals used a bullhorn to demand that everyone in the building come out. When there was no response, he signaled the police, who began rushing through the door. The reporters surged forward but were barred from entering.

"If you want, you can come in with me," Garrett said.

I followed him through the crowd to the entrance.

"She's with me," Garrett said to one of the cops who tried to block my way. Inside, the police stomped about in the dark in a frantic search. I followed Garrett and a flashlight to the kitchen, through a door that led down a flight of steps to the basement. The two marshals stood with several other cops, training their flashlights into a huge hole in the concrete floor.

"This is how they got out," one of the cops said.

"Where does this lead?" one of the marshals asked, as a rumbling noise came from below.

"Probably close to the subway system."

"I don't get it. Why go to all this trouble when all they had to do was walk out the front door?"

"They obviously didn't agree with you over which exit was the safest," Garrett said.

The marshal gave him a look of total incomprehension.

"Well! What are you going to do?" the marshal asked.

"Didn't they vacate the building peaceably?"

"But what about this vandalism," the marshal said, pointing to the huge hole in the floor.

"That would be a matter for another police unit other than mine."

"I'll be filing a report about the way this whole operation was handled."

"That's a good idea. It's always better to get everything in writing."

The marshal shook his head and walked back up the steps of the basement.

"So what do you think?" Garrett asked me as the other cops followed the marshals.

"About what?"

"Why your friend, Lucius and his buddies preferred to travel below street level?"

"Why are you so interested in a simple eviction?" I asked.

"Because you are. And because you seem drawn to men who have a strong inclination toward making themselves scarce."

"Oh! We're back to that again."

"Of course! But just for my own curiosity—what do you make of their hasty retreat to the underground?"

"I have no idea. I was as surprised as everyone else."

"You disappoint me, Muriel. I thought you of all people would have figured it out. But I guess like most of these antiwar activists, you know very little about the Vietnamese and even less about what's happened to the men sent ten thousand miles to fight them."

"What are you talking about?"

"Your Grunt Collective got very close to the Viet Cong but they never knew how close until they found the tunnels the Vietnamese dug underneath U.S. air bases. From the looks of the escape route your friends took, it appears the Vietnamese tunneled their way inside their psyche."

"How do you know so much about Vietnam?"

"Because I was there too."

"Why are you telling me all this?" I asked.

"I just thought I'd pass along some information that might help you. And who knows? Maybe you'll remember that when you hear from Theo."

Garrett read my mind before I could speak it.

"I'm not trying to get you to set him up. Just tell him I want to talk with him."

"Does Theo know you?" I asked.

"He's acquainted with me. I've questioned him a few times."

"What about the Grunt Collective?" I asked. "Do you intend to question them too?"

"No. I'm much more interested in Theodore Sutherland. Same as you."

RAYMOND

1970

GERALD STARTED HANGING OUT with Frank and me after the Jimi Hendrix New Year's Eve concert at the Fillmore East. We would usually meet at the Riviera, a bar in the West Village, for endless postmortems on the Sixties.

"I still believe Hendrix missed an opportunity to push himself and the rest of us to a much more dangerous place," Frank said.

"And where would that be?" I asked.

"How the fuck should I know? He's the one who made everyone believe he could catch lightning in a guitar. Maybe he could've created an amp overload that might've knocked out the power all over New York City. That would've put Hendrix and his Strat in the same company with David and his slingshot when he went up against the mighty Goliath."

"That's just what he wants to get away from—all the expectations people have. They just want him to do something outrageous that has nothing to do with the music."

"It's still about the music. But the presentation has to change to hold people's attention. It's like the war. There really wasn't that much opposition to it until the killing was shown on TV as the shit storm of guts and brains it always was!"

"So you're saying people won't be interested in Hendrix unless he substitutes one form of outrage for another?"

Frank tilted back in his chair and drained a full mug of beer, which I interpreted as a yes.

"I don't agree with you," Gerald said, startling us. He hadn't said a word since we sat down.

"Gandhi counseled his followers to abstain from using violence even in self defense against attacks by the British," Gerald said. "He proved that there was a power at work in the world more formidable than the rule of force. But in order to prepare himself to receive this spiritual energy, it required extensive fasting, meditation, celibacy and isolation."

"That only proves everything I've been saying," Frank said.

"How's that?"

"Think about it! What could be more outrageous than what you just said about Gandhi! The only problem I have with his philosophy is the belief that denial and restraint lead you to the big brass ring. I've done some study of Eastern thought myself. And I'm much more attracted to the Buddhist practice known as *sekti*. It goes back to 13th-century Java and says the most effective way to avoid losing ourselves in our sexual appetites is indulging them to their fullest."

"Your logic never fails to astound me," I said.

"Don't give me the credit. I'm only repeating what minds greater than our own have said—namely, restraint in the presence of temptation leads to self-mastery."

"I don't see how this has any relevance to Gandhi's philosophy," Gerald said.

"The relevance is in the result. So as long as we get to the same place, it shouldn't matter how we got there."

"I know you don't believe that bullshit," I said.

"Who said anything about believing." Frank grinned. "I'm just knocking back some beers with a couple of friends."

"If what we're talking about doesn't matter to you, then what does?" Gerald asked.

"A few things. But they have nothing to do with the hand job you intellectuals give to any thought that enters your mind."

"Oh, right! And you're just a disinterested observer," I said.

"Hey! Vietnam cursed and cured me of ever letting ideas get too close to me. Most of the guys I knew in the 'Nam had room for only one idea, which was to get the fuck outta there!"

"That's just what those vets in the Grunt Collective did the other day," I said.

"I like the move they made," Frank said. "It was the last thing anybody expected. But now they have to decide what to do next."

"Why do they have to do anything?" Gerald asked.

"You're an artist. Why do you think? There always has to be a *next*! Otherwise, why bother making a *didi mow*."

"What's that?"

"It's a dink expression for a quick get away."

Gerald reacted as though he'd been hit in the face.

"I guess I won't have to tell you what dink means," Frank said.

"Why do you call the Vietnamese that?"

"What would you call people who are trying to kill you?"

"They weren't all trying to kill you."

"I had a lot of buddies who ended up in body bags because they believed that."

Gerald didn't say a word. So it looked as though it was up to me.

"You know that's the same as the *all whites are suspect* argument that drives you up the wall when blacks use it?"

"Oh come off that shit, Raymond! This ain't no abstract conversation about what some faceless white people feel about blacks, but about real life and fucking death situations where you don't know if the crying infant you pick up won't turn into a human booby trap and all that's left of you is a pile of blood and shit!"

"Well..." I felt the anger trembling in my voice. "It's a comfort to hear that what whites feel about blacks can never be a life and death matter."

"That's not what I meant and you know it!"

"So you can presume to tell me what I mean but I can't return the favor."

"You're making this about race but it's not," Frank said. "If those black guys from the Grunt Collective were here, they'd know what I'm talking about."

"They'd also know why they were scuffling for their lives in an abandoned building and why you own a business."

I knew I'd done some damage before my words registered in Frank's eyes.

"Why don't we change the subject," Gerald said.

"We can never seem to get away from it. Can we?" Frank said, speaking directly to me.

"What's that?" I asked.

"You know...*La via vecchia.*"

"Oh," I said, suddenly feeling drained. "The old way."

"You remember the rest?" he asked.

"Not in Italian."

"*Chi lascia la via vecchia per la nuova, sa quel che perde e non sa quel che trova.*"

We finished our beers and paid the bill, each of us wanting to leave the site of the disaster. Gerald and I walked to the subway. It was too much to hope for that he would take my silence as a cue that I didn't want to talk.

"What was it that Frank said in Italian?" he asked.

I blew air out of my mouth to steady myself.

"*Whoever forsakes the old way for the new knows what he is losing but not what he will find.*"

"So what was his point?"

"Maybe that sometimes the flow of tribal blood is thicker than friendship. So I guess he was trying to stop the bleeding."

"It seems to me, he should've known how we'd react to him, calling Vietnamese *dinks*."

"How we'd react seemed to end up being mostly me."

Gerald shrugged. "I didn't feel I knew him well enough to say that much. I mean, he's your friend. Isn't he?"

"That's right! And you're not! Which means Frank's got more of a claim on my loyalty than you do!"

"Wait a second! If you're feeling guilty about the way you came down on him, that's on you, not me. And if he's got no problem with spouting racial slurs, I guess I assumed that you would! But if I was wrong, don't worry. I won't make that mistake again."

Gerald's assumption was right. In the three years since Frank had returned from Vietnam, I challenged him less about the quicksand of rage he so willingly immersed himself in. I would watch him lash out at everything in the war that had hurt him—beginning with the civilian and military command, the anti-war protesters, and the Vietnamese whom, surprisingly, he respected. Maybe the demands of being Frank's friend had simply exhausted me. Now it was just easier to distance myself, which I began cultivating after I saw Uncle Aubrey killed by that cop—and that was part of my work as a historian. I wasn't proud of being distant, but I also had to admit that I felt a bit smug that I'd avoided the psychic fallout that had twisted Frank in Vietnam. My anger in the bar wasn't about what Frank had said, just at Gerald having heard it. And I responded out of fear at what Gerald would think if I kept quiet. I was still furious. And I reached out for the most available target.

"Have you ever wondered," I said, "why people who pride themselves on being black often lead the most contradictory personal lives?"

In one movement, Gerald stepped away from my side and faced

me without any hint of aggression.

"I don't want to make the mistake of being presumptuous again. So why don't you tell me what you meant by that, Raymond?"

Of course, we both knew what I meant. And his calm exposed and shamed me as no other gesture could have.

"Whatever I meant, I'm sorry," I said.

He walked away without another word, leaving me as out of touch with the comforts and dangers of tribal blood and friendship as I had ever been.

M U R I E L

1970

I CALLED KHADIJAH as soon as I left the building that Lucius and the Grunt Collective had been occupying. After dialing her number at work several times and getting a busy signal, I went directly to Naomi's law office. Khadijah was at her desk. She looked up at me without speaking and kept typing.

"I guess you know?" I asked.

"Unfortunately, I do."

"Have you spoken to Lucius?"

Khadijah stopped typing, pushed herself away from the desk and squinted as though she had noticed something strange about me.

"Do I look stupid to you?" she asked.

"What do you mean?"

"Do you know that *Ne-e-gro* called me asking for help after he didn't have sense enough to leave that building through the front door? I mean, I thought their reason for moving there in the first place was to do what the city had no intention of doing—turning an eyesore into a place that was livable. But instead of using the presence of the television cameras to show the police arresting men still trying to serve their country like they did in Vietnam, Lucius bails out through a hole in the basement floor like a thief in the night! Theo would've never..."

Khadijah smiled and shook her head slowly. "I guess it's going to take longer than I thought."

"What is?" I asked.

"Getting Theo out of my system."

"Don't be so hard on yourself."

"Why not? Somebody has to."

"Did he say what he's going to do?"

"No! And I didn't ask."

"Why not?"

"Have you forgotten? I'm on probation! The last thing I need is to be involved with some reincarnated Che Guevara."

"I don't know if it's possible for us to understand what the war has done to men like him," I said.

"You're absolutely right! And since I'm not a journalist or a lawyer, I'll leave it to you and Naomi to figure out whether he needs a shrink or to join Theo among the missing in action."

"Why are you so upset? I thought you said there was nothing going on between you two?"

"It doesn't matter whether I was fucking him. I'm just tired of being around people who attract ambulances or chase them!"

"Do you think I'm one of those people?" I asked.

"I wouldn't press me for an answer right now, if I were you."

I couldn't tell if she was serious, so I backed off and walked down the corridor to Naomi's office.

"Close the door behind you," she said as soon as I got to the doorway.

"I guess you heard what happened?" I asked as I collapsed in a chair.

"Pretty much."

"Khadijah thinks Lucius should've taken advantage of the media presence and not made it look like the Collective was defying the police."

"I don't think he was that interested in symbolic gestures."

"Have you talked to him?" I asked.

"Yes. Just before you arrived."

"What'd he say?"

"He wanted to know if the police intended to arrest him. So I did some checking and the worst he's looking at is a fine for trespassing on city owned property and vandalism. That's of course, if they stick to the letter of the law. But as a law professor once told me—the letter of the law and its application are separated at birth."

"So what's Lucius going to do?" I asked.

"I guess what he learned to do so well from the Viet Cong—stay hidden by becoming one with the elements."

"Is there a way for you to reach him?"

"Only when he calls me."

"When you talk to him again, let him know that I need to see him."

"Why?"

"When I met those Vets, I saw how much they care for each other. It reminded me of how it was when I worked in Mississippi. I never imagined that we would have so much in common. I just don't know which side of things I'm on anymore."

"Well, you may have to wait in line to find out."

"What do you mean?"

"There's someone from your side of things who's resurfaced and he wants to see Lucius too."

I opened my mouth but the words didn't follow.

"That's right," Naomi said, "Theo."

"Why did he leave like he did?"

"He didn't get into that. All he wanted was for me to put him in touch with Lucius."

"Did he mention me at all?"

"He said to tell you he was sorry about Walter, that he liked your articles and he'd be in touch."

"Be in touch! So he'd rather speak to a perfect stranger than talk to me?"

"What can I tell you, Muriel? He's on the top of your list but you're not on the top of his."

"What about Khadijah? Where is she on his list?"

"Let's just say she's not a priority."

"I guess I shouldn't be surprised," I said.

"I guess not, since he wants to see Lucius as badly as you do. But probably not for the same reasons."

"And you know where you can put that tasty little remark." I felt a flash of anger burning in the back of my head as I stood up to leave.

"I'll let you know the moment I hear anything from either one of them."

I was tempted to storm out like the most fearsome opera diva. But Naomi's buttery farewell, "*See ya, boobee*," took all the fury of my melodramatic exit. It was all I could do just to keep from laughing.

•••••

A few days later, Naomi called to tell me that Khadijah had quit her job. As bothered as she was by Lucius' latest move, Theo's call to Naomi completely unnerved her. I called Khadijah several times but she was either never at home or not answering the phone.

Finally, I found out Khadijah now had an unlisted number. I went to her apartment and after ringing the bell over and over without getting a response, I decided to wait in front of the building until she returned. After about twenty minutes, I saw her walking toward me from the corner. When she saw me, she didn't look pleased.

"Khadijah! What's going on? I've been trying to reach you for over a week."

"Let's go upstairs," she said.

Once we were in her apartment, we must have sat for ten minutes before either of us spoke.

"So are you going to let me in on what's happening or not."

"I've decided to become a midwife."

"A midwife! Why?"

"Listen to yourself, woman," Khadijah said. "You make it sound like it's something scandalous."

"It's just that you've never mentioned anything about it. In fact, I feel like you've been deliberately trying to cut me out of your life."

"Muriel, I don't understand my life anymore. I needed some time away. And I began to think that if I learned more about life at its very beginning, which didn't include giving birth myself, maybe my own life might begin to make more sense."

"And you think becoming a midwife will do that for you?"

"It's something I can learn to do, where the end result will be a lot more promising than anything I've done so far. Look at it this way...being a midwife will let me remain committed to the philosophy of Push Comes to Shove."

"Aside from that pitiful attempt at humor, where does this leave us?" I asked.

"It leaves you searching for something even more elusive than Theo. And me wanting to learn how to do one thing well that doesn't lead to destruction." She smiled. "We should be able to keep up a friendship in between all of that."

RAYMOND

1970

I WAS WORRIED WHEN I HEARD that Lucius Braxton and some other black Vietnam vets had disappeared without a trace into the subway. I expected Muriel to try to find him, but I didn't expect her to succeed. When she told me a meeting had been arranged at some underground location in the subway system, I was upset. My unease stemmed from a childhood fear of being buried alive. I hated tight, enclosed spaces.

When Uncle Aubrey was killed, I'd never been to a funeral and had never been in the presence of someone who was dead. At the wake, I stared intently at my uncle in his plush boxed bed while my father explained to me that the body was merely the house where the soul resided. But if the house collapsed prematurely, as in Uncle Aubrey's case, the soul would have to seek new quarters. I was relieved to hear that his soul would not be trapped in a body sentenced to eternity in a box, especially after the casket was closed and lowered into the grave. Then Uncle Aubrey's wife, Aunt Alice, jumped on top of the coffin, grabbed it and began screaming that she would not let him leave without her. It took two of my uncles to pry Aunt Alice's fingers off the casket.

It was all very confusing. If Uncle Aubrey's life had vacated his body, why was my aunt behaving like there was still someone alive inside him? But this hair-raising clawing and scratching at coffins continued at the funerals of other relatives I attended.

So my childhood was plagued by the question—*Was the life that left the body buried in the box along with the corpse or not?* Although, I'm no longer haunted by that question, I rarely ride the subways or spend extended periods in rooms with the doors closed. Not surprisingly, Muriel didn't know quite what to make of all this.

"Look Raymond!" she said, as we discussed her meeting with Lucius. "I think your reasons for not wanting to be behind closed doors are more than a little eccentric. But what has any of this to do with me?"

"It has everything to do with you, if you remember the closed door the police broke through right before they murdered Walter."

"And so what do you think is going to happen when I meet Lucius?"

"It's already happened. You were trapped in that room with Walter. It became his tomb and you're still locked in there with him. You won't be able to get out until you give up this obsession to find Theo!"

"You sound like the one who's obsessed," she said.

"You're impossible!"

"Not impossible, Raymond. Just difficult." A smile slid across her face.

"What's so funny?" I asked.

"We're having an argument. I like that."

I didn't. I'd grown up being frightened of having strong feelings because they inevitably led to being upset, having an argument and somebody getting killed, like Uncle Aubrey. I wanted to find out if this had always been the case. And I discovered that the past was infested with arguments, resulting in unimaginable violence and carnage. But instead of erasing the evidence like my parents did, I chose to immerse myself in the world of hurt, hoping that knowing about it would be the best way for me to protect myself and others.

While I had known people who seemed very much at home riding their emotions, like kids on a high-flying swing, I'd never been that close to any of them except for Frank. I had to admit that my attraction to Muriel had been my usual curiosity about people whose arguments with the powerful had almost gotten them killed. But the fact that she saw our disagreement as a hopeful sign of things to come made me wonder if getting close enough to hurt someone might not lead to mutual destruction.

Still, it bothered me that Muriel could so easily dismiss my warning about how rooms become tombs. That's where my understanding of the world has led me—from a fear of the soul living on in a sealed box after death to an even greater fear of the coffins we make of our lives long before our bodies fail us.

M U R I E L

1970

WHILE I WAITED FOR NAOMI to contact me about meeting with Lucius, a Greenwich Village townhouse blew up. The police said it was a bomb factory for the Weather Underground. The *Times* did a feature story on this breakaway faction of SDS and linked it to Push Comes to Shove and the Grunt Collective as examples of groups who had lost touch with the political realities in America and the most effective ways to bring about meaningful change.

Two days after the explosion, Naomi called to say she wanted to see me. Lucius had agreed to meet me in lower Manhattan at midnight near an entrance to the Holland Tunnel. I killed time before the meeting by going to the last show of an overrated B movie classic at the Bleeker Street Cinema. I got a cab to Canal Street and walked from there. The late-winter frost of March was starting to thaw but the wind pressing in on me had not entirely lost its sting.

I stopped at the corner where I was told to wait. I noticed a man walking toward me from the other end of the block. As he came abreast of me, the burning tip from the cigarette in his mouth highlighted his face. He was white. I expected him to walk past me but was startled when he spoke.

"Stay put, Muriel," he said softly.

He kept walking, disappeared around the corner and then reappeared just beyond the curb. He took a long drag of his cigarette and flicked it into the street. Then he stamped his foot down several times on the cover of a sewer and stepped away. The cover rose and the man pushed it away from the hole.

"Come on!" he said.

I moved warily to the hole and a beam of light hit me in the face. I was helped down the iron rungs by the man on the street and whoever was holding the flashlight. When I reached the bottom, the cover slid back over the hole.

"Follow the light!" a man's voice said.

I walked down the tunnel behind him, watching the light aimed no higher than our knees. He stopped suddenly, turning off his light just as another came on. As I shielded my eyes from the glare, the footsteps of the man I'd followed echoed off to the left and faded away completely into dark vastness.

"Could you get that light out of my eyes?"

"Just wanted to make sure it was you." Lucius pointed the light back to the ground.

"Were you expecting someone else?"

"No. But Vietnam taught me to be suspect of whatever I expect to happen."

"Why would my wanting to talk with you make me suspect?"

"You've been taken by surprise once before, Muriel. If it happens again, I don't want it to be on my turf."

"Do you really live down here?"

"Why not? It's a lot safer than where you live."

"How long do you intend to stay?"

"There are Viet Cong who've spent years in underground tunnels, stretching from North to South Vietnam. From them, I learned how to get to a point where there was no difference between where I was and who I was."

"Who was the guy waiting for me up on the street?"

"Another grunt from the war."

"I didn't expect to find someone white involved with the Collective."

"There you go again with those expectations of yours. The one thing that all the men who fought the war on the ground have in common is trying not to die. Those of us who understood that didn't have time to fight any other wars."

"Aren't you worried about being arrested?"

"The police don't seem to be that interested. Not like you and a few others."

"What others?"

"Your friend Theo."

"Have you talked to him?"

"Done better than that."

"You've seen him! When?"

"A few days ago."

"What did he want?"

Lucius didn't speak right away. It was as though he was waiting for the memory of Theo's physical presence to materialize out of the pitch dark before continuing.

"I don't think even he knew. He wanted to talk about the Vietnamese and how they'd been successful fighting a war against a much more well-armed adversary. I told him that wasn't hard to figure out since the VC weren't worried, like we were, about getting back home because they were already there. Theo said he never believed that shit about the advantages of waging a war in your own backyard. He said he could go a mile from where he grew up in the Bronx and feel like he was in another world. He didn't think the Vietnamese were any different as far as that went. But I told him, maybe that was the genius of Ho Chi Minh's brand of communism—convincing enough people that they could feel at home anywhere in their own country."

Lucius paused, remembering. "After I said that, it seemed like Theo didn't have so much of an attitude. He asked me if that was why we were down here in this sewer. I told him that was as good a reason as any. Then he surprised me by saying he wanted to join up with us but we'd have to teach him how to survive down here. I told him he was welcome to stay but he'd have to pull his weight like the rest of us and learn how to live down here by *being* down here. He said that was fine with him because that meant we could start making new plans for Push Comes to Shove. I asked him what he meant and he said he wanted to help us plan an underground offensive against the city government. I thought he was kidding at first but when I realized he wasn't, I asked him why would he think we'd be interested in doing anything like that. He looked like I'd questioned the fact that one was followed by two. Then Theo said, *Why else would you be hanging out in a sewer?* And when I told him we were there to get a better perspective, he looked at me like I was crazy. He asked me if I was serious and I said I was about to ask him the same question. He wanted to know what I meant. And I asked him if he was in the war. He said he was in the one over here and would put his commitment up there against anybody's. I told him I didn't doubt his commitment but that we were committed to different things."

"What did he say to that?"

"He got really pissed off. But I tried to explain that we'd just got through fighting for the U. S. of A. and weren't interested in starting a fight against it. He told me we might not have a choice since we were on the run from the police, just like him. I said it wasn't the same because he was in the world, but not in the war. He agreed but said there were things about us that were the same. I thought he was going to say that we were all black. But that wasn't it. What he meant was that he and the Grunt Collective had worked for the uncle of us all. I asked *what uncle* and he said *Uncle fucking Sam!*"

Lucius' words jolted me in a way similar to the electric cattle prods used by police in Mississippi. And I spoke more as a reflex than for any reason having to do with thinking. "What did you say to that?"

"Nothing."

"Theo was a cop?"

"No. Just an informer. He was going to get prosecuted for armed robbery unless he cooperated."

"Did he know about the police raid?" I asked.

"Not until after it happened."

"Why did he split?"

"He said the police tried to get him to plant explosives in your building, so they could bust everybody. When he used them to fire-bomb the police precinct instead, he knew they'd figure out he'd done it."

"So it was Theo and not Walter they intended to murder!"

"That's how he sees it."

"But what made him turn against the police? And why didn't he let the rest of us know what was going on?"

"You'll have to ask him that yourself."

I felt lost in a maze far more complicated than the cavernous subway system.

"Where is he now?" I asked.

"Who knows."

"What do you mean? I thought you said Theo wanted to become part of the Collective."

"He did. But when he realized we weren't willing to turn ourselves into the Viet Cong, he said we'd end up being part of his guerilla war against America anyway."

"What do you think he meant?"

"I don't know. But right before he climbed up the rungs leading to the street, he told me to remember that Marcus Garvey once said *Look for me in the whirlwind or the storm. Look for me all around you.*"

"Oh that's great!" I said. "I won't have any trouble finding him now."

"Don't worry. I don't think you'll have to wait very long before he contacts you. Theo may not want anyone to know what, where and when he'll do damage, but he definitely wants everyone to know he's the one doing it."

"What about you? Will I have to look in the whirlwind to find you again?"

"I'm in touch with Naomi from time to time. You can reach me through her."

"What about Khadijah? Have you spoken with her?

"No. Have you?"

"Yes."

"Then I should be asking you about her and not the other way around."

"What do you want to know?"

"Nothing really. I think Khadijah has had more than enough of me."

•••••

As Muriel crossed Hudson Street and walked up Sixth Avenue, she only had a vague recollection of having climbed out of the sewer. She called Raymond from a phone booth and asked if she could come over. At Bleeker Street, Muriel took a few steps into the subway, but recoiled at the thought of going back underground. She turned around and hailed a cab that took her to Raymond's apartment on West 21st Street.

After Muriel told Raymond what had happened, they sat on the couch for several minutes without speaking.

"So. Are you done?" Raymond asked.

"With what?"

"Looking for Theo."

"I haven't found him yet."

"Maybe not. But it's more important that you've found him OUT! He's become an outcast who's cut himself off from all authority except his own."

"I still want to know what made him come over to our side."

"The only side Theo's interested in is his own!"

"I don't care! I need to talk to him!"

"You think talking will give you some clarity about Walter? It won't. Nothing Theo tells you will. In fact, the more you dig into this, the messier it's going to get. Remember, I told you about the cop who killed my uncle? Well, years later, I tracked him down. He was working at some afterhours club in Harlem. And I actually expected him to explain why he shot my uncle. He looked at me like I was speaking a foreign language. Finally, he said he'd never given any thought to why he did it. He killed my uncle and was punished. That's all that mattered to anyone. So, he didn't see much point in thinking about why he'd done it."

"What's your point?" Muriel asked.

"Just that if you see Theo, you'll either be disappointed by his explanations or you'll find out things you wish you hadn't."

"That's a strange thing to say, coming from someone who studies history."

"I don't think so. I didn't become a historian to find out why things happen."

"Then why did you?"

"To know what's going to hit me before it does. And, if I'm lucky, to know when to duck."

"What about using history to eliminate the things that make you a target in the first place?" Muriel asked.

"You obviously haven't studied enough history."

"And you've become paralyzed by studying too much."

Muriel could feel herself perspiring and noticed sweat glistening from Raymond's hairline. They were both surprised that their argument had summoned up lust with the anger. They were almost out of breath without having moved.

When they'd first made love, Muriel was unable to take the full pleasure of herself and Raymond into her mouth and hands. There was always a reminder of the bloody taste and smell of Walter. But the excitement of arguing rekindled Muriel's readiness to allow passion to overtake her in the presence of someone willing to do the same.

They had stumbled across intensely held beliefs in each other, which they both found disagreeable. While Muriel and Raymond had different views of the world, they were also moved to look for flaws in the flesh. Rather than hurl their clothes about in a frantic rush for the bed, they undressed each other slowly, folding their clothes neatly and placing them on the sofa. It didn't take them long to find the blemishes they were looking for. Muriel licked a scar above Raymond's right eyebrow as his damp fingers tried to entice the reluctant nipple of her left breast. She whispered her thirst into his ear; and with a fully open mouth tasted his whiskey-soaked tongue. Craving the smell of what they disliked in one another, Muriel and Raymond trembled as they savored the funkiness of their sweat-washed skin.

MURIEL

1970

IT WAS INFURIATING SOMETIMES how Raymond challenged all explanations for why things happened in the world, whatever their source—especially if it was me. I couldn't understand why I felt so drawn to someone who wasn't particularly outraged when the U.S. sent troops into Cambodia or when the police and National Guard fired upon and killed student demonstrators at Jackson and Kent State. Unlike Raymond, I found it difficult to accept, that regardless of our best intentions, human beings continued to find resourceful ways to hurt one another. One would have thought this attitude would have made him cynical. However, I was more susceptible to the moodiness and despair brought on by these events. Raymond was able to take pleasure in a world he didn't expect would change very much for the better. In this respect, he reminded me a lot of Walter, who also accepted me as I was. Without realizing it, I became committed to not losing another man who wanted to keep me safe in spite of myself.

It made perfect sense to me that the only way to go on believing I could remake the world, and have a man in my life who didn't, was for us to get married.

RAYMOND

1970

I HAD NEVER MET ANYONE QUITE LIKE MURIEL—someone whose convictions burned even more fiercely when all the evidence suggested otherwise. At those moments, she would shrug and say *It's easy to refute what I'm saying when you're only interested in examining the basis for my argument and not your own."*

"Does that go for you too?" I would ask.

"Only if I'm wrong!"

I loved that Muriel could laugh at how ludicrous her response sounded and still defend it. Nothing I've learned from observing people up close or from a distance has helped me bring the meaning of events into sharper focus. Baseball has come closest to giving me the clarity I haven't found anywhere else. It's the only game where the team on the offensive doesn't have the ball or fate in their own hands. If I had to express my idea of the drama of being human that would be it. Because between the moment the pitcher throws the ball and the catcher prepares to receive it, anything can happen.

I couldn't help but envy how easy it was for Muriel to see all the way through the things she believed. They came out of her as a burst of light I couldn't imagine in myself. I saw the beaming light of an oncoming train. Muriel saw the dawn at the end of the dark night.

It didn't matter whether I believed what she said, most of which I didn't. What mattered was my need to protect in her what I could never find in myself.

MURIEL

1970

IT DIDN'T TAKE LONG for Theo's mysterious parting words to Lucius to become all too clear. In the wake of the police attacks against Push Comes to Shove and others, there were retaliatory acts and sniper fire that wounded several New York City police officers. Statements were sent to *Out In Left Field* and other major newspapers by groups calling themselves By Any Means Necessary and the Black Peoples' Liberation Army, who claimed responsibility for the shootings.

And then one evening, two cops, one white and the other black, were patrolling Mount Morris Park in Harlem not far from the brownstone where Walter was murdered. The newspaper accounts said two black males walked past the officers, turned, drew their weapons and shot them both in the back and continued firing into their fallen bodies before running off. The black cop was pronounced dead on the scene and the white cop died in the emergency room.

Within hours of the murders, a statement to UPI announced that the guerilla arm of Push Comes To Shove and The Grunt Collective was responsible for what they called the Peoples' Revolutionary Vengeance, carried out in retaliation for the murder of the revolutionary, Walter Armstead.

The statement also said that the police could expect the peoples' vengeance to continue for as long as law enforcement officials behaved like an occupying army, providing punishment instead of the protection of the law. The manifesto ended with some impassioned lines from the poem "If We Must Die," by Claude McKay:

> *Oh kinsmen! We must meet the common foe*
> *Though far outnumbered, let us show us brave*
> *And for their thousand blows deal one death blow*
> *Like men we'll face the murderous cowardly pack*
> *Pressed to the wall, dying but fighting back!*

There was no doubt in my mind that Theo wrote the statement. I was relieved that Lucius had gone underground. The whole city was a coiled serpent, bracing itself for an attack or waiting to strike back. The police stopped black men randomly and took them into custody for questioning. Thanks to Theo, Lucius would be at the top of the interrogation list. I wrote a piece in *Out In Left Field* about the harassment received by many black men I interviewed in the weeks following the police murders.

So I wasn't surprised to look up and see Detective Garrett standing in front of me as I ate a sandwich on a park bench during my lunch break. He held an ice cream cone but didn't eat it.

"I've been expecting you," I said.

"Glad to live up to your expectations."

He sat down beside me.

"Don't get too comfortable, Detective. I already know what you're going to ask me, so we can get this meeting over with very quickly."

"If I were you, I'd do everything possible to make me comfortable. In case you've forgotten, a word from me and you're serving your five years probation from inside a state prison."

"Is that what you threatened Theo with to get him to infiltrate Push Comes to Shove?"

How did you find out?" he asked.

"Through an acquaintance."

"That acquaintance wouldn't, by any chance, be Lucius Braxton?"

"I'd rather not say."

"What are you prepared to say—other than what you wrote last week about police harassment?"

"Not much, except that Theo said you gave him explosives to plant in our house, but he used it to bomb the police precinct instead."

"Well, Theo is a convicted felon with delusions of revolutionary grandeur. So I wouldn't put too much credence in whatever stories he told that acquaintance of yours."

"What've you got to say that's any more believable?"

"It's very simple. In order to avoid prosecution on several extortion charges, Theo agreed to become involved in Push Comes to Shove."

"But why did you choose him?" I asked.

"He's the kind of character who can convince himself and everyone else of just about anything. Obviously, he suckered both of us."

"Since you're here talking to me, does that mean you think he's behind the murder of the two cops killed in Mount Morris Park?"

"I think he's behind the rhetoric but not the murder. Basically, he's a half-ass actor in search of a stage."

"He may have become a better actor than you think," I said.

"If he is, that means I'm on the hook until I find him."

"Why don't you explain to your superiors that, unlike Theo, the black men they've ordered you to harass aren't interested in pretending to be assassins!"

"This isn't about race! It's about a group of hate-filled individuals who've declared open season on all cops. And as far as a bit of over-zealous questioning of black men by the police, if you had seen the bodies, you'd..."

"I don't need to see them! In case you forgot, I was in the bedroom when the police broke in and blew the face off Walter Armstead!"

I was so upset that I didn't realize I had mashed the sandwich inside my fist. Garrett stared at me with what looked like concern.

"The whole police force didn't kill your friend Armstead," he said, taking a bite of the ice cream cone.

"And all black men aren't responsible for the dead cops."

"Look, I know that. But because of these murders, detectives like me, who have informants working under cover in black militant groups, have to bring them in for briefings. I'm in the very embarrassing position of having the only informant who's been turned around. I'm under a lot of pressure, which means so are you."

"Are you aware that the cops who murdered Walter may have been out to get Theo instead?" I asked.

"There's no evidence to support that." Garrett's voice was empty of conviction.

"Why do I have the feeling that Theo may not be the only gifted actor I've had the chance to see in action?"

Garrett got up from the bench. His face stiffened with anger as he stared down at me.

"I don't think you really want to see me in action."

"What do you want from me?"

"You know what I want."

"I won't set him up."

"Just get me close enough, so I can talk to him, face to face."

"How am I supposed to do that?"

"You'll figure it out." Garrett finally took a big bite of the chocolate ice cream just starting to melt, then threw the rest in a garbage can as he walked away.

Garrett was right—I figured it out. I decided to do a series of articles on self-described black and white revolutionaries who were in jail or, if I could locate them, living underground. I hoped the series would get Theo's attention, since his craving for notoriety had compelled him to surface before. The editors liked the idea of putting a human face on individuals whose bombings, kidnappings and plane hijackings seemed without rhyme or reason to most Americans.

RAYMOND

1970

MURIEL AND I WERE MARRIED in a civil ceremony at City Hall with Naomi and Gerald acting as witnesses. Frank refused to come; he gave us his blessing but said that everything that had happened to him after pledging to serve his country made it impossible for him to ever participate in another oath-taking ceremony again. Even though we'd known each other less than a year, Muriel and I had become extremely close and felt strongly that our commitment to one another should be validated by law. We were well aware of the past and continuing violation of the spirit and letter of the law all around us. But Muriel had brought me around to admitting that I still believed in the rule of law, even while remaining skeptical of the protection it was supposed to provide. She also reminded me that we were the only ones sworn to uphold the pledge we were making under the law.

"You better be careful!" I said. "Someone's liable to accuse you of practicing law without a license."

"Well, they'd be wrong. The only thing I'm practicing is marriage. And now I have a license for that."

After the ceremony, Naomi and Gerald took us out to dinner to celebrate. I hadn't spent that much time around Gerald since our altercation. We kept up the appearance of friendliness whenever we met. But neither of us went out of our way to be friends apart from our connection to Muriel and Naomi. Most of the dinner conversation was taken up with Muriel's meeting with Detective Garrett.

"Do you think the D.A. knew about how the cops use people like Theo to infiltrate radical groups?" Muriel asked.

"Probably not," Naomi said. "Unless Garrett was making a case against Theo, there would be no reason to get the D.A.'s office involved. The less people knew about Theo, the more useful he'd be to the cops."

"Right now, I don't know which one of them was more truthful about their relationship," Muriel said.

"If I were you, I wouldn't waste time worrying about which one is telling the truth," I said. "What you should be concerned about is how you're going to get Theo to meet with Garrett."

"How much time is Garrett giving you?" Gerald asked.

"More than enough and too little," Muriel said.

"What do you mean?"

"No matter what I write, it could be quite a while before Theo tries to contact me. If that happens, Garrett may get impatient and decide to cut his losses by coming after me."

"Let's talk about something else," I said. "We're supposed to be celebrating!"

"You're right!" Naomi said. "I'd like to make a toast."

We raised our champagne glasses.

"To Muriel and Raymond! May your lives be full, using up all the time you have together and not saving any of it for a rainy day."

Naomi's remarks made us pause for a few seconds.

"Too bad Crystal isn't here," Muriel said. "She would probably perplex us even more by trying to explain what you just said."

"Speaking of Crystal," Naomi said. "She's been posing for Gerald."

"Are you working on a painting of her?" Muriel asked.

"No. I'm just doing some nude studies. My real project is a painting that attempts to capture the Jimi Hendrix Experience."

"I don't think I could do that," Muriel said.

"I'm not sure I can either, but it's doubt that's the challenge for an artist."

"No. I mean pose nude."

Irritation knitted Gerald's forehead.

"Have you ever posed for Gerald?" Muriel asked, looking at Naomi.

"No. He never asked me."

"You've never shown any interest in posing for me," Gerald said.

"You're right."

"Would you have done it if he wanted you to?" Muriel asked.

"Of course," Naomi said. "Wouldn't you, or are you too modest?"

I could see a muscle tensing in Gerald's jaw. I must say, I was enjoying watching him bristle as the conversation shifted away from his work.

"It's not modesty," Muriel said. "I'd just be concerned about how my body would look."

"It would look the way the artist sees you," Gerald said.

"That's exactly what I don't want—someone trying to define me."

"When an artist does it, it's different."

"In what way?" Muriel asked.

"As an artist, I'm not interested in defining anyone. It's my impressions of what I see that I'm after."

Muriel smiled. "Sounds like you want to take hold of something in people so you can play God."

"You're right. But unlike other people who do that, I'm not causing any harm, except, hopefully, to the powers that be."

"I'm just wondering what happens to us when we take ourselves that seriously."

"Muriel, I think you're confusing playing God with acting as though you are, which is what you and all your friends in Push Comes to Shove were doing."

"Well, honey," Naomi said, "there goes your disclaimer about the artist not causing any harm."

"That was the artist, baby, but not the art!"

"Okay," I said. "Why don't we have some more champagne while both our marriages are still intact."

That was the last time the four of us went out together. Although Muriel never said anything, I assumed she and Naomi decided their friendship was better off without Gerald and me around.

MURIEL

1970

MANY OF THE CLOSEST TIES I'VE HAD WITH PEOPLE have at some point been threatened and then destroyed by violence. It's not surprising that I thought violence might be a way for people to get back what had been taken from them. This belief led me to join Push Comes to Shove. But there was something else that attracted me. Like so many of the people I met when I worked in the South, Theo and Khadijah had convictions that poured out of them in torrents. And I felt at home in the company of all that passion, something Miss Mattie and Mister Percy were never able to give me. Even though Push Comes to Shove no longer functioned, its very name defined what had become a fact of life in an America at war with itself. Theo was still a combatant and I hoped it wouldn't be too long before I enticed him to come out of hiding.

My first article was on a woman named Imani Touré, who Naomi was representing in connection with one of the recent attempted murder cases of cops. She was a high-profile member of By Any Means Necessary and had made very inflammatory statements, calling on black people to use the only language the police were capable of understanding or respecting.

Touré was shrewd enough not to name the language directly, leaving it to her listeners at rallies to fill in the blank. She was being held at the Women's House of Detention in Greenwich Village. Once again, Naomi worked her magic, getting me permission to enter the prison and convincing Touré to talk to me.

My nerves were grinding in the pit of my stomach as I walked into the visiting room. I'd been on the other side of that bulletproof partition little more than a year before. I had just sat down when a woman I recognized from newspaper photographs came in. Her eyes leaped out at me instantly, I froze like deer in her headlights. The rest of her was less intimidating. With the exception of her head, crowned by short, frizzy hair and her bony hands and forearms, she seemed lost inside the baggy prison-issue clothing. When

I picked up the phone on my side, she was already talking.

"...but I'm not quite sure."

"What aren't you sure about?" I asked.

"Whether I should've agreed to talk to you."

"Maybe I should tell you a little about myself."

"I know who you are."

I smiled and was reminded of my first meeting with Naomi.

"I say something funny?" she asked.

"No. I'm just glad that you agreed to the interview."

"Good for you. But just because I know about you doesn't mean I want to talk to you."

"Then why did you agree to see me?"

"So I could make up my mind."

"What can I do to help?"

She bristled and sat up straight. "It's that kind attitude that bothers me. It's like you're looking in on trouble from outside of it. You of all people should know better than that! After watching the police blow Walter Armstead's brains all over your bedroom, you oughta know that our people will always be in trouble in this country until we take the fight to the troublemakers!"

"Do you think it's a fight that can be won?" I asked.

"What do you think?"

"If you decide to let me write a story on you, people will read it because they want to know what you think. What I think isn't important."

Imani leaned in closer, touching the partition with her forehead. "It's important to me," she said.

"No. I don't think it can. Do you?"

"I know you have your own reasons for wanting to do a piece on me," she said. "But if I agree to let you do this story, it's because I feel you're really interested in what I have to say. Since all this shooting back and forth between black folks and the police started, not many of my brothers-in-struggle have been interested in listening to my opinions on anything. So when someone finally wants to hear what I have to say, it turns out to be two women, first Naomi and now you."

"Does that surprise you?" I asked.

"Yeah. And that surprises me even more."

"Well, now that I have the element of surprise on my side, how about answering my question about the struggle."

She waited for a long moment, savoring her answer. "I agree with you," she said finally. "I don't think a guerrilla war against the police can be won. But it's really not about winning as much as it's about forcing the cops to consider paying the price with their own lives if they continue treating our communities with disrespect."

"Does that mean you're in favor of guerrilla tactics like the ambushing of the two policemen in Mount Morris Park?"

"Ah, there it is! That's a reporter's predictable trick question. You disappoint me, Muriel."

"Like it or not, it's a question I have to ask."

"And like it or not," she said, obviously enjoying herself, "the only answer I can give is that I believe, as Malcolm did, that if your thought pattern changes, then a change in your behavior will follow."

"And of course, that change in behavior must be brought about..."

She nodded her head, anticipating where I was going, "...by any means necessary!" she said.

We both laughed and Imani seemed surprised by the sound. She lowered her head slightly, averting her eyes from me. When she looked up again, I saw fear.

"You know, when people told me that the legendary Muriel Pointer had turned in her terrible swift sword for a typewriter, I didn't want to believe it."

"Do you believe it now?"

"I know that those of us who looked up to you have problems with you putting your doubts out there in everything you write, for everyone to see."

"But they're mine and no one else's."

"You're not talking to yourself when what you say reaches thousands of people. That's more than the rest of us can."

"But what could I possibly write that would be of value to those men you said are no longer interested in what you have to say?"

"It would be different with you," Imani said. "In Push Comes to

Shove, you and Theodore Sutherland raised the bar for what was permissible when responding to the power of the state. And with Sutherland underground, the hope was that you would continue in his absence."

"Well, if I'm to believe what I read, Theo and the rest of you seem to have done quite well raising the bar without me."

"We've raised it all right, but may not have left ourselves any place to go except over a cliff. Or turn on ourselves. It's already started. People arrested are accusing each other of betrayal and cutting their own deals with the D.A."

"What are you going to do, Imani?"

"Try to get out of here without betraying myself or anyone else. And I want you to finish this interview as soon as possible."

"Why?"

"I can't afford the luxury you have on that side of the glass of thinking out loud about what I don't know. If I'm going to come out of here with any sanity, I need to project arrogance and not ignorance, just like the brothers have been doing."

"You could say that arrogance is just a cover for the other," I said.

"Maybe from where you sit. But from where I am, it feels like survival."

"Still want me to write the article?"

"As long as you don't try to get me to reveal things I'm uncertain about."

"All right. But you'd come across much better if you did."

"Muriel, at the moment, I don't have the slightest interest in your idea of what would be better for me."

•••••

After I left the Women's House of Detention, I went to see Naomi at her office.

"Imani reminds me a lot of you," Naomi said.

"How's that?"

"The way you deal with fear. You both move toward it."

"Well, how do you intend to keep her away from her fear of a lifetime residency, paid for by the State of New York?"

"It depends on who the police informants have targeted as having conspired to murder specific police officers. She says she never had any private conversations with anyone about killing any cops. If she's telling the truth, then somebody may be implicating her to save themselves. Or she's part of a clean sweep of the leadership that the D.A. ordered, hoping to destroy the organization, even if he can't convict everybody who's indicted. It's not clear yet. So how did the interview go?"

"Imani's making it hard for me to portray her in a sympathetic light. She refuses to reveal anything about herself beyond rhetoric."

"Brace yourself! There may not be much more than that to get."

"I don't believe that."

"Maybe not, but some of the people I'm defending from By Any Means Necessary are off the charts with this death dance they're doing with the police. And the police and the F.B.I. are worse. I consider myself a committed radical. But the Feds and some of these local law enforcement people have an intimacy with radical movements that I can't begin to approach. Look at this thing between Theo and Garrett. They're like jilted lovers and each has convinced himself that he's the injured party."

"Speaking of injured parties," I said, "I'm sorry about my part in that little row you had with Gerald at my wedding dinner."

"Don't worry, we'll get over it."

"So you're not over it."

"We haven't figured out what it is yet. Seems like we both have an itch of some kind. Of course, the obvious thing to do is scratch, but that hasn't made it go away."

"Maybe it shouldn't be scratched at all," I said.

"You may be right."

"Have you and Gerald ever thought about having children?"

Naomi put her elbow on the desk and made a cradle of her hand, then rested her chin in it, a cliché of thoughtfulness. "Oh Muriel. How is it that someone who wants to remake the world can be so remarkably predictable?"

"I just asked a question!"

"We've thought about having children but that's not the source of the itch."

"Are you saying that you and Gerald don't want children?"

"I know you're a very busy person, Muriel. But have you ever actually looked at our lives? Gerald's paintings are the only offspring he's got room for in his life. And mine are right here on my desk—case records, legal briefs and appeals. Whatever's going on with us, not having children ain't it."

"So if children aren't the problem, is it the race thing?" I asked, unable to stop the words from coming out of my mouth.

Naomi rolled her eyes. "This is what friends are for?"

I kept quiet, knowing she wasn't interested in having me answer her question.

"To say our problem is Gerald's being black by way of Baltimore, South Carolina and who knows where in Africa and me being a sometimes not-so-nice Jewish girl from the Bronx and the daughter of Russian immigrants would be like complaining about the weather. I'm sorry to disappoint you, Muriel. But don't worry! The instant I know what the trouble is, you'll be the first person I tell."

"I didn't mean to badger you."

"Oh yes you did!"

"Yeah, that's what friends do."

"Think our husbands will get there?"

"Doesn't look like it."

"Do you have any idea what it's about?" she asked.

"No. Raymond says they just don't click."

"Gerald said the same thing. When I pressed him about it, he got pissed and accused me of trying to get the two of them together just because they're both black."

This time I kept my mouth shut.

"Well?" Naomi said.

"What?"

"You don't have anything to say?"

"No!"

"But you're *thinking!*"

"If it pleases your grace, I am entitled to do that, am I not? Or has the distinguished jurist from the Bronx decreed to do my thinking for me?"

"All right! It's just that they're two very intelligent men and it would have been nice if they could've become friends."

"I guess that's their loss," I said.

"And our gain."

"How's that?"

"We get to have them and each other!"

"Yeah, I guess we do," I said.

RAYMOND

1970

I LOVED THE WAY the substance of my days thickened as I got used to moving in and around the same space with Muriel. Whether it was navigating around our different work schedules, cooking (which I did most of), cleaning the apartment, doing laundry, making love, arguing, getting on each others nerves, leaving one another alone while we did our own work or just not wanting to talk, I was enlivened by all of it! I even enjoyed the aggravation of having too much to do and not enough time to do it in.

I had made a world with Muriel; it was chaotic but intact, something the turbulent events outside our apartment couldn't give me. I didn't think it could get any better than this until Muriel began complaining of exhaustion and not being able to hold down any solid food without throwing up. She chalked it up to a stomach virus brought on by overwork and hoped more bed rest would take care of it. It was apparent that the middle-aged, church-going black couple who raised Muriel gave her what they had to give, but not what they couldn't. That evening before Muriel and I went to bed, I broke the news to her that she might be pregnant.

•••••

I hadn't seen very much of Frank lately, so I went by his apartment to do a little crowing about the contribution Muriel and I would soon be making to the population of New York City.

"Well, I have to give Muriel a lot of credit," Frank said, while restringing one of his electric guitars.

"Why's that?"

"She's given you the opportunity to make history in the only way you ever will."

"I'll take that in the perverse spirit in which good wishes from you usually come."

"I think it's the ultimate WOW, myself," Crystal said from a yoga position on the floor.

"Crystal, you are the one person living in this apartment whose good cheer doesn't come across like you're asking me to take out the trash."

"Hey, you never know what you're liable to find in the trash," Frank chimed in. "Just because it's used don't mean it has to be refused."

"I know. That's how you outfitted your cafe." I said.

"Maybe..." Crystal said, breathing in deeply, "trash is the stuff that dreams used to be made of."

"You got it, babe! And even though they're a little messed up, at the Far Out, I can sell dreams to you wholesale."

"Frank, you make P.T. Barnum sound like a shill who's lost his touch," I said, bowing in mock reverence to the master.

"Thank you, thank you. But please be seated. I stray a bit from my customary humility when people stand for too long in my presence."

Frank gestured with his hand in the direction of a chair and I pushed him, playfully, as I sat down.

"All kidding aside, Raymond. I hope you know I think it's great that you and Muriel are having a kid."

"Who knows. Maybe it might become contagious?" I said with a wink.

His eyes cut into me as if I'd threatened him. Ever since returning from Vietnam, he'd sometimes have bizarre mood swings that came without warning.

"Not me," he said, still staring at me. "Kids mean you have to believe in the future."

"What's wrong with the future?"

"Nothing! Bring it on! Just don't ask me to believe in it!"

"Well, believe it or not, but the future definitely had you in mind because it brought you back from the bad boonies."

"That wasn't the fuckin' future! That was me and the guys who had each other's back, rolling the dice in our hide-and-go-seek with the VC and hoping we'd never crap out."

He was shaking.

"I'm sorry, Frank. I didn't mean to upset you."

"If you didn't mean it, then why the fuck did you say it?"

"Crystal! How do you live with this guy?" I said, trying to lighten things up a bit.

"It ain't about how she lives with me," Frank said. "It's how I live with myself."

I started to say something but decided against it, hoping Frank's mood would pass more easily with silence.

Crystal sat motionless, her eyes closed, legs crossed and each foot resting on the opposite thigh. After several seconds, she opened her eyes.

"Is it okay, Frank, if I tell you what I think about you in front of Raymond?"

"Say whatever you think you need to say."

"You're like my name, Frank. And you're broken in so many places, there's no way to seal up all the cracks to put you back together the way you were before. And that's what's hurting you more than being broken, that no matter what, you can't be like you used to be. I think if you could let go of yourself and not try to hold on so tight, then much more of what's hurting could get out. It's still going to hurt a lot when it comes out but the pain'll be much worse if it stays inside. I don't know much about the future, Frank. But right now, I feel like you're a fist; but I believe there's a future inside you trying to pry that fist open so you can become an outstretched hand."

I didn't know that Crystal had stopped speaking until I heard Frank move. As he walked slowly toward her, there was a blankness in his eyes that made him look half-asleep. He stood in front of her and extended his arms to pull her up from the floor. He then released her and opened his right hand.

Crystal smiled. Then Frank slapped her across the face.

"Well, babe, there's the fuckin' future! Hurts, doesn't it?"

Crystal had no reaction except to touch her cheek gently with her hand.

"What the fuck's the matter with you Frank? Have you lost your mind?"

"I've been trying to, but it keeps coming back."

Crystal raised her hand as a sign for me not say anymore. She picked up her coin purse from a chair and walked out of the apartment. In frustration, I made a lunge at Frank and he shoved me away.

"If you come at me again, I'm gonna have to turn back into a fist."

His words sounded almost like a plea for me not to push him any further than he had already gone on his own. I left him looking down at the palms of his hands. I caught up with Crystal about a half a block from the building and we stepped into a nearby coffee shop.

"Are you okay?" I asked.

"I'll be all right."

"Has he ever hit you before?"

"Not like that."

"What do you mean?"

"He has a hard time letting me touch him. And sometimes he gets angry."

"I've known Frank a long time and I never known him to be like what I just saw."

"I know Frank's your friend, Raymond. But I live with him. You don't have to cover for him in front of me."

"I'm not saying I've never seen him get angry before."

"Frank's trying the best he knows how."

"What are you going to do?" I asked.

"About what?"

"I mean, are you going to stay with him?"

"If he wants me to...I feel a lot of things, Raymond. But Frank does things; and he helps me believe I could do things, too."

"What if he hits you again?"

"Then I'll leave."

"Where're you from, Crystal?"

She tilted her head up slightly as though trying to recall.

"I sometimes think that in a past life I..."

"I mean in this life."

"You probably think I'm pretty dizzy, don't you?"

"No! I think you're...different."

"I'm from Lake Ronkonkoma. You know, on Long Island. You ever been there?"

"No. I can't say I ever have."

"It's a place that's not quite white bread, but more like rye."

I nodded as though I understood the distinction.

"Crystal's not the name I was born with. It was Millicent. But I never felt like that was really the name for me. When I first saw a piece of crystal, I didn't know what it was called. But seeing myself reflected in it told me that it was something I could hold on to that might tell me who I was every time I looked into it."

"I see what you mean...You know I've been meaning to ask you how it's been working out, posing for Gerald?"

"Oh!" she said, her back straightening. "That's been just beyond real! I mean I sit there without moving and every once in a while Gerald asks me to shift positions. And then he tells me to do it natu-rally without him having to ask. And I feel the pulse at every pres-sure point in my body...And that's how the drawings look when Gerald shows them to me. It's like he's captured my whole body breathing."

"What does Frank think about all this?"

"He likes it that I'm doing something I enjoy. He's come to Gerald's studio with me a few times. They seem to get along pretty well."

"Oh! They do?"

"Yeah, they've become kind of drinking buddies."

I could feel a blood vessel in my neck throbbing. "So it doesn't bother you having someone you don't know that well studying you while you're naked?"

"Not really. But it would bother me if someone I didn't know was studying me while I was naked and I didn't know they were doing it...That's sort of what historians do, isn't it? But you do it to both the living and the dead."

"Like I said, Crystal, you're different."

MURIEL

1970

WELL, IF I LIKED TO SWEAT, having this child promised to give me all the perspiration I could handle. I was reminded of my craving for physical touch as a child, which only increased after my parents were killed. I came to feel that I needed some expression of affection, whether an arm around my shoulder or a hug. I realize now that what drew me to the South were the photographs and TV coverage of civil rights workers linking arms at church rallies and holding onto one another when they were attacked by mobs. I found myself gravitating toward groups of people under threat who offered comfort to one another. I didn't believe this need could be satisfied in any other way. But now my desire for closeness and touching was being fulfilled through something coming only from me. And I wasn't in any immediate danger! So when I felt that first surge of life, it was as though my childhood outcry over the loss of the two who made me, was finally being answered by the life I was making. And my wail grew fainter the more the child within me churned.

•••••

Other than Raymond, the person I most wanted to share my pregnancy with was Khadijah. The last time we spoke, she mentioned a move to another apartment. Not wanting to lose contact with her, I insisted, over her mild attempts at secrecy, that she give me the new address, in the West 80s near Riverside Drive. The weather was balmy for October, so we decided to sit in the park. Khadijah's mood was the best I'd remembered since before the police raided our brownstone. She was taking midwifery classes and offered all kinds of advice.

"Go easy on the spicy food if you're feeling nauseous. Whole wheat toast and apricot nectar helps."

"I want you there when I deliver."

"I won't be fully accredited by then."

"I want you there anyway. I haven't forgotten what you said about deciding to become a midwife. Your wanting to be more connected to life at its beginning is something I've thought about a lot since I got pregnant."

"How's Raymond taking it?"

"He's more excited than I am."

"Hope he can keep that enthusiasm going after the birth."

"I was wondering if you'd lost that whiplash of yours when men come into the conversation."

"I like Raymond."

"Which is high praise coming from you."

"What can I tell you? I didn't invent the shit men do."

"So what are you doing when you're not studying?" I asked.

"I'm working with a support group for poor women and women who are political prisoners at the Women's House of Detention."

"Did you read the piece I did on Imani Touré in *Out In Left Field?*"

"Yeah. She's one of the women this group I'm working with is trying to help."

"I thought you'd given up on groups."

"I have. But I haven't given up on people."

"Do you know Imani?"

"Not very well."

"What do you think of her?" I asked.

"I think—like some other people we know—she lets her rhetoric get ahead of her common sense."

"She seems to think that's a price we should be willing to pay."

Khadijah put her hand on my stomach and rubbed it gently. "I can't pay it anymore. And I don't believe you can either, especially now."

"The thing is, I'm still entangled with people who are," I said.

"Like?"

"Theo, of course."

"I'm not following you."

"That Detective Garrett has threatened to have my probation revoked unless I help him to draw Theo out of hiding."

"How're you supposed to do that?"

"Well, he did get in touch with Naomi after the piece I did on the Grunt Collective. I'm hoping this series I'm doing on radicals like Imani will make Theo want to contact me about doing a profile on him. He likes that kind of attention."

"You're going to help the police bust him?"

"I told Garrett I won't do that."

Khadijah shook her head. "Do you think what you want and don't want really matters to Garrett? He'll use you to bust, or more likely, kill Theo whether you think you're helping him or not."

"If he tries to reach me, I can have Naomi warn Theo about Garrett. Then if he decides to meet with me it, at least he knows the situation."

"Theo and Garrett are opposite sides of the same coin. I wouldn't want to be caught between them."

"Not much else I can do."

"I guess not."

"Whatever Theo decides to do, it won't take him very long."

•••••

I was right about the wait not being long, but not about what was coming. I heard the news on WBAI, a leftist radio station that I listened to constantly. A special tactical police unit had trapped the Grunt Collective where the subway lines converged below Houston Street. The city discontinued train and bus service in lower Manhattan and streets were sealed off to pedestrians and all traffic. The police were evacuating buildings in the area. Soon after the first news report, Raymond arrived home from teaching. He'd already heard what had happened. We stared at the radio transfixed, listening to sketchy details about the negotiations between the police and the Collective. Our radio vigil was interrupted by a call from Naomi, wanting to know if we'd heard the news and saying she was coming right over.

"What've you heard?" I said, when Naomi arrived.

"The police have them surrounded in the underground tunnel where they've been holed up for hours. I'm not sure what they're being charged with but it's related to the cop killings in Mount Morris Park."

"Damn, Theo!" I said.

"Are Braxton and the other vets armed?" Raymond asked.

"Probably," Naomi said. "But it wouldn't matter with the siege mentality the police have adopted. I talked to some of my contacts in the D.A.'s office and offered to represent the Collective in the negotiations. But they told me no one else gets near them until they surrender."

"What do you think it'll take to get them to come out?" I asked.

"Maybe they don't want out," Raymond said. "Remember? They refused to come out of that building when the threat was much less than it is now."

The radio coverage continued with live interviews on the scene but no new developments. The telephone rang and Raymond answered it.

"Hello...who's calling?" He covered the receiver with his hand. "It's for you, Muriel. It's Detective Garrett."

I took a deep breath, as I got up to take the phone.

"Yes...So I've heard...You've spoken to him...All right...I'll be there as soon as I can," I said, hanging up the phone.

"What do you mean, you'll be there!" Raymond said.

"Lucius says he won't talk to anyone else until I meet with him."

"You can't agree to that! They'll use you as a hostage. Garrett must know that."

"Lucius won't do that. He just wants to talk with me."

"About what? His last will and testament!"

"I'm going, Raymond. And I want you and Naomi to come with me."

"Think, Muriel! You have no idea what you're walking into or what Braxton's state of mind is!"

"I owe it to Lucius. What I wrote is partly responsible for bringing him to the attention of the police and Theo."

"But you're not responsible for what he's done!"

"It's very risky, Muriel," Naomi said. "These situations can go bad really fast."

"I know. But I have to go."

"What about us and our child? Are you willing to jeopardize it all for this group of fucking kamikazes!"

Whenever we argued like this, Raymond fought for me as well as with me. I loved him so much at that moment that I almost gave in.

"I don't want to fight with you, Raymond. I'm going. You can come or not."

"This is fucked up! And so are you!"

He didn't say anymore but picked up his house keys and stood at the front door. We left the apartment and were greeted by the swell of noise and people hanging out of windows and packed along the sidewalks. Horns blared from cars hip-hugging their way up 8th Avenue. All traffic, we were told, was being diverted at 14th Street and redirected north from 1st to 12th Avenues up as far as 57th Street. We wended our way south through the carnival-like atmosphere along 8th Avenue. Street vendors had moved their carts into the vicinity of 14th Street, peddling everything from gyros to Grunt Collective t-shirts. The street talk was ripe with rumor and opinions on how the showdown could be solved.

"I've heard those vets have booby-trapped the entire subway system. They've threatened to blow it up unless they're allowed to live permanently below street level in an area away from the subway lines."

"Hey, I say *give 'em what they want*. And if they know the subway system so well, let them run it. Couldn't be no worse."

"That's not what I heard. The word I got is that they took some people from the Veteran's Administration hostage and won't release them until they get benefits for every vet."

"Hey, I say agree to whatever they want. Then kill em! All of em! That's the only way to deal with people who wanna go one-on-one with the U.S. of A., whether it's here or in fuckin' Vietnam!"

When we got to the police command post at 14th Street, I gave my name and told the officers that Detective Garrett was expecting me. They told us to wait behind the police barricades with the throngs of people pressing in behind us. Raymond hadn't said a word to me since we'd left the apartment. I glanced up at him but he refused to look at me. I felt Naomi press against me and squeeze my arm. Another officer approached the one I'd spoken to, and after talking with him briefly, walked over to us.

"Miss Pointer, come with me please."

He moved the barricade aside for me to pass through, but blocked Raymond and Naomi.

"Sorry, you two can't go beyond this point."

"This is my husband and my lawyer," I said. "I want them with me when I speak to Detective Garrett or I don't go any further."

He hesitated and then let them through. We were led through a sea of uniformed and plainclothes police to a huge trailer. We went in and saw Garrett seated inside.

"I appreciate you coming down here, Miss Pointer."

"What do you want me to do, Detective?"

"Like I told you over the phone, Braxton wants to talk with you. He refused to tell us why. He respects you. We were hoping you might be able to, at least, get him to start talking with our negotiating team again."

"What kind of risks will my wife be taking?" Raymond asked.

"Our assault team tells us they're heavily armed."

"And you're asking her to walk into that?"

"It's her choice."

"But you can't guarantee her safety."

"No. I can't."

"I'll do it," I said.

"Muriel!"

"Raymond! I said I'm going to do it."

Fuming, he left the trailer, slamming the door behind him.

"So. What now?" I asked.

"We'll contact the assault team and Braxton to let them know you're coming down."

Garrett, Naomi and I left the trailer. I looked around for Raymond and saw him not far away with his head down, pacing beside another police van.

"I'll be right back," Garrett said.

"I hope your instincts about Lucius are right," Naomi said.

"So do I."

I glanced back over toward Raymond, who was deliberately not looking in my direction.

"You can't blame him for being upset," Naomi said.

"I don't. I just hope he doesn't stay angry for too long. He doesn't handle being upset very well."

"You ready?" Garrett said.

"Guess so."

Naomi and I hugged and I gave a little wave to Raymond just as he glanced over at me. Garrett and I walked west on Houston toward Varick Street, deserted except for police in bullet-proof vests, carrying assault rifles. I could feel a heightening of tension around me as we left the roar from the huge crowds behind us. We walked down the empty street, evacuated warehouses on either side of us.

"I thought it was Theo you were after," I said.

"I still am. But our interest in the Grunt Collective increased once they issued that statement, you know, the one implicating them in the murder of the two cops in Mount Morris Park. And the higher-ups in the department didn't look good when these blacks disappeared without a trace into subway tunnels. That's why we're committed to finding them."

At Varick and Hudson, armed police crouched behind patrol cars and panel trucks at both ends of the block. Shooters on roofs and in warehouse windows aimed down at a solitary sewer cover in the street.

"How'd you find out they were here?" I asked.

"I was wondering whether this was the same area where you met Braxton after he disappeared."

"What are you talking about?"

"I was just curious...Don't worry, he wasn't being sought when you met with him...But to answer your question—You forget, I served in Vietnam too and know a little something about tunnels myself..." Garrett gave a thin smile. "Well, enough fun and games. This is it. Last chance to change your mind, Muriel."

"I haven't changed my mind."

"All right. Whatever else you talk with Braxton about, you have to make him understand that he and his buddies can walk away from this. And by walk away, I mean they're going to do some jail time for creating this reckless extravaganza. But they won't have to give up their lives. I know they didn't kill those cops. But they're gonna have to get jerked around as though they did until the folks who run the show feel like they're back in charge. The same thing happened to you, Imani Touré and now the Grunt Collective."

I nodded.

"Braxton has got to understand that it ends here! No trains, buses, boats or planes are going to take him and his crew somewhere in exchange for you or anyone else. There's only one move for them to make—come out unarmed, and give up their freedom for a while in order to have it for the rest of their lives. Checkmate!"

"I'm ready, Detective," I said.

Garrett walked me through the fortifications at the corner of Varick to the sewer. He stamped on the cover and another cop with a crowbar pried it off. A cop helped me onto the rusty iron rungs that led down into the hole. Just as I reached the bottom, the cover was replaced.

"Come this way, Muriel," someone said in the darkness, not far away. "Follow...the...sound...of...my...voice."

I moved carefully in the dark toward the voice. After going a short distance, the space in front of me glowed with the crisscrossed beams of flashlights. And there, lit by shafts of light, I saw Lucius and six other men, dressed for combat and cradling automatic rifles. They sat in a semi-circle. Stacked in a corner were several canvas satchels.

"Sorry to have gotten you into this mess, Muriel," Lucius said. "But we all agreed you were someone we could trust."

"I don't know what I've done to earn your trust."

"You let us tell our story without trying to do it for us," one of the men said.

"Since we got back in the World," another said, "people seem more interested in how they feel than how we're doing."

"Yeah," a third shouted, "Some wanted us home with honor. Others said they wanted us home period! But what difference does it make? All them people up on the streets is the most attention we've got since we came back."

"Maybe my articles started all the trouble," I said.

Lucius smiled. "Any trouble we're in started long before then."

"What can I do to help?" I asked.

"First, tell us what's going on up on the street," Lucius said.

"The block is completely surrounded and apparently they've got assault units down here blocking off the tunnels."

"That's what we've been told. From the sound of their voices, they're only about twenty meters from here."

"There's a Detective Garrett who you know about from Theo. He seems to be one of the people in charge. He says he doesn't believe you killed those cops, so you're only looking at the jail time for the trouble you've caused down here. He wanted me to tell you that there's nothing to discuss except how you're going to surrender."

"Did he say how much jail time?"

"No."

"Any time in jail is too much," one of the men said.

"Heard that," Lucius said. He leaned closer to me.

"This Garrett. Do you know if he was in the war?"

"He says he was."

"That figures."

"Why?"

"Some folks land on their feet. Others land any way they can."

"Muriel Pointer!" a voice called from a distance not too far from where we were.

"Yes!" I yelled back.

"Are you all right?"

"I'm fine!"

"Muriel, we want you to do us a favor," Lucius said.

"If I can."

He handed me a small leather pouch.

"Inside are some personal items we'd like you to hold on to for safekeeping until we're released. Or not."

"Is there anything else?"

"What about it, grunts?" Lucius called back to the others.

"What time is it?" one of them asked.

"The only time!" they all shouted back in unison.

"You can tell Garrett that we'll be ready to surrender as soon you get back up there," Lucius said. "This circus is leaving town."

Rising, they trained their flashlights around and gathered the satchels, their weapons and other gear in a pile.

"Miss Pointer is leaving!" Lucius shouted down the tunnel. Then turned to me. "It meant a lot to us that you came."

Not knowing I would do it until the second I did, I threw my arms around his neck, holding him tightly.

"Hey, this isn't goodbye," he said. "You're keeping that pouch for us, remember?"

He pulled away from me.

"You should go on up now. Do you remember me telling you what Theo said to me right before he left us?"

"No I don't."

"Don't worry. It'll come to you."

Lucius trained the flashlight ahead of me so I could see my way to the iron-rung ladder. Before turning to follow the beam, I saw the other men sit around the pile of weapons and combat gear, cross their legs and bow their heads, as if in prayer. The cover to the hole was removed and I climbed up the ladder to the street.

Garrett was pacing nervously when I reached him.

"Well, you took long enough...Are they coming out or not?"

"Yes. Lucius told me to tell you that they want to have a few minutes to themselves before surrendering."

"What are they doing down there?"

"Praying."

"What the fuck for? They're going to jail, not to church...What's that you got there?"

"Oh, some personal items they wanted me to keep for them."

"Let me see!"

I handed him the pouch. He opened it up and pulled out a tangle of dog tags and chains.

"Oh shit!" Garrett yanked the walkie-talkie from inside the patrol car. "I want everybody out of the tunnels now! That's right! Get the fuck out of there!"

Then he grabbed my arm and pulled me away while yelling to other officers, "Get everybody out of this area! It's gonna blow!"

We stumbled in slow motion. We didn't get very far before a thunderous rumble from under the streets shook the block, throwing us to the ground. Sewer covers flew out of their holes and then slammed back down on the street with a dull gong. Dazed, I got up slowly and saw water suddenly burst through the sidewalk a half a block away, gushing up in geysers. Then I remembered what Theo had said to Lucius: *Look for me in the whirlwind or the storm. Look for me all around you!*

•••••

When I reached out and held Lucius, my body must have known what my mind refused to admit. Once again, violence had rushed in to claim someone dear to me. It took all night and part of the next day for the bomb squad and rescue workers to thoroughly examine the site for more explosives, clear away the debris and retrieve the seven bodies. There were injuries to several police in the assault units but none were serious. Garrett explained to me later that the Grunt Collective used explosives packed into satchels, each one having the power of a grenade. Lucius learned to make them from the Viet Cong. But the Collective had constructed the bomb packs to have a reduced impact, causing damage to a much smaller, concentrated area. It was as though they had performed their version of self-immolation, like Buddhist monks in Vietnam. In a way, the Collective had followed Garrett's ultimatum to surrender. But rather than giving themselves over to the temporary confinement in this life, they chose eternity.

The families of the seven black men claimed their bodies and had private funeral services. There was some opposition from the VFW to requests by three of the families to have their sons buried in military cemeteries, but ultimately the wishes of the bereaved prevailed. I went to a memorial service for the Grunt Collective organized by a few local Vietnam veterans groups in New York, which Frank had been instrumental in bringing together. During the quietly moving ceremony, one veteran stood up and said the men of the Collective had been trained as hounds to go off to protect the flock from the wolves, only to return home and be set upon by the flock.

Afterwards, I met the families of the men. I gave them the dog tags entrusted to me by Lucius. His mother thanked me for being a friend to her son but wanted me to have his dog tags, adding that after what the war had done to him, keeping the dog tags would be too painful.

My role in the tragic events between Varick and Hudson Streets earned me notoriety that varied depending on which part of the political spectrum was judging me. To some, I was the missing link in the effort to build bridges between the left, the anti-war movement and returning Vietnam veterans. To others, I was a lapsed revolutionary, turned ambulance-chasing journalist and police informant. I refused all interviews, making the article I was obligated to write for *Out In Left Field* the largest selling issue in its history, which fueled even more speculation about my real agenda.

I got heat from Raymond and my friends for what I did and didn't do. And throughout the immediate aftermath of the deaths of the Grunt Collective, the only person who left me alone was Detective Garrett. But I knew, soon after most of these others finished the meal they'd made of me, he would be back as usual for the feast. And I had to admit, I was looking forward to it.

RAYMOND

1970

MURIEL WASN'T HURT but I was furious with her for putting herself and our baby at risk. I was surprised when she refused to come back at me, like she usually did, when we argued. She absorbed all my attacks, passively admitting her thoughtlessness. Her silence was very disappointing, since she had been the one who convinced me that arguments were healthy and didn't have to end with either of us beaten and battered to within an inch of destroying our love. Muriel seemed to have retreated into some inner sanctum of grief for Lucius that kept my rebukes and attempts to comfort her at bay.

She was in her fourth month of pregnancy and I began to worry. I tried to rally Naomi to help out. She did what she could but was often tied up with more cases involving activists. There was Khadijah, of course. I had avoided calling her since she was usually distant and not particularly friendly. But when Muriel became pregnant, they were drawn even closer together.

I was desperate for someone who could help Muriel out of her deep funk. I called and another woman answered the phone. When Khadijah got on the line, she was aloof at first but gradually echoed my concern that Muriel's health and the well-being of the baby might be jeopardized unless she was able to snap out of it. Khadijah agreed to come over to see Muriel in the next day or two.

•••••

I was interested in the possible repercussions after the Grunt Collective deaths. Their story was covered internationally and triggered a rash of bombings of banks around the country, particularly those heavily invested in Third World countries, as well as induction centers in federal office buildings where draft records were kept. These bombings were carried out at night when the buildings were empty. But in cases where security guards and janitors were present, calls were made to alert the building or the police. Sabotage is not an exact science. On a number of occasions, warnings arrived too late or were not taken seriously and people were injured. And in one instance, a man working late was killed.

In the midst of the bombings, I was asked to participate in a symposium on "The Use of History in a Time of Political Turmoil" at the New School. During my remarks, I pointed out that events were occurring with such dizzying velocity that it made sense to pause and examine political action in light of how people behaved under similar circumstances in the past. A black man in the audience rose from his seat and interrupted me.

"Since you're a professor of history, you should know that Lenin said that *it's more useful to go through the experience of revolution than to write about it.*"

"Lenin knew what he was talking about," I said. "While he was writing in Switzerland, he almost missed the revolution."

"Is that supposed to be a joke?"

"No. I was merely doing what we all need to do more of, which is to look at the circumstances."

"Yeah, well I'm looking at *the circumstances* in which you said what you just said. To me, it all adds up to you being a petty bourgeois Negro aspiring to be bourgeois!"

"If that's true, then it's my problem. Isn't it?"

"No, my ideologically uncultivated brother! It's not just your problem! It's mine 'cause you're in my way!"

I moved to the side of the podium, stood tall and brought my arm down across my body in a flamboyant arc worthy of a matador as I said, "Olé!" Scattered laughter broke out in the auditorium but not from the man it was directed at.

"Sure, I'll get bullish on you, motherfucker," he said, rushing the podium.

Fortunately, others restrained him.

Shaken by the whole incident, I walked to Frank and Crystal's apartment. He had made up with her and our short-lived confrontation seemed to have been settled by neither of us bringing it up. Like planning events at the Far Out, organizing the memorial for the Grunt Collective had given Frank something to channel his anger into. If the war gave him anything besides the camaraderie he shared with other vets, it was the ability to be at his best in a crisis. The absence of the war's life and death intensity was harder for him to handle.

Frank was alone when I arrived. Crystal was at a dance class and he was feeling a little stir-crazy, since he hadn't left the apartment all day. We hit the streets. The Lower East Side below 14th Street had a grunginess and under-the-arms ripeness that set it apart from the rest of the Village. The streets didn't breathe as much as heave with an urgency that wanted to do everything at once. But I'd sensed a change in recent years. The buoyancy capable of lifting possibility beyond skyscraper heights had fallen to earth. Now people moved as though stun-gunned by dreams that had turned into boomerangs, hitting them right between the eyes.

Everything seemed to be going bad: the drugs, the scene and the karma. But Frank, having lived to tell the tale of his own catastrophe through the Far Out, was loving every minute of it.

"*Olé!*" he shouted, at a local bar, after I told him what happened at the symposium. "You've always been a master of the quick comeback. But are there any situations where you'd stand and deliver?"

"I like to think I do a bit of that every day. But if you're talking about close order knuckle drill, it would depend."

"On what?"

"On the situation."

"See! That's what that guy meant when he called you an aspiring bourgeois. You think you can choose the situations when you have to fight. That's always been the difference between us. The way I came up, the situations chose me. And I accepted that because I didn't believe there was any other way."

"But you don't believe that anymore."

"Most of the time I don't. But then there are the other times."

"Well, it's those other times," I said, "when people feel they're not being allowed to choose that are tearing this country apart."

Frank looked into the thick glass of his beer mug as he mulled over my words. "Wonder if the Grunt Collective believed they made their own choice or had it made for them?" he asked.

"Muriel says during her whole time with them, they never acted like they were desperate."

"You know, Crystal asked me the other day if I knew any guys who committed suicide in the 'Nam? And I didn't know of any."

"Crystal does have a way of sneaking into your mind without you even realizing it," I said. "When I followed her out of the apartment that day, we talked for a long time. She had some interesting things to say about what it's like posing for Gerald. She also mentioned that the two of you have been hanging out."

I felt Frank's tempo stop for an instant and then pick up again.

"Yeah, we've hung out a bit."

"That's quite a turn around from the first time we were all together."

"Well, we got to talking when I'd go over to Gerald's studio with Crystal. I had a chance to see his work. It really impressed me. He's been working on something he calls *The Jimi Hendrix Experience*. It's just about finished and I offered to let him use the café to show his new work and to have Excess and Crystal perform at the opening."

"Sounds great," I said, without any enthusiasm.

"I get the impression that you two ain't likely to share a candied yam any time soon."

"Fuck you, Frank...and the cannoli you rode in on!"

"Oh that's sweet, Ray," he said, the laughter beginning to crackle. "Really sweet!"

MURIEL

1970

MY WAIST THICKENED and swelling was beginning to show below it. I also didn't have the energy I used to. My editors at *Out In Left Field* let me lighten my schedule. This had less to do with being particularly sensitive to my pregnancy, than it was their willingness to accommodate a writer who had become a valued commodity. My moods swung from exhilaration over the baby to despair about Lucius. I was withdrawn and not easy to live with. Khadijah called and asked how I was. I hadn't spoken to her since right before Lucius' death. I understood her not wanting to get sucked into the circus atmosphere swirling around me. So I was pleased when she said she would come over to see me.

"You don't look so good," she said, making concern sound like an accusation.

"How good am I supposed to look when I'm barefoot and pregnant?"

"You know what I'm talking about."

"Yeah, but I know you don't want to get into that."

"I'm here aren't I?"

"I'm glad you are."

"Whatever it is about Lucius that's got you turning yourself inside out, you need to let it go."

"But I knew what they were going to do! Same as I did when those cops broke in on Walter and me. I couldn't stop them. But at least I could've tried with Lucius!"

"From what you wrote in *Out In Left Field*, they just wanted to be done with their lives."

"That's the way it seemed."

"Then accept it and ask yourself why you're spending so much energy on folks who're beyond your reach."

"What do you mean?"

"Do you want this child?"

"Of course I do!"

"Then start treating yourself like you want to be in this world enough to want this child to be in it too! You said you couldn't stop those cops from killing Walter and Lucius from killing himself. Well, here's your chance to stop yourself from killing the relatively calm journey this child could have from now until you give birth. You'll never be able to give this kind of protection again. So, relax-the-fuck-up! And don't add insult to the hurting that living in the world is gonna put on this child."

I sulked a bit, not liking that I was on the receiving end of so much that made sense.

"Yeah," I said, finally, "I guess you're right. I sure don't want to bring a child into the world with an attitude like yours."

"Not if you can help it, you don't."

"How'd you get to be so smart so quick?" I asked.

"Carrots!"

"Oh! You and Bugs Bunny."

"And you know how smart he is."

"Maybe I should study to become a midwife."

"Forget it. You're too hung up on the trouble that comes *after* birth," she said.

"What else is there?"

"I don't know but I'm sure whatever's there, you'll find it."

"You seeing anybody?" I asked.

Khadijah nodded.

"Who is he? Anybody I know?"

"Yeah, but the *who* ain't a *he*."

I felt a blinding light erupt in my eyes like the flash from a camera. I stretched my legs out, putting them on the coffee table.

"You all right?" she asked.

"Just a little stiff...So who is she?"

"Imani Touré."

"I didn't know she was out of jail."

"She made bail a couple of weeks ago."

"So how long has this been going on?"

"A while."

"Have you always been attracted to women?"

"Not to my knowledge."

"So when did it start?"

"You mean, in relation to the longstanding hots I've had for men?"

"Look, I know things haven't gone that well with the last two men you've been involved with."

"Oh! So that's what you think it's all about."

"I don't know, Khadijah. You tell me."

"I just did. I'm living with Imani."

"Yeah, I know but..."

"But what? If I'd told you I was living with a man, we wouldn't be having this conversation."

"We don't have to talk about it, if it bothers you."

"Oh, I don't think I'm the one who's bothered," she said.

"You think I am?"

"You must be. Otherwise, why would my telling you I'm living with a woman become a discussion about men?"

"It's not about *men!*" I said. "It's about *two men* you've had a relationship with."

"Truth be told, Muriel, you've had more of a relationship with them than I ever did."

"But that's different."

"You're right," she said. "All I did was fuck them! You obviously thought they could do a lot more for you than I did."

"What's that supposed to mean?"

"Look! You're trying to find the one man who can help you understand something about yourself and some other men, which is fine if that's what you need to do. But my being with Imani has nothing to do with men or anything they may have done to hurt me."

I didn't know quite what to do with all this. What was I to make of my assumption that Khadijah and Imani could only have been brought together through the pain inflicted on them by men? And if I believed that, how much more pain did I expect men to put me through in my search for Theo before my questions about Push Comes to Shove were answered?

•••••

As Frank and Crystal continued preparations at the Far Out for the opening of Gerald's exhibition, which he was calling The Jimi Hendrix Experience, the news arrived from London that Hendrix had died at the age of twenty-seven. He had apparently strangled on a mixture of sleeping pills and alcohol, which he vomited while asleep. Just as the depth of Hendrix's loss was only beginning to sink in, Janis Joplin died of a heroin overdose two weeks later in Los Angeles.

There was already a great deal of anticipation in the East Village leading up to the exhibition of Gerald's paintings. These two deaths raised it even higher. At Crystal's suggestion, Frank and Gerald agreed that the opening reception would include a musical tribute to Joplin. On the Sunday afternoon of the opening, the overflow crowd at the Far Out was beyond Frank or Gerald's expectations. It was as if all of downtown had been waiting for an opportunity to celebrate and grieve for Hendrix.

Those who were not turned away were greeted by Hendrix's unmistakable, strange foghorn baritone singing, "Are You Experienced?" And the answer was provided on several huge canvasses on which Gerald explored various stages of Hendrix's brief musical pilgrimage. One painting showed a blues hydra, three heads (bearing a likeness to Robert Johnson, Leadbelly and Muddy Waters) atop one massive body. A long-fingered hand pressed against the strings along the neck of a guitar followed by a stream of birth fluid in the form of musical notes. Another painting showed Hendrix with his Strat, writhing in an ecstatic blur of colors. A microphone protruded from his open fly and a throng of white male and female figures hovered around the mike with their mouths open as though singing into it. The last painting presented Hendrix as the physical equivalent of water. It showed Hendrix as porous and not confined by the borders of skin and bone; and his dispersed body seemed to undulate across the canvas in waves. And like the sea, the mood and temper of his many parts were inconsistent, floating between brush strokes of turbulence and calm.

When the recording of Hendrix singing ended, everyone stood as though the flesh had curled up their backs.

The silence was shattered by Joplin's voice shouting, "Went down on me..." just as Crystal leaped to the floor from a rope hanging from the ceiling. People moved out of the way as Crystal threw her body around with the same abandon that Joplin sang. And with every repetition of the words, "Down on me," she gave her body over to the double entendre by curling herself into a protective ball then snapping open boldly with her legs gapped wide. As Crystal's body went limp and slid to the floor, the sizzle in Joplin's voice cooled. But not before leaving a bruise in every throat.

The performance ended with Frank leading the house band, Excess, into its own rendition of Hendrix's version of "The Star Spangled Banner." The amplifiers exploded with the deafening feedback of "the rockets red glare, the bombs bursting in air." From within the café, drenched in darkness, Frank's voice rang out:

"They can kill the sound of the instruments but not the power behind the sound!"

A few people began to scream and were joined by more howls, serving notice that the loss of Hendrix and Joplin, who burned so brightly and quickly, did not put an end to the sweet and raucous thunder they left behind.

MURIEL

Late Autumn, 1970

WITH MY ATTENTION FOCUSED ON MY PREGNANCY, it was a while before I realized the effect of Gerald's opening exhibition on Raymond and Naomi. I was never into either Hendrix or Joplin, so Crystal and Frank's performance didn't move me all that much. But I was quite taken with Gerald's paintings, particularly the one giving Hendrix the physical qualities of the sea. Now in my second trimester, I realized I was made up of mostly water.

Oddly enough, Raymond and Naomi didn't talk much about Gerald's paintings. There was something other than art that seemed to be troubling them that neither seemed willing nor able to speak about right away. But I suspected it had something to do with the performances that Frank and Crystal gave at the reception. I had put this out of my mind until one afternoon, during my long daily walk, I stopped by Naomi's midtown office. As usual I could barely see her behind the avalanche of case files on her desk.

"You look like you need a break," I said.

"I need more than that!"

"Don't tell me about needing *more*. No matter how much I eat, this baby gets it all and leaves me hungry!"

"Hunger is definitely the operative word with me." Naomi looked in my direction but her thoughts were clearly elsewhere.

"What is it, Naomi?"

"Remember when I told you a while back about a kind of an itch that had grown between Gerald and me?"

"What about it?"

"It's become this appetite for something—something that being with Gerald isn't giving me."

"What is it you're not getting?"

"I'm not sure."

"Why don't you take some time off from all this." I made a sweeping gesture across her desk.

"I don't need to get away. I need to GET THE FUCK OUT!"

"When did all this happen?"

"I don't know exactly. But I remember at Gerald's opening, Crystal's performance gave my pulse a rush that had me trying to catch my breath."

"Are you telling me she turned you on?"

"If you wouldn't interrupt, I'd tell you."

"All right! But get on with it!"

"What I'm saying is that what she did gave me a taste for something I've never had before."

"Are you telling me you want to be with women now instead of men? Seems to be a lot of that going around," I said.

"I'm saying I want that feeling in my life no matter where it leads me."

"What about Gerald?"

"You know, when Gerald and I first started going out, we talked a lot about the thing that white women and black men are supposed to have for each other. Well, that thing never seemed to happen with us. We genuinely admired each other and were relieved when the fixation on white and black flesh never materialized. When we decided to get married, none of the looks or cracks from strangers mattered because we were confident that what we felt for one another had nothing to do with what anyone else thought. But we were so intent on having our attraction to each other not be about lust that we didn't make enough room for passion. I mean, it's been in our work but not for each other. And now it's not even in my work."

"What is it? The workload?" I asked.

"No. It's not the amount of work. It's the very fact that what I do has become a load. I know what Khadijah meant about doing something where the result of her efforts actually mattered. That's how I felt when I was involved with civil rights law in the South. What I did helped to change the laws. You were there. You know. We all felt uplifted by whatever we were asked to do. But now I'm just a glorified bailbondsman."

"So that's what you wanted to tell me?"

"No. This morning I got a call from someone who told me that Theo wants to meet with you."

I rose out of my chair.

"Why didn't you tell me before?"

"Because you need to know you're not the only one looking for something."

RAYMOND

Autumn, 1970

NO ONE LEFT INDIFFERENT to what they saw or heard at Gerald's opening. If I'd been on better terms with Gerald, I would've discussed his work with him rather than go through the meaningless exchange we had at the reception after the performances. Frank had no such problem. The two of them were becoming fast friends, which meant that Frank was often not around when I dropped by his apartment.

One afternoon I was walking through Washington Square Park on my way to get something to eat before my next class. I caught sight of Frank and some members of Excess performing a skit of some kind in front of a small crowd. As I moved closer, I noticed they had their jeans and coats on backwards and were speaking disjointed nonsense. It took a few minutes before I realized they were doing a parody of Nixon meeting with members of his cabinet and a few military advisors as they casually discussed the decision to invade Cambodia and the number of casualties that could be anticipated for such an invasion. As they spoke gibberish and went through their slapstick antics, I wondered whether the crowd's laughter, including my own, was in response to the absurdity of the decision to invade Cambodia? Or was it just about how ridiculous Nixon and his cabinet were?

"Thank you for your kind indulgence," Frank said to the crowd. "But we hope you won't continue to indulge a government that is worthy of the mockery we've been making of it. We see ourselves as the *servants of misrule*, giving you examples of the ass-backward ways of our government. We intend to stay on the government's ass, pointing out the paper trail behind it that leads to all the bullshit!"

"Not bad," I said to Frank after the crowd had dispersed.

"I thought I saw you, but I wasn't sure. How's the expectant father?"

"Fine. But I'm a bit concerned about my would-be friend."

"What do you mean, *would be?*"

"I haven't seen much of you lately. And you never call."

"Yeah, I know. I've been into a few things like what you just saw. And Gerald, Crystal and me have been talking about working together again on something."

"So what's all the *servants of misrule* stuff you were talking about?" I asked.

"Well, I've been reading a lot about the Middle Ages and how there were families that would choose one of their own to impersonate people who had the most status and position in the village. Everything would be turned upside down during the Christmas season. Folks who didn't have much more than their pride got a chance to change places with those who took pride in their permanent misrule over others. It was all done in the spirit of fun and after a few weeks everything went back to the way it was before."

"So, does that mean that what I just saw will be part of the Yuletide cheer you'll be spreading this year?" I asked.

"Yeah! But I want to take it beyond the government and expose the kinds of misrule that we all practice against ourselves and each other."

"Do you think any of this will change anything?"

"As fucked up as I am, I can't worry about that. My best chance of not losing it is to keep moving instead of just watching everything moving around me."

"That's what I like about you, Frank."

"What's that?"

"I can always depend on not knowing what you'll come up with next."

"I don't deserve the credit for making it up as I go along. My teachers were the people who sent me to the 'Nam. Difference is, they don't have to live in the shit they make up!"

Fury rose up in Frank's voice and we both waited for it to pass.

"Speaking of making things up," I said. "I've been meaning to ask if you've talked to Gerald about the painting of Hendrix with the microphone poking out of his fly?"

"Yeah, we did. It was inspired by the story that's made the rounds. You know, the one about Jim Morrison going up on stage while Hendrix was playing, kneeling down in front of him, unzipping his fly and sucking him off without any reaction from Hendrix."

"You don't believe that do you?"

"Could have happened. But Gerald isn't interested in whether it actually did or not. He sees what Morrison may have done as a fantasy that had already taken place in people's heads."

"Sounds like a fantasy that's clearly in the head of the artist," I said.

"Gerald said the same thing to me. He hopes the painting makes us see that we all, including Hendrix, may have diminished his music by playing it up, at the beginning, as an extension of his dick and the reputation he had as a cocksman. The painting is Gerald's admission that he was misruled by that fantasy. He's challenging us to consider that we may have been guilty of the same thing."

"He told you all this?" I asked.

"Not in so many words. But that's my take on what he said."

"I'm impressed, Frank."

"What the fuck you impressed about? You think I can't have any insight into anybody black except you?"

I had to admit that had been my fantasy. I liked the fact that I had, for many years, been the only black person who Frank really knew well. I knew it was possible that he'd gotten close to black guys in Vietnam. But if he did, he never mentioned them when he returned. As long as Frank saw black people through his friendship with me, I had a special, even exotic status, which gave me an unspoken advantage of knowing more about his tribal secrets than he knew about mine.

I remember my father once telling me that the best way to get over any feelings of inferiority regarding white people was to spend time with them. He was right about that. But what he didn't prepare me for was how much I enjoyed the mystique I derived from being around whites who either feared me or, like Frank, treated me better than their white friends because I was the only black friend they had. This wouldn't necessarily change if Frank and Gerald were friends.

But what I feared already seemed to be happening. I sensed a lessening in his attention toward me.

MURIEL

Late Autumn, 1970

MY MEETING WITH THEO was arranged through a series of messages sent to me through Naomi. I took the Broadway local downtown to the last stop, got on the ferry to Staten Island where I waited an hour and then turned around and came back. A few days later, I

received a note to take the train to Coney Island where I was supposed to stand at a certain section on the boardwalk. This was followed by directives to go to Yankee Stadium in the Bronx and
Flushing Meadow Park in Queens where I also waited for an hour
and then left.

Finally, I was instructed to go to the Riverside Drive approach to
the George Washington Bridge in Manhattan. When it looked as
though I had once again waited in vain, a van went by and stopped
about fifteen feet beyond me. An arm reached out of the rolled down
window on the passenger side and waved me inside. The door
opened and slammed shut behind me. Before I could settle my very
pregnant self into the back seat, the van surged forward, almost
throwing me to the floor. A white woman with shoulder-length hair
pulled back and tied in an elastic band was driving. A white man,
mouth smothered by a thick mustache, sat beside her.

"I was beginning to wonder if anybody was ever going to show
up."

"You would've waited a lot longer, if you hadn't followed our
instructions," the man said.

I looked out the window and realized we weren't going across
the bridge to New Jersey. We were on the parkway, heading north of
New York City.

"Don't worry about where we're going." The woman stared at me
through the rear-view mirror. "All you should be thinking about is
who not where."

"All right, then. Who are you?"

"We're Maggie's Farmers."

"What?"

"We took the name from the Dylan song. Like it says, we ain't
gonna work on Maggie's farm no more."

"That's right!" the man chimed in.

"So what do you do now that you're done working on Maggie's
farm?" I asked.

"We're committed to bringing about a redistribution of the wealth
in this country among the people who have labored the most to pro-
duce it."

I squinted at them. "How do you propose to do that?"

"We never discuss our methods before we put them into action. That's a mistake Push Comes to Shove made."

"Tell me about yourselves," I asked.

"He just told you," the woman said.

"I mean, before you decided not to work, as you say, on Maggie's farm."

"My life as a revolutionary began almost a year ago," she said. "Anything before that is of no importance."

"Maybe not to you. But how do you expect anyone to follow your example if they don't know how you got there?"

"No one knew much about Jesus' life before he began to preach the gospel. And he was able to cultivate disciples to spread his movement among the masses."

"There's a difference," I said. "Unlike Jesus, you're not visible to the people you're trying to reach. You need someone like me to describe your lives, so they can connect your actions to real human beings."

Neither of them said anything for a while, as the high rising steel buildings gave way to hovering trees and vines.

"We were under the impression that you wanted to talk to Theo," the woman said softly.

"I was under the impression that Theo wanted to talk to me. But I'm interested in anyone who is allied with him in the way I was."

"Since you speak in the past tense, does that mean your alliance with him is over?" she asked.

"It's not over but it's changed. And I'd like to find out what happened to both of us to cause that change."

"It's no mystery what happened to you," the man said.

"That's interesting. Because I'm still trying to figure that out."

He paused for a moment, then spoke slowly. "You pawned your soul because of your fear of jail."

I leaned toward them. "You don't know me! How would you know anything about my fear or what it might make me do?"

"Come on! You were released without being tried," the woman said. "You must have cut a deal to avoid prosecution."

"What about the fact that they had no case?"

"That only proves your complicity with the system," the man said. "If you were a true revolutionary, they would've been able to make a case against you because you would've done something that disrupted the state's ability to carry on business as usual."

There it was again: the charge that I wasn't a revolutionary. I couldn't quarrel with that. What could I say definitively about myself now, other than that I was married and pregnant?

We kept driving north for another hour before pulling off the main highway and onto a two-lane road. After a few miles, we turned onto a gravel road hemmed in by woods.

The woman slowed the van and turned left onto a path. We hadn't gone very far when two women in combat fatigues stepped out from behind a tree with automatic weapons slung over their shoulders. Their faces were smeared with what looked like shoe polish and they nodded as we passed them. The trees gave way to an open field of tall weeds, leading up to a cabin. Three people stood up in the high grass; their faces were also darkened and the military greens and browns made them indistinguishable. The van stopped in front of the cabin.

"You wait here," the woman said, as she and the man got out of the van, entered the door of the cabin and closed it behind them. I turned around but couldn't see any of the people I'd passed in the van only a moment before. The door of the cabin opened and the man who'd driven up with me walked back over to the van.

"You can go in now," he said, pulling the sliding door open for me.

I walked a bit unsteadily, as much from nervousness as from my bulk and entered the cabin. Theo was seated, moving backwards and forwards in a rocking chair. He was wearing a beret and army fatigues but was pretty much as I remembered him except for his eyes, which seemed vacant as a doll's. On either side of the rocker leaned a spear and a pump shotgun.

Looking at Theo reminded me of that famous photograph of Huey Newton sitting in a wicker chair while holding a spear and shotgun. I had a feeling that Theo had deliberately placed himself among these familiar props. The woman who had driven the van stood a few feet away from him with her arms folded.

"Well, Muriel, we meet again at last."

"Up until this moment, I had my doubts that it would ever happen."

"You're going to have to let Cynthia search you."

A flash of anger swept through me as I recalled the hundreds of searches I'd been subjected to in the South and by the police and prison guards at the Women's House of Detention after Walter was killed. The hands of all those men would crawl over my flesh, not with the intention of discovering something I'd concealed, but with full knowledge of what they were looking for and where to find it.

"I'm sorry," she said. "This won't take long."

I braced myself for the touch of her hands; and while I didn't like it, I didn't feel violated.

"How many months are you?" she asked, smiling to reveal a crooked front tooth.

"Seven and a half."

"I thought you were looking quite full of yourself," Theo said.

He started to say something else but didn't.

"It's not Walter's. I'm married. It's no one you know. His name is Raymond." I suddenly felt very tired.

"Why don't you sit here?" Theo got up and helped me to the rocker.

His sensitivity moved me, as it had when he, gently, removed my hands from my ears after bursting that man's eardrums. Cynthia opened up two folding chairs that were in the corner. Theo sat down in front of me and Cynthia moved her chair over by the window.

"Hope you don't mind Cynthia being here. We have a policy that at least two of us have to be present if we meet with anyone from outside the group."

"That's fine with me."

"It's hard to know where to begin," he said.

"Why don't you explain your being a police informant."

He shrugged.

"What can I say? I had a long rap sheet and the police were

threatening to bury me in prison for years if I didn't cooperate. I was also incredibly naive about what was going on in this country. But the things I saw once I got involved in Push Comes to Shove educated me in a hurry."

"Detective Garrett doesn't think you're naive at all."

"Figured he'd come out of the woodwork sooner or later."

"He's done more than that. He's the one who led the effort to flush the Collective out of the subway. And he also threatened me with a probation violation unless I helped him get in touch with you."

"That why you're here?"

"No. I needed to talk to you for my own reasons."

"Well, go ahead and talk!"

"Why did you send out those press releases, saying the Grunt Collective was responsible for those police killings?"

"What makes you think I did that?"

"It seemed likely when Lucius didn't want to join you in declaring war on the government."

"Did it ever occur to you that maybe Garrett was responsible for linking the Grunt Collective to those police killings?"

"So you had nothing to do with those stories?"

"If Maggie's Farmers announced any action we'd taken against the police, we wouldn't implicate anyone but ourselves."

"What do you think of what the Grunt Collective did?"

"Well, all I can say is that for a group with their resourcefulness and imagination, I was disappointed that they didn't put both to better use."

"What do you mean by better use?" .

"I think I'll leave it at that."

"Was it Garrett's failure of imagination that made you break with the police?" Theo smiled.

"That's an interesting way of putting it. But like I just said, playing at being a revolutionary made me see why someone would become one."

"So if you're no longer playing a part, what do you stand for?"

"I stand for one thing: *I ain't gonna work on Maggie's farm no more*. Not Maggie's. Not Garrett's. Nobody's except my own!"

"What about the rest of Maggie's Farmers." I glanced over at Cynthia. "Do they work for you?"

"They work with me. We all want to get rid of the Maggies of this world."

"But aren't you their leader?"

"In a way, but we follow the example of the Lakota Indians. They're an independent people that never allowed anyone to lead them anywhere they didn't want to go."

"So did Maggie's Farmers kill those cops?"

"Those who know the answer to that question won't tell. And those who do tell are either liars or fools. What I will say is that I've been reading a lot about the Lakota warrior, Crazy Horse. I'm learning how to be more persuasive and taking into account what others want, not just what I want. The trick is to have both be one and the same or at least close to one another."

"So have all of you been able to pull that trick off?" I asked, turning to Cynthia.

"We're pretty much agreed on what we want, but haven't worked out how to go about getting it yet."

"And what have you agreed on?"

Cynthia looked over at Theo, who smiled.

"We want to begin to destroy America as it's presently consti-tuted and start remaking it at the same time."

"How are you going to do that?"

"You're part of how we intend to do it," Theo said.

"Oh, really?"

"Through your article, we want to unveil Maggie's Farmers' plan for redistribution of the nation's wealth. This will involve the estab-lishment of a trust fund administered by a group of distinguished Americans who have a proven record of humanitarian service on behalf of the have-nots. Donations to the trust fund would come from the most affluent sectors of the country—banks, insurance companies, brokerage firms, industrial and retail organizations, the medical and legal professions and the entertainment industry. The amount of these donations would be a percentage of the gross

earnings of these various corporations. We know they all camouflage their profits, so it's not like they'd be putting themselves in a
financial bind."

"I know you've already considered this," I said, "but what are you
going to do when they reject your proposal, which you know they'll
do?"

"If that happens, we'll start identifying *targets of opportunity*
from among the prospective donors I cited."

"Does that mean you'll kill people?"

"Let's just say, they'll be targeted. Just like Walter was."

"Theo, I hope you haven't embarked on this *plan* of yours with
me anywhere in your mind. Because I don't need you to be my personal avenger."

"Don't worry. What we're involved in has nothing to do with settling personal scores."

"I'm curious about how you intend to remake America while
you're occupied with these targets of opportunity?"

"By changing the way we live together as Maggie's Farmers,"
Cynthia said. "As women and men, we'll all be doing whatever
needs to be done, whether it's cooking or targeting. Every day we
come up with ways to root out our willingness to accept hierarchies
of all kinds. Any decision affecting the group as a whole is arrived at
by consensus. Emotionally, we open ourselves to experiencing each
other sexually, whether it's between races, between women or
between men. We believe that in order to make a different world
than the one we were born into, we have to experience ourselves and
our relationship to others differently by imagining what it's like to
be someone we're not. And we have to begin to do that now."

Cynthia's words reminded me of the way many of us in the
Movement used to talk about our vision of a beloved community
before it was beaten out of us. Events had led me to focus on power
and how to take it from people who had it, rather than on what could
be achieved with people who had much to give.

While listening to Cynthia, I watched her face slowly open up. I
couldn't say the same for Theo. His opaque eyes took in everything
but gave up nothing in return.

"I was thinking," I said, still looking at Cynthia. "If you believe a better world could be created by trying to understand someone unlike yourself, then how could you justify killing someone just because they're rich?"

The muscles in her face tightened. "We'll give them every opportunity to act in their own self-interest. But if they refuse to give up a portion of the wealth they accumulated at the expense of others, they'll have to forfeit their most precious asset."

"So do you have a problem with the execution phase of our plan?" Theo asked.

"I guess I do. I believe people should be held accountable for what they do. But I'm not in favor of vigilante justice."

"You know, Muriel, you're as naive as I was. A black man who steals a loaf of bread will go to prison but a corporate executive who embezzles millions will get probation and an opportunity to make restitution. That's vigilante justice! I saw this tendency of yours when we were in Push Comes to Shove. You never wanted any harm to come to people who would crush you without giving it a second thought!"

"So to be a revolutionary I have to become as evil as they are?"

"No. But sometimes you have to do what they do before they do it to you."

"What you're planning doesn't sound like a sometime thing."

"You say you came up here because you're writing about us for *Out In Left Field*, Muriel. But what do you really want from me?"

"I thought you could help me figure out why those of us in Push Comes to Shove were so shocked when the police came after us just the way we said they would. Maybe I was more naive than everyone else and didn't really believe my own rhetoric. But I thought I did. My husband Raymond told me not to expect any answers from you. But in the short time I've been here you've taught me that in order not to be shocked by something horrible, you have to believe in nothing!"

"I take that as a compliment. But it's not entirely right. I believe in myself and the rest of Maggie's Farmers." He paused for a moment. "You know, you're worst than naive, Muriel. You're pathetic!

Most people try to go through the eye of a needle, and failing that, spend their lives looking through it to the other side. But you want to stand on the head of the needle and be above it all. Well, I've seen the view from both places. And I don't wanna be above the needle's eye—or look through it. I wanna take that needle and poke out the eye of every fucking Cyclops that gets in my way! So Muriel, why don't you run along and have your baby and let Maggie's Farmers make the world a fit place for your child to live in."

"Anything you want me to tell Detective Garrett?" I asked.

"Tell him I've made my own pact with the devil. So I won't be needing him as my go-between anymore."

"He may feel you owe him for all the time he spent cultivating you."

"He may have put in the time, but I did all the work. Tell him if he wants to know what we'll do next, he should remember some of the ideas I used to come up with to entrap black radicals. As far as the when and the where goes, he'll have to figure that out for himself and start earning his detective's salary for a change."

"Is it okay if I talk to some of the other people in Maggie's Farmers before I leave?"

"If they want to talk with you, that's up to them."

I got up slowly from the rocker and Cynthia opened the door for me.

"What do you hear from Geneva?" Theo asked.

"Her name is Khadijah now and she's studying to become a midwife. She'll be assisting the delivery of my baby."

"She with anybody?"

I nodded.

"Who is he?"

I took a deep breath before answering. "It's...a woman."

"Damn, Muriel! There you go again, saying something like you're worried about how I'll take it. Why should you care? Maybe in your next life you'll come back as a painkiller!"

Theo started laughing and kept laughing even after the cabin door slammed shut. I looked around. Except for the guy who came up with me in the van, I couldn't see any of Maggie's Farmers.

"Where is everybody?" I asked.

"They're around," he said.

"Can you let them know I'd like to talk with them?"

He put two fingers in his mouth and whistled. The high grass rustled and five figures draped with weeds and leaves stood up in different parts of the field. They moved toward the cabin as though tall green stalks had uprooted themselves from the earth. When reaching the small clearing surrounding the cabin, they sat down in a semicircle. I joined them, sitting down and leaning back against a tree. Despite their elaborate efforts to conceal themselves, I recognized the two women I saw on the way in, along with two other men and another woman. I tried to get a sense of the racial composition of the group. But given their camouflage job, they could have been from anywhere from Beirut to the Bronx.

"Why are you dressed like that?" I asked.

"It's part of our training to hide ourselves in whatever environment we're in," one of the women said.

"How would you hide in a city?"

"We have exercises that teach us how to achieve a level of stillness in a room full of people or on a crowded street that allows us to go unnoticed while still being visible."

"Theo tells me you have patterned yourselves after the Lakota. Why is that?"

"They were nomadic people who lived off the land. We've taken on a similar existence out of necessity."

"Theo says he's been studying the life of Crazy Horse," I asked.

"It's not just Theo," one of the men said. "We're all into Crazy Horse! Because of his character and courage, he was among a select few chosen by the elders to live simply and look after the welfare of the tribe. We chose Theo to fill that role. And if any of the rest of us prove ourselves worthy, we may be chosen one day as well."

"What has Theo done that the rest of you haven't done?"

"We don't talk about that even among ourselves. But when things happen, we make note of them and wait for the next sign."

"What sign?"

"Crazy Horse had a recurring dream that predicted events in his life to come. Theo has shared a dream of his own with us and we've already seen evidence of it in things that have happened."

"Can you tell me anything about the dream?"

Maggie's Farmers turned to exchange glances. As if on some intuitive cue, they all rose to their feet, turned around and walked out of the clearing to blend back into the tall weeds, swaying to the pressure of a stiff breeze. The cabin door opened behind me and Theo and Cynthia walked out on to the porch. I looked over at the guy who came up in the van with me. He'd been sitting a few feet from me but hadn't joined the semi-circle.

"What was that all about?" I asked.

He looked at me but didn't speak.

"Why don't you tell her, Greg," Theo said.

"I used play in this rock group and there's a rule that any musician who's ever been on the road knows. One that you break at your own peril—never let any civilians on the bus."

"So why did you let me on the bus in the first place?"

"Well, we decided to do it just once," Theo said, "since we needed someone, as you said, to put a human face on the seriousness of our intentions. But to answer your question about my dream, it goes like this. All of Maggie's Farmers are in a cave but I'm on one side of a pit and they're on the other, which is the way out. My escape to the other side is blocked by a huge serpent. It begins to wrap itself around me and I try to get a stranglehold around its neck before its fangs can sink into me. But I can't see because my forehead blends into my cheeks, covering the place where my eyes are supposed to be. I cry out for help from the rest of Maggie's Farmers but they can't speak because the flesh between their noses and chins covers the area where their mouths would be. I have the power of speech but can't see what the serpent will do next. And they can see the serpent but can't speak to warn me when it will strike."

•••••

Cynthia and Greg drove me back to the city. No one said very much. But I did catch Cynthia looking back at me periodically through the rear-view mirror.

"I've been wondering," I said, breaking the silence, "what it is about Theo that made you join Maggie's Farmers?"

"It's the way he explained things that made me see exactly what he was saying," Cynthia said. "There're not many who can do that."

"Yeah," Greg chimed in. "He showed me that once people understood why terrible things were happening to them, they wouldn't get hurt as much."

"So what do you understand about Theo's dream that will stop you from getting hurt?" I asked.

"It's a dream in progress, like Crazy Horse's," Cynthia said. "We just have to wait and see how it develops."

"Don't you think it's risky, allowing your fate to be determined by one person's dreams?"

"Theo's dreams aren't dictating what we do," Greg said. "They're just telling us where our actions are likely to lead us."

"You don't have to wait for Theo's dreams to tell you that."

"That's what you don't understand about Theo," Cynthia said. "Before meeting him, I'd cut myself off from people because everything I tried to do was ignored. But all I did was hide. Theo convinced me there were things I could do that would get people to take notice."

"So you want to end up like the Grunt Collective?" I asked.

"That won't happen to us," Cynthia said. "But if we do go down, there're a lot of people who'll be keeping us company."

I didn't say anything after that. It was understandable why neither Cynthia nor Greg wanted to think about the implications of Theo's dream. It spelled disaster for Maggie's Farmers just as Crazy Horse's dream predicted catastrophe for the Lakota. But I was still moved by the world that Maggie's Farmers were trying to create among themselves. And while the doom awaiting them seemed obvious, I envied how they were trying to live, and saddened that I couldn't be a part of it.

They dropped me off at the subway station at Broadway and 157th Street.

"Thanks for what you said about your beloved community," I said to Cynthia, as I got out of the van. "Were you in the Movement in the South?"

"Summer of '64," she said. "Good luck with your baby and I hope things work out for you on the head of that needle."

I wasn't sure how to take what she said. Her remark seemed generously seasoned with both empathy and mockery. If Cynthia intended her words to be ambiguous, maybe she also had doubts about what she and Maggie's Farmers were about to do.

•••••

During the last weeks of my pregnancy, I wrote feverishly, trying to finish the article about Maggie's Farmers before I went into labor. I'd gotten huge and avoided full length mirrors so I wouldn't have to look at the body that made me look like an aspiring sumo wrestler. When I wasn't writing, eating, sleeping or going to Lamaze classes with Raymond, I did my breathing exercises and chewed ice chips. There were times when I felt like I had an ocean inside me and would brace myself for the tide to come in, which it did with greater frequency. Khadijah came over regularly to help me practice various breathing techniques and boiling roots for tea to make my contractions more bearable.

"How'd you find out about all these different roots you bring me?" I asked while drinking a cup of sassafras tea.

"This old black woman I study with told me about them. She learned from her mother who was also a midwife. She told me that tea made from hen feathers works even better than sassafras, but it's not used anymore by women who live in cities."

"I don't think I'd want any tea made from hen feathers in my system, no matter how good it's supposed to be," I said.

"It'd be a lot better for you than all this writing you're doing."

"What do you mean?"

"You obviously didn't learn anything from all the grief you got when you did that piece on the Grunt Collective. And it'll be worse for you once people read about Theo and this group, that should be called *jive Maryland Farmers,* who pretty much admitted they've killed cops and are threatening to kill more people."

"I'm writing about them, not in support of them," I said.

"Doesn't matter. You're still going to get hit from all sides. And with a baby coming, you don't need that. You're asking for a post-partum depression from hell!"

"I think it's important that their story gets told."

"No you don't. You think it's important that *you* get to tell it."

"I don't deny that. But I'm closer to the story than most people."

"That's my point! You're too close to it. It'll be years before you have the distance to understand everything that happened to you in Push Comes to Shove."

"And what am I supposed to do in the meantime?"

"Seems like that decision's been made for you," she said, looking at my stomach.

"I know that. But I'm talking about trying to figure out why so many of us were surprised when the terrible things we predicted actually happened."

"Maybe we were just young and foolish. And how else were you supposed to react when you saw Walter get his head blown off by those cops?"

"But there's something else nagging at me that has to do with the things I've come to believe or, at least, thought I did."

"Like what?"

"The belief that the world tips in favor of the few and not the many. And how to balance things more fairly than they are."

"I don't see anything wrong with that."

"But Theo once told me that I identify too much with the pain that people go through, even those who mean to do me harm. Do you think that's true?"

"I don't know, Muriel. But I wouldn't spend a second on some insight that Theo thinks he has about me."

"But there still may be something to it."

"What if there is?"

"Then what do I do about it?"

"See! This is one of the reasons why I decided to study mid-wifery. There are things I have to do in preparation for a delivery. But I don't worry about everything that could possibly happen and whether I'll be able to handle it. I like to think I'll be at my best. But there ain't no telling. That kind of certainty is for people like you who believe what they think has to conform to how they behave. Things hardly ever work out that way for me. That's what I learned from Push Comes to Shove."

"I hear you but I'm not sure if I believe it."

"Good! That's a start, not believing something I said just because it makes sense to me. Now, if you can begin to apply that to yourself, you might start to make some progress toward whatever the hell it is you think you're looking for."

"I hate it when you make sense because you'll never let me forget it."

"Then stop talking foolishness and do your breathing exercises. You know the one I'm talking about."

I gave Khadijah my mock homicidal stare and then began doing the exercise where I took four panting breaths and on the last one I'd blow out with greater force. It was boring and I never liked it, which was why she always made me do it. After about ten minutes of this, the doorbell rang.

"I'll get it," Khadijah said.

When she returned to the living room, Imani was with her. I hadn't seen her since interviewing her for *Out In Left Field*. Imani was radiant now. She had sprung open like a butterfly, a far cry from my memory of her cocooned in a chair on the other side of a bulletproof partition. And as she walked into the living room, her flowing bell bottoms gave her a lighter than air grace. I looked from her to Khadijah whose mouth was curled in a snide expression, which was about the best she could do when it came to showing that something pleased her.

"It's good to see you outside of that fiberglass box," I said.

"You and me both!"

"What've you been doing?"

"Thinking mostly."

"That's something you two can't seem to take a breath without doing," Khadijah said.

"And how many breaths can you take before a thought crosses your mind?" Imani asked.

She had fired back at Khadijah before I did. I liked Imani even more already.

"Any plans?" I asked.

"I may go to law school."

"Muriel!" Khadijah cut in. "Since you've exhibited a lot of peculiar behavior in your post-Push Comes to Shove life, maybe you can help me understand this perverse aspiration of Imani's. I've listened to her talk about it, but I don't get it. After flaunting the law in such grand fashion, why would you then want to uphold it?"

"You've probably known this for some time, Muriel," Imani said, "but there are many things that Khadijah just doesn't get. One is that if you work to have the laws applied fairly to every one and try to change those that protect the privileges of only a few, then you wouldn't have as much defiance of the law. Another thing she doesn't get is that, as a soon to be full-fledged midwife who'll be delivering newborns, she won't be able to deliver those of us who're already out of the womb!"

I liked the way they talked to me about each other while we were together in the same room. I was so tickled that I went into a laughing spasm that left me panting.

"I don't know what you think you're doing," Khadijah said, "but that's not one of the suggested breathing techniques I showed you."

RAYMOND

Winter, 1971

As MURIEL ENTERED HER THIRD TRIMESTER, my apprehension increased when I realized she was determined to finish the article on Maggie's Farmers before giving birth. I didn't want her to tax herself too much but my efforts in that regard were useless. When

Muriel turned in the article, I worried about the public's response, remembering the attacks leveled against her after the piece on the bombing deaths of the Grunt Collective. I even tried to get her to ask the editors at *Out In Left Field* to delay publishing the story until well after the baby arrived but she refused.

During those final weeks, I also began to feel an unexpected distance stretching between Muriel and myself. I never missed a Lamaze class, felt the baby's movement under my hand when I rested it on Muriel's stomach and listened to its heartbeat regularly. But the experience of what Muriel was going through, as the life inside her made its presence felt, was something I could only share indirectly. I sometimes saw what I thought was a gloating expression on her face that seemed to take pleasure in what I could never really know. At other times, I would get a stinging glance, which I read as anger at the biological fate that spared my body from the burden of carrying our child. I was too afraid of being mistaken, so I never attempted to verify my suspicions by asking Muriel about them.

Part of me envied not only her obvious euphoria over the physical sensations of life moving inside her, but also the discomfort of an altered body, even the nausea, vomiting, night sweats, cramps in the legs, swelling of the feet and hands, contractions and frequent mood swings. I imagined myself telling this to Muriel and heard her laughing herself to the brink of going into labor and saying: "*Pull-eeeze*, Raymond! Get real! That's just like a man, wanting everything you can't have until you get it." And if Muriel was right about that, I didn't intend to be *just like a man* when the child I wanted, and was about to have with her, entered my life.

It would have helped if I could've talked to someone about all this. But other than Frank, who was busy with his *servants of misrule* performances, there wasn't anyone else I felt comfortable enough with to confide in. That realization startled me and I began to wonder if my feelings of separation from Muriel were symptomatic of something much deeper. I remembered a story I'd heard about someone asking Charlie Parker if he had any really close friends. And Parker said he'd had a very close friend as a child who had done him a terrible wrong. He had died. When I thought about it, I had no real confidantes as a child. And after Uncle Aubrey was killed, I began to align myself with those who were dead and buried in books. The people among the living whom I felt closest to were baseball players. And my intimacy with them was solely on the basis of the stats that I kept in my head.

Sometimes, after teaching my classes, I would spend afternoons walking the streets between the East and West Village, pondering the source of my isolation and oblivious to the people rushing by me in the winter chill of late December. On one of my existential day-dreaming excursions, I found myself within a few blocks of Frank and Crystal's apartment. I decided to stop by and see if they were around. As I approached the building, I saw Naomi coming down the front steps. She began walking toward me with her head down and her right hand holding, tightly, to the neck of her overcoat.

"Hey, Naomi! How you doing?"

She met my eyes with surprise that quickly dissolved into what looked like dread.

"Are Frank and Crystal at home?" I asked.

"That would be an understatement."

"What do you mean?"

"I'm not quite sure."

"Naomi? Are you all right?"

"Not really."

"Did something happen to Frank and Crystal?" I asked.

"Yes, but it didn't happen to me."

"Naomi, I have no idea what you're talking about. I'm going up."

I started to walk toward the building and Naomi grabbed my arm suddenly.

"Raymond, please don't go up there."

"Why not?"

"Just don't!"

"I'm going unless you tell me why I shouldn't."

Naomi's eyes became glassy. She stared right through me and opened her mouth but nothing came out.

"They're up there. All three of them—together," she said.

"Three of them? Who's the other person?"

"Gerald."

"You mean that...?"

"Yes."

I began to feel the cold, standing there. But it didn't seem to bother Naomi. She was so disoriented that I had to guide her to a nearby coffee shop. We sat silently over our mugs of coffee for quite a while before it occurred to me that Naomi might not volunteer any more information. This upset me, a bit, because I felt my sympathy obligated her to be more forthcoming about what had happened. But I also had to admit, with some embarrassment, to more than a little voyeuristic curiosity, which I wanted satisfied regardless of the pain it might cause Naomi.

"Did you have any suspicions that this was going on?"

"I didn't need any suspicions. Gerald told me what they wanted to do."

"Why did he do that?"

Naomi stared into her coffee mug. "Because he wanted me to join them."

"What did you tell him?"

She looked up at me. "I agreed, but then changed my mind."

"And what did Gerald say?"

"He still wanted to go through with it. And so did Frank and Crystal. So I left and ran into you."

"And Frank was comfortable having Gerald make love with Crystal?"

"That's not all he was comfortable with."

"What do you mean?"

Her eyes flashed disbelief. "You're unbelievable, Raymond! What do you think group sex means? Do I really have to spell it out for you?"

Whatever I imagined about Frank, Crystal and Gerald being involved, it didn't include Frank and Gerald having sex. I didn't think it was because they were men. I just wasn't prepared for the men to be Frank and Gerald.

Walking home after Naomi and I left the coffee shop, I felt anger sizzling on my skin. But I was either unable or unwilling to identify its source.

I ran into Frank a few days later in Washington Square Park. He and Crystal were with five other people, who were all disguised as some part of an animal. The men wore the horns of a ram, a lizard's tail and their chests protruded, revealing the breasts of a woman. The women had beards, goat hooves for feet and bat wings. They stood still briefly and then began to mime exaggerations of talking, teasing and taunting between the sexes. It was fascinating to watch how the women and men, taking on the role of the opposite sex, inhabited space with their bodies so differently. They also imitated people walking down a crowded street and sitting or standing on a bus or subway. I was struck by how much these ordinary daily routines revealed about the discomfort men and women carried around when we were near one another.

Afterwards, Frank, Crystal and I sat on a park bench, warming up with cups of coffee.

"Who came up with the idea for what you were doing?" I asked.

"I did," Crystal said, obviously pleased.

"At first, it didn't make any sense to me," Frank said. "But when I started paying closer attention to the way people behaved, I could see that Crystal wanted to show how foolish men and women can be by having us imitate each other's body language."

"But Crystal, what about the way people moved like they didn't have enough room?" I asked.

"I was just trying to show how I can be on a stage filled with dancers and feel like I have more space than if I'm walking among only a few people on the sidewalk. Dancing allows me to make room for myself in a way that I don't do when I'm not performing. I believe we all need to make a space for ourselves. But not by pushing other people out of the way."

"Are you saying men push women out of the way?" Frank asked, as though issuing a challenge.

"Some men do."

"Am I one of them?"

"Not when you try real hard not to be."

"Oh! Well, what about women? They don't push anybody around?"

"It's unhealthy, no matter who does it." Crystal stood up.

"Where're you going?"

"I have to go to work."

Frank grabbed her arm. "You sure you're not leaving because of what I said?"

"Not this time." Crystal's eyes were as translucent as her name. And as she looked at Frank, staring back at her, I noticed that something in her eyes had jarred him. It was as though, when she said, "Not this time," her eyes punched the words into his like the keys of a typewriter.

Frank let go of her arm.

"Keep the peace, Raymond," she said.

"You too, Crystal."

As I watched Crystal leave the park, I was surprised by the slow drip of pleasure I felt over the rift between them.

"Let's get the fuck out of here," Frank said. "I'm freezing!"

We walked over to Frank's apartment where he rolled a few joints. He kept to his habit of offering me one. And I kept to mine of refusing.

"There's something I've been meaning to talk to you about."

Frank looked over at me and I felt everything slowing down from the heady reefer haze, settling into the apartment. He took a drag from the joint, held his breath and then exhaled without ever taking his eyes off me. He seemed ready for and resigned to whatever I was about to say.

"I heard about the scene you had over here with Crystal, Gerald and Naomi."

He took another drag on the joint.

"Aren't you going to say anything?" I asked.

"What's there to say? You're telling me something I already know. I was there. Remember?"

"That's my point, Frank. I might never have known, if I hadn't run into Naomi leaving your apartment."

"So? What are you, my fucking priest?"

"No. I'm just a friend who thought we shared what was going on in our lives."

"Friendship means I gotta tell you who I'm fucking?"

"It does if it means ignoring the hurt you can cause by sleeping with friends and their spouses."

"Hey, I didn't think this up all by myself."

"All right," I said. "Why don't you tell me about the part you did think up?"

"So this is about me confessing."

"No, Frank. Unlike a priest who you get shut in with, you've shut me out."

"If you felt that way, why didn't you come on up after Naomi told you what was happening. I can't speak for Gerald but I know Crystal and I would've been happy to see you." Frank poked his lips out and made a sucking sound.

"You know that's not what I'm talking about."

"You're not! And here I thought you loved me," he said and started laughing.

"You think this is all a joke?" I asked.

"Don't you?"

"And what do you call the scene you were in with Crystal and Gerald?"

"I call it interesting until something better comes along."

"And what about Naomi? How did her change of heart figure in to your plans?"

"It didn't."

"Didn't it bother you that she was upset?"

"We all agreed that if any one of us changed our mind, it wouldn't affect what the others wanted to do."

"But Naomi's your friend! The fact that she didn't want to go through with it should've mattered to you."

Frank shook his head. "Where are you going with this, Raymond?"

"The point where you started disregarding your friends in favor of someone you hardly know."

"Not knowing Gerald all that well wasn't a problem for me."

"Why not?"

"Because knowing too much about anyone or anything has

fucked me up enough already."

"I can't believe you really mean that," I said.

"You better believe I mean it! While you were in the friendly confines of some institution of higher learning, I was up to my eyes in the elephant grass acquiring an education I didn't want. Like not learning soon enough that getting close to a buddy might mean having to connect the pieces of what was left after a land mine was through with him. Or learning that the VC weren't the only ones trying to keep me from getting out of 'Nam alive. I had a lot to fear from these kickass, BB-brained officers, trying to lose their cherry in the bad-boonies. And like every other grunt, I didn't want to end up with my shit on their dicks! But there were lots who weren't as lucky as me...And since I've been back in the world, I don't get strung out on what I feel about anybody."

"Where does all this leave Crystal?" I asked.

"Crystal's incredible! Whatever she feels finds a way to come out of her mouth. Every time I think I'm about to catch her saying something she doesn't feel, she surprises me. I love that about her. But that means she's capable of putting a world of hurt on me."

"Are you looking for a way to discard me too?" I asked.

Frank had smoked the joint down to the end and sucked what was left of it into his mouth and swallowed it. "That's up to you," he said.

"What kind of bullshit is that?"

"Don't look so surprised, Raymond. You've been running the same scam on me since we were in high school. And it wasn't until I got back from the war that I understood what seeing your uncle killed had done to you. Cuz the same thing happened to me in the 'Nam. And the other thing I realized, after being around a lot more bloods while I was there, was how you used being black to keep white people at a distance, the same way I've learned to. So now it's my turn to be the militant, to be even blacker than you!"

Frank's words were body blows, knocking the wind out of me.

"You know, Frank, I hope you enjoy being blacker than me while you can because it won't last long."

"That's not true. Look how long our friendship has lasted."

Something snapped inside me and I bolted out of my chair. I stood over him, shaking.

"Get the fuck up!"

"Why?"

"So you can try to knock me down!"

"Rough sex? I prefer what went down between Gerald and me. At least we both liked the same thing."

With no thought of what I was about to do, I punched him in the face. Blood streamed out of Frank's nose.

He wiped it away with the back of his hand, stared at the smear and sucked it. "Looks like I came before you did." Frank got up from the couch, went into the bathroom and closed the door behind him.

I stood for quite a while, without the energy to move. When I finally dragged myself out of the apartment and into the street, my whole body ached.

M U R I E L

Early 1971

RAYMOND AND KHADIJAH took me to the hospital in a cab. Once I was admitted to St. Vincent's Hospital, Dr. Lawrence was called, the woman obstetrician Khadijah suggested. The contractions were coming more frequently and the numbing pain from the thuds in my chest made me wonder if this child would come into the world kicking and screaming with combat boots on. I thought about how important it had always been for me, after my parents were killed, to be close to people in danger or in pain. Now that I was in pain, I refused to allow myself to consider the possibility that I might be anywhere near the life-threatening situations on the far side of pain that had been so much a part of my life.

I remember sitting up with my legs raised and bent at the knee with Doctor Lawrence and Khadijah pushing against the heels of my feet. I tried to push as Raymond, who held my hand, urged me to do. But the paralyzing contractions, sending my body into spasms, took whatever strength I had left. All I could do was give myself over to the tremendous pressure inside. Khadijah, Doctor Lawrence and Raymond spoke but I could barely make out what they were saying. I must have been delirious by then because I had the sensation of something expanding just below my breast bone, making me feel like I was being entered and opened up from inside. And through the blur of sweat streaming into my eyes, I saw myself open and become a band around the crown of a head which brought the rest of the body out through the place that had given me so much delicious pleasure and now pain.

A girl! Raymond and I decided to name her Tasha because Khadijah said that the sound *Tah-sha* came from the back of my throat once the baby was completely out of me. And with the birth of Tasha another kind of birth took place in Raymond. From the moment she was separated from me, he attached himself to her. When I was breastfeeding Tasha, I sensed Raymond's desire to get her back in his arms. It was as though he was trying to make up for not having carried her in his body. The only way to do that was to take hold of her as much as possible, so Tasha would become as familiar with his touch and smell as she was with mine.

I loved it that Raymond wanted to connect immediately with Tasha in his own way without me being the go-between. But I was troubled by his inability to connect with anyone else. Raymond was often sullen and distant. When I asked him about it, he dismissed my concern as a symptom of the letdown that comes after pregnancy. I talked to Khadijah and she said it sounded like Raymond was the one suffering from postpartum depression.

A few days before my scheduled release from the hospital, Naomi called, making it clear that she wanted to visit me when no one else was around. I hadn't seen her at all in the last weeks just before I gave birth. She arrived, looking very tired after what had probably been a long day; but that was typical for Naomi. What alarmed me was her appearance: a missing button on her blouse, hair that was more than a little dishevelled and a lacerating run in one leg of her black tights. And when she kissed me on the cheek and looked admiringly at Tasha, asleep on my chest, it all seemed perfunctory.

"Damn!" I said. "You look like you're the one who just had a baby."

"I'll remember that, if I ever get foolish enough to consider having children."

"What's going on, Naomi?"

"Everything but me, it seems. But I didn't come up here to kvetch. How does it feel to be a mother?"

"I don't know yet. And I may not get many chances to find out, if Raymond has anything to say about it."

"Why's that?"

"He just about devours Tasha. If he had breasts that lactated, I'd have been a bystander the moment the doctor cut the cord."

"That probably means he'll be a great dad," she said.

"I guess. But I'm worried about him not wanting to be anything but that."

"You should count your blessings. For a lot of men, it's the other way around."

"Maybe you're right. But I can see something's bothering Raymond the moment Tasha's not in his arms."

"Have you talked to him about it?"

"I've tried but he says I'm looking for trouble where there is none."

"He may be right."

"I don't think so. But there's not much I can do about it either way, if he won't talk."

"And if he did?" Naomi asked. "What would you really be able to do to help him?"

"Oh! That sounds like a line from your recent *disenchantment with the law* speech."

"It's getting older every day."

"Well, to follow your lead—have you talked to Gerald about it?"

"Not in so many words."

"Listen to you," I said. "You can't even follow your own advice."

"That's not the only thing I've had trouble following."

"What do you mean?"

Unfortunately, she told me. Naomi also said that she and Gerald had agreed to a trial separation. He'd moved in with Frank and

Crystal. Of course, all of this explained why Raymond was completely out of it except when focused on Tasha. Once again, my efforts to make a place for myself in the world with people I cared about was unraveling.

"Have you decided what you're going to do?" I asked, more as a way not to scream than with any desire for an answer.

"No, I haven't."

"There's one thing you can say about walking out of Frank and Crystal's apartment," I said. "At least you know what you won't do."

"I don't know about that."

"Why not?"

"Something else happened before I left the apartment that I don't even want to admit to myself..."

I took a deep breath, glanced at Tasha in blissful sleep and wished I could join her.

"When I turned to leave, Gerald and Frank were already in bed together. Crystal was sitting on the carpet in the middle of the living room floor with her legs crossed and completely naked. As I walked by her, she grabbed the heel of one foot and then the other and crossed them both behind her neck. When I closed the door, she was looking directly at me, rocking back and forth, fingering herself. I was so dazed, I had to brace myself against the wall in the hallway to keep my balance. My stomach muscles tightened up as I stood completely still. And my skin felt like steam. I couldn't get my hand inside my clothes fast enough...I must have stood in that hallway for at least ten minutes, listening to myself breathe, before I could move."

"Naomi," I said, thoroughly disgusted with her. "Why are you telling me this?"

"Because I've spent years representing people for things they've done and haven't done. And I don't know if I can do it anymore, since I don't know what I will or won't do in my own life!"

"I'm really tired, Naomi. I think I want to take a nap."

"If you want me to leave, just say so."

"All right. Could you leave? I don't need you coming in here telling me you don't know what you're doing anymore, especially right after I've had a baby."

"What does your having a baby have to do with what I just told you?"

"I don't have many friends, but I'd like the few I've got not to be freaking out on me when I need them."

"That's why I'm here. To support you."

"Yeah, but you're a mess!"

"Muriel, I'm sorry I couldn't delay what's been going on in my life to accommodate Tasha's arrival. I'll try to do better next time."

"If Tasha was beyond the sound of my voice, I'd tell you what you could do with your sorry."

Naomi got up from her chair.

"You know," she said. "You're right. You should take a nap."

•••••

When Raymond came by later that day, his face went through its instant switch from distress to delight when he saw Tasha. We took our usual walking tour around the maternity ward. While he held Tasha, I waited for him to get his jollies with his bill and coo routine before I interrupted.

"Why didn't you tell me about all this stuff that's been going on with our friends?"

The joy in his face began to flicker off and on. "You talked to Naomi."

"That's right. So were you going to tell me at all?"

"Of course. I just felt it could wait until after you had the baby and things calmed down a bit."

"Naomi didn't sound calm this morning."

"She just needs some time to sort things out with Gerald. They'll probably get back together."

"Oh! You think so?"

"Don't you?"

"I wouldn't know. I haven't had as much time as you to mull it all over. But since we're on the subject, what about you and Frank?"

"What about me and Frank?"

"You used to be such good friends. Think you'll be able to sort out what's happened between the two of you?"

"What makes you think there's anything to sort out?"

"Look, I know there's no love lost between you and Gerald. So those sad sacks under your eyes can't be from any sleepless nights you've had, wondering whether Naomi and Gerald will get back together. Something else must have happened."

"What happened was Vietnam. And since Frank got back, he hurts people to keep them from getting too close."

"Surprised?"

Raymond shrugged. "Not really."

"So why are you in such a funk?"

"Because I let him bait me and behaved even worse than he did."

"Why don't you talk with him about it?"

"I think the mess we've made of things is beyond talk."

"As long as you and Frank have known each other? I find that hard to believe."

"Look at the state the world is in, then tell me what talk can do."

"I'm not talking about that! I'm talking about you and Frank."

"The last time I checked, we were all living in the world you're not talking about."

"Tell me, Raymond! How do you intend to communicate with our daughter, if you don't believe words matter?"

"That's interesting coming from a veteran of Push Comes to Shove. You used to be all about direct action, not talk. But I wasn't saying words are useless, Muriel. Only that mine failed me when I needed to talk with Frank."

Raymond turned to Tasha, still asleep in his arms, whispered into her ear and rubbed his nose against her cheek.

"You don't have to worry about Tasha and me," he said. "I won't have any trouble communicating with her."

I went home with Tasha the following morning. During those first weeks, I was pretty much apartment-bound, going out only to take walks with Tasha. Raymond was tireless, doing food shopping, cooking meals, and getting up in the middle of the night to change or comfort Tasha if she woke up. All this was done without a word of complaint. In fact, he seemed energized by it all. Khadijah visited regularly, coming alone or with Imani. Naomi and I only spoke on the phone.

One morning when the front door bell rang, I hoped it might be Naomi. I'd told her whenever she wanted to visit, to just come by. I looked through the peephole and saw Detective Garrett. I put the night latch on and cracked the door.

"This isn't a good time."

"I know. But admit it, there'll probably never be a time when you'd want to see me."

"I'm really not up for talking with you right now."

"Well, I can always have a squad car come by and take you and your baby over to the precinct."

I unhooked the latch and let him in.

"This won't take long," he said, sitting down in one of the armchairs in the living room.

"I don't believe that and neither do you."

"You're right. But you know, it's almost as interesting for me to watch your life evolve as it is tracking down Theo. Enjoying motherhood?"

"Yes, I am. And I can't wait to get back to it when you leave."

"You know, Muriel, sometimes you're such a disappointment to me. Since you're a writer, I'd hoped you'd have the same appreciation for the slow, unfolding of this exchange between us as you did when you wrote about your conversation with Theo. But I guess not...So did you put in a good word for me with him?"

"I told him you wanted to talk."

"What did he say?"

"He said he'll pave his own way to hell without any further help from you."

Garrett shook his head.

"What do you make of his talk of *targets of opportunity?*" he asked.

"Haven't thought that much about it."

"Do you think he's serious?"

"You know him much better than I do."

"Yeah, I know him. But you've seen him! Does he sound like someone capable of doing what he's proposing?"

"I don't know how someone who said what he did is supposed to sound. I think he's convinced himself that he'll do what he says he'll do. And I don't think it matters to him how he sounds."

Garrett looked away from me and gazed up at the ceiling as though trying to grasp some thought just out of his reach. "No matter what he told you, whatever he does, he's going to need me."

"That's wonderful. I hope you two will be very happy."

"Oh, we will. I'm convinced of it. I'm the only one, including Theo, who really knows the meaning of that recurring dream he talked about in your article. I'm the serpent in the pit. I'm blocking his way, but not to the other side where his comrades are waiting. I'm the obstacle, keeping him from digging deeper into the pit he wants to make for himself. The fact that Maggie's Farmers can't speak for themselves should tell you how little Theo thinks of them. And his inability to see is the shadow I cast over everything he does. I'm the blindfold he has to remove to see himself with his own eyes. So this whole elaborate plan of Theo's to force the rich to redistribute their wealth among the have-nots is a diversion from his primary objective—me. I'm the only target of opportunity he's truly interested in. All the rest means nothing to him."

"Look! This has all been very informative. But I don't want to be involved."

"You're more involved than you know."

"How?"

"You haven't figured it out yet?"

"Figured what out?"

"Why do you think Theo disappeared the same day the police busted into your bedroom and killed Walter?"

"Garrett, I'm sick of playing this game."

"Muriel! You never played the game! You got played!"

"What are you talking about?"

"After the fire bombing of the police precinct, Theo broke off communication with me. Even before that, I began to suspect that the high he got from playing at being a revolutionary in Push Comes to Shove had opened his nose up big time. I thought I could turn him around before he fell in love with his new image of himself but it was too late. I was ordered not to make any further contact with him and another plan was devised, without my knowledge, to get rid of the problem Theo had become. I knew the plan was to murder him, which I wouldn't have gone along with. Theo knew he was on borrowed time once he broke with the people who invented him. But somehow he found out when the raid was going to go down and split before the cops arrived who botched things up further by forgetting the description they were given of what Theo looked like."

"There's no need to go on, Detective. I know the story."

"No you don't. And neither did the cops who killed Walter."

"What are you trying to say?"

"You were probably right when you said Walter was murdered because those cops only saw that he was black. Unfortunately, what you and they didn't know, but Theo did, was this—Walter was one of us."

I winced as though I'd been struck. I sat perfectly still; and not wanting to be hurt by anything else Garrett might say, I began to will my mind to distance itself from my body.

"Are you telling me Walter was a cop?"

He nodded.

"I don't believe you."

"If I were you, I wouldn't want to believe me either."

"Why are you telling me this now?"

"I figured it was time you realized that being deceived is only possible if you're capable of deceiving yourself."

"Does that apply to you too?"

"Of course. The difference is: I know it and you don't."

"What about Walter? Why didn't he know what was going on?"

"I was never in communication with him. So I can't answer that question. But Theo must've figured out who Walter was and set him up to be killed in his place."

"You don't know if any of what you've said is true. You're just making up shit the way Theo does. Lucius was wrong about you being one of those vets who landed on their feet when they got back from Vietnam. You obviously landed on your fucking head!"

"It doesn't matter how you land, sweetheart, as long as you ain't killed by the fall."

Garrett stood up.

"I probably won't be back. So you won't have to worry any longer about whether the tales I'm spinning are made up of more of the truth than Theo's. But what I said about Walter being a cop wasn't me trying to turn straw into gold. Believe that if you don't believe anything else. Have a nice life, Muriel. You and your family."

After Garrett left, I double-bolted the door. I went into the bedroom, lifted Tasha, who was asleep, out of her crib, placed her on my bed and lay down beside her. I began inhaling Tasha's milky breath and didn't move again until Raymond came home.

THEO

1971

Dear Naomi Golden:

When I went underground, I knew Garrett wouldn't rest until I ended up like Walter. And once I was out of the way, I would be dismissed as a parasite who failed at everything—being a thief or a paid informer. So I'm giving you my version of who I am and what I've done. And by the time you read this, whatever I intend to do will be over. Garrett may be hunting me down, but I'm leading the chase.

I never knew my mother and father, and spent my childhood in too many foster homes to keep count. I didn't think much about being abandoned and had no interest in looking for my parents when I became an adult. In a way, having no one to point to who was responsible for me being in the world was an advantage. I could dispense with getting all exercised about who to credit or blame for how I got here and move on to the more important business of making up my own life.

There's one thing I've always known about myself. Once I commit to something, that's what I become. And if I believed what I committed myself to, I never had a problem convincing anyone else. As a kid, I figured out very quickly that if I was good at saying what I felt strongly about, I could manipulate other kids who wanted to kick my ass on a regular basis. I learned that those who believe in physical strength and nothing else are no match for someone with the gift of gab. In time, I realized I didn't want to be tied to any particular way of thinking but was drawn to rolling the dice and seeing where any number of beliefs might lead me.

Actors fascinated me. They could become different people and not limit themselves to being one person. But when I learned more about their lives, even the best of them were completely lost when they weren't acting. The only way not to be like those actors who didn't know what to do when a movie was over was to be someone different every day. That's how I've lived most of my life. But there was a problem with living this way. If you weren't in the movies, you'd probably end up in jail—which was how I met Detective Garrett.

Garrett recognized my talents immediately. Up until I met him, I went back and forth from being a small-time street hustler, tricking people out of their pocket money, to passing myself off as a front man for some bonafide business in order to get people to go into their bank accounts. My mistake was I quit working alone. I hooked up with this guy I knew as a shill in a fool-proof real estate scam I had going. But he overplayed his hand with these marks I'd worked my ass off to cultivate. After meeting my guy once, they got suspicious and called the cops. He got busted and gave me up.

I was looking at some serious jail time when Garrett entered the picture. He told me he respected my work, which was legendary among detectives dealing with extortion. I was even compared to Lee Marvin, not only for my acting chops but for my big lips as well. Garrett also said that performances of my caliber would've usually earned me an award in a penitentiary in upstate New York. However, I was in luck. He needed an actor of my range and experience to take on the role of a lifetime—a dynamic black man who infiltrates a dangerous black revolutionary group that the government had targeted for destruction. Garrett gave me five minutes to make up my mind. I didn't need that much time.

The thing Garrett never understood about me was that I couldn't be his stooge for very long. Like Steve McQueen in "The Thomas Crown Affair," I woke up every morning wondering who I would be that day. So having become an informer impersonating a revolutionary, it was inevitable that I would want to become one. As I graduated from words to action, like scaling a windowless school building and shattering a man's eardrums, I realized my real enemy wasn't the state but doubt.

As a kid, there were moments when questions about the two people whose juices made me would force their way into my thoughts. When this happened, I would lie down on my side and curl into a ball until I was sure of myself again. Later, I had other moments of doubt, like when a cop grabbed hold of me on that windowless school building and when a landlord challenged me near the courthouse. I knew my life was in that cop's hands and I wanted him to give me what his job called for and what I never allowed myself to expect from anyone—protection. And when that landlord yelled: "Get out of my way," it was like I was a kid again, being scolded by an adult voice of authority. I felt myself wanting to do what he said. I opened my arms and it took all my willpower not to curl up before I smashed his eardrums with my hands.

I firebombed a police precinct station not too long after. And I split the same day the police broke into our house and killed Walter. I couldn't trust myself to control my body every time my faith was shaken. I needed to woodshed for a while to rebuild my defenses with actions that took me further than I'd ever gone before. And given what Garrett and his cut buddies in the law were up to, I had a model for the extremes I could aspire to and maybe even go beyond.

RAYMOND

1971

WHEN I GOT HOME, I called Muriel's name several times but she didn't answer. I went into the bedroom; Muriel was lying in the bed, holding Tasha. She stared at me and her eyes were swollen from crying. As Muriel explained what had happened, the muscles in my shoulders and neck began to clench. I reached out to touch her arm but she pulled away.

"You can get through this," I said.

"How can you be sure?"

"Because I know you."

"Yeah, just like I knew Walter."

"What you didn't know about him shouldn't change you at all."

"If that's true, then why do I feel so stupid and unsure of everything?"

"It'll pass," I said.

"Oh yeah! Like the way you've gotten over what happened between you and Frank."

She'd actually shouted and taken me to task! The Muriel who convinced me that the world wouldn't come tumbling down from the hurt we might cause one another was back. And given what had happened between Frank and me, I needed her more than ever.

A few weeks later, my parents called from Florida to say they were coming to New York to visit their new grandchild and daughter-in-law. They were both permanently unhinged by Uncle Aubrey's death but developed ways of banishing the memory of that terrible day. My mother made it clear to my father and me that if we expected any further attention from her, she needed to feel taken care of. My father was much better at it than I was. And I assumed that was because he was a grown-up and I wasn't. But over the years, I discovered that taking care of my mother was the one thing my father did better than anything else.

MURIEL

1971

WE DIDN'T HAVE ENOUGH ROOM for Raymond's parents to stay with us. So they got a room at the Sheraton Hotel further uptown on Seventh Avenue. I had assumed that we would all get together at our apartment. But apparently that hadn't occurred to anyone but me.

Raymond's father, Cecil, opened the door to their hotel room.

"There you are!" he said, giving me an affectionate hug without squeezing the breath from my body. I appreciated Mister Bonner for not acting as though he knew me. I was also quite moved by the way he approached Raymond who was holding Tasha. He kissed him on the side of the mouth and then took Tasha into his arms, holding her gently in hands that were slabs of flesh with fingers as thick as knockwurst.

"Estelle! She's beautiful!" he said, walking into the room.

I hadn't noticed her before he spoke. Mrs. Bonner was sitting in a chair on the other side of the room. Her honey-glossed legs were crossed with the hem of her dress riding across the middle of the knee. Her face was absolutely breath-stopping—not a trace of makeup, an unblemished complexion and a sun-kissed radiance.

Mr. Bonner leaned over slightly to give her a better look at the baby. Mrs. Bonner gave Tasha the once over but made no move to take her from him. She lifted her eyes from Tasha and let them settle on me.

"Raymond! Aren't you going to introduce me to my daughter-in-law?"

"Of course."

I felt his hand on my elbow and moved toward her without sensing any exertion on my part. Raymond bent over to kiss his mother and she turned her cheek to him. I reached out for her hand, expecting her to do the same. But she merely held it out for me to take hold of instead.

"Mom, this is Muriel."

"I know that son. Who else could it be? Well Muriel, I'm glad we've finally met."

"So am I, Mrs. Bonner. Raymond has shown me photographs of you, but they don't do you justice."

"That's very kind of you. And if Raymond hasn't told you already, you should know that flattery will get you somewhere with me."

Raymond and Mr. Bonner smiled. Raymond's was sheepish embarrassment in the presence of his mother's vanity, while his father's was unapologetic proof of where flattery had gotten him with the woman he adored.

"Now, let me have my granddaughter," she said.

Mr. Bonner handed her the baby. Tasha had become a bit agitated by all handling by different people. But once she was in Estelle Bonner's arms, Tasha fastened her gaze onto her grandmother and settled into a calm that only occurred when she was being breastfed.

"Raymond," Estelle said, "Why don't you show your father around mid-town, so that we females can get better acquainted."

When they left, Tasha was completely under Mrs. Bonner's spell and I wasn't far behind.

"How are you holding up?" she asked.

"Except for being tired a lot, I'm fine."

"I'm not talking about having a baby. What about the catastrophes you've lived through?"

"I'm coping. I guess that's what everybody's got to do."

"That's not going to be good enough."

"I'm not sure I understand, Mrs. Bonner."

"I've been a social worker for twenty-five years and have had many clients who were traumatized. But none of them were fine like you seem to think you are."

"I don't know what else to say."

"You don't have to you say anything, as long as you do right by my son and granddaughter."

"That's what I thought I was doing."

"You're fooling yourself. I had murder thrown up in my face, just like you have. And if you don't find a way to get it out of your head, you won't be any good to Raymond or Tasha."

My face turned hot and I fought to keep my voice down. "What about Raymond seeing his uncle murdered? Did you ever have this conversation with him?"

"He was very young; and like any child, he had a much more fertile imagination than most adults. So he was able to digest what happened and put it to better use than you have."

"How do you know I didn't do the same thing. I was even younger than Raymond when my parents were killed."

"Look, honey, my job is to read people and encourage them to act in their own best interests when they don't want to. You and Raymond are both attracted to danger. But he only wants to study it in a book, while you seem to want it in your life as much now as you did when that young man you were living with was killed."

My look became a stare when she mentioned Walter.

"Did you think I wasn't going to find out about the person who married my son? I've read all your articles, especially the one about your meeting with that maniac who was in that group you used to belong to. And I also heard about that dangerous stunt you pulled while you were pregnant of agreeing to meet with those Vietnam veterans just before they blew themselves up. Now, if you were me, what would you think about the future of a marriage between your son and the woman with that resumé?"

"I see your point." I had no interest in defending myself.

Mrs. Bonner leaned forward and handed Tasha back to me. She rested her elbows on the arms of the chair and folded her hands.

"But what's your point, Muriel?"

"I don't understand what you mean."

"What I mean is, what in the world are you doing?"

"Trying to figure out what I should do," I said.

"That's simple! You need to be a wife to my son and a mother to my granddaughter. If you do that, you'll be the daughter I'd move heaven and earth for. And trust me, you don't want to know what I'm capable of if you fail to do right by either one of them."

"That won't be a problem for me," I said.

"Then what is the problem?"

"I was beginning to care a lot about him. And I thought he had feelings for me. But I found out that he might've been a cop."

"So what! If it's true, you can stop grieving over someone who wasn't the person you thought he was."

"Mrs. Bonner, my grief isn't for him. It's for myself."

"That's a waste of time. So you made a mistake in judgment. Get over it!"

"I don't know if I can."

"Then do what that young man you lived with did before he was killed—fake it!"

"Is that what you did?" I asked.

"You're damn right! All you young people seem to want to make a virtue out of how much you know. There're many things I wish I didn't know. When my brother was killed, I tried to ignore the things you're determined to notice. We're both acting. But your performance is obviously taking a greater toll on you than mine."

"That's because you've had more practice," I said.

"Then I suggest you start doing something about that."

I had to admit, I was touched by the way Mrs. Bonner had gotten all up in my business, just the way a mother would have. And an intense desire for her approval shivered through my skin.

RAYMOND

1971

THE DAY BEFORE MY PARENTS RETURNED TO FLORIDA, I had lunch with them at a restaurant near their hotel. As usual, my father was upbeat, telling me how wonderful Muriel and Tasha were. He continued priming me up for the moment when I knew my mother would break her silence and launch into what they really wanted to talk about. Ever since I was in college, the strategy for getting me to comply with their wishes had become more subtle. Instead of just telling me what to do, they tried to convince me that doing things their way would work out better in the long run. However, on this particular afternoon, my father's grin seemed to be straining to hold its place on his face.

"Your father and I are worried about Muriel."

"What are you worried about?"

"It's more concern than worry, son," my father said.

"All right! What's the concern?"

"She's carrying a burden that's going to make it difficult for you both to hold your family together," my mother said.

"We'll work it out."

"Not if Muriel keeps digging up ghosts that are better off left alone."

"Sometimes it's the ghosts that won't leave you alone," I said.

My mother rolled her eyes. "That's an excuse used by people with weak minds."

"It seems to me that doing everything in your power not to remember, is no better than not being able to forget."

"Raymond! Are you talking about me?" she asked.

"Estelle! Why don't we let all this alone for right now," my father said.

"I'm more than happy to do that Cecil. I just hope my daughter-in-law can do the same. Otherwise, our granddaughter will have to carry the burden of what her mother refused to leave alone!"

"Mom, I have tell you," I said. "Everything you've done to forget has made me want to remember even more."

"If saying that is meant to hurt me, your father has taken very good care of me. So that won't happen. We're only trying to look out for you, Raymond, because it's quite obvious there's no one else to do it."

"Muriel takes care of me!"

"How does she do that, son?"

"She helps me see that *living my life out loud*—being out in the world—doesn't have to hurt me or the people I care about."

"It's not your life that worries me. It's hers."

"I won't listen to anymore of this criticism of Muriel," I said.

"But Raymond, I was only doing what you said Muriel encourages you to do—living my life out loud. I'm sorry if I hurt your feelings."

"What about Muriel's?"

"We both care a great deal about Muriel and Tasha," my father said. "They're part of our family now."

I was relieved that my father intervened before the living my mother and I were doing got too much louder.

MURIEL

1971

AFTER PUTTING HIS PARENTS IN A CAB to the airport, Raymond came back to the apartment and told me about their conversation.

"I hope you didn't upset them too much," I said.

"They'll get over it."

"Yeah, but what about me?"

"What do you mean?"

"It's me they have a problem with, not you. And after what you said to your mother, she may end up making me pay for it."

"That's what I get for coming to your defense."

"You weren't defending me. You used me to hit back at your mother about things that only involve the two of you."

"I don't understand you, Muriel. After what she said about you, why are you taking her side?"

"Because no matter what, she'll always be on your side. But I have a ways to go to get her on mine. Don't make it more difficult for me than it already is."

I was surprised at how pissed I was with Raymond. And he was pissed at me for being pissed. Sensing something was wrong, Tasha began to cry in her playpen. Raymond reached in, picked her up and began murmuring words of comfort that we were hard-pressed to use with one another.

Later that day, I got a call from a friend of Miss Mattie's telling me that Mister Percy had passed away. I hadn't seen either of them in almost two years. But I did call when Raymond and I were married and right after Tasha was born. Neither Mister Percy nor Miss Mattie had mentioned any health problems he was having, and wouldn't have even if there were. And I hadn't bothered to ask.

Raymond, Tasha and I took the train up to Yorktown for Mister

Percy's wake. When we got to the funeral parlor, there were ten or twelve people standing or seated in the dimly lit area around the casket. Everyone looked to be around the same age as my stepparents, though I didn't recognize anyone. Miss Mattie was sitting in the row of chairs to the right of the casket. A man and a woman were speaking to her so softly that I couldn't make out what they were saying. Miss Mattie hadn't changed very much except for the lines of grief in her face.

I walked over to Mister Percy laid out in his casket and realized I had never seen anyone dead this well-preserved. They were always damaged, in pieces. I could finally appreciate Raymond's childhood worry that the spirit might be trapped inside a body that bore no resemblance to the departed loved one. This was true of Mister Percy. Nothing about his body seemed to have ever been alive. He looked like he'd been stuffed, zipped up and painted over with a dull ashen finish.

When the couple talking to Miss Mattie stepped away, her gaze found me.

"How're you, daughter?" she asked.

"I'm fine...Miss Mattie, this is my husband, Raymond. And this is our daughter, Tasha."

Her face gave no hint of what she might have been feeling as she looked at them and held her hand out to Raymond. She held the baby for a while, staring intently at Tasha's rapidly changing facial expressions. Raymond finally took Tasha and Miss Mattie and I sat without speaking for some time.

"What was ailing Mister Percy?" I asked.

"The usual aches and pains that finally wore him out."

"But was it anything in particular?"

"Ain't being tired particular enough for you?"

"Miss Mattie, I don't mean to upset you. I was just wondering if Mister Percy had been complaining about anything bothering him."

"What difference would that've made?"

"Just that if he had gone to a doctor, maybe something could've been done."

"I don't see what a doctor could've done to keep his heart from stopping while he was asleep."

"You're probably right. But it might've been worth several more years with you for him to have gotten a check-up once in a while."

"I'm not complaining."

"You never do."

"And you still think that life is something you can fix when it's broken."

"I don't want to fix life, Miss Mattie, just make it better."

"Sounds like the same thing to me."

"What do you have against making things better?"

"Nothing! Except you don't seem to have gotten much satisfaction from trying."

"That's because it's difficult to get people to change their ways."

"Does that surprise you?"

"No! But it upsets me!"

"Why should it, if they're doing everything you expect them to do?"

"I guess I want to believe human beings can always do better."

Miss Mattie smiled for the first time.

"I feel blessed when they don't do no worse."

"What did you and Mister Percy think about the way I turned out?"

"He would've been pleased with how you've settled down with a family."

"Is that the way you feel?"

"Percy and me didn't disagree on much that really mattered."

"Does that mean you agreed with him about me?"

"Oh child! You've spent so much time disapproving of what others do. And yet you want everybody to approve of you."

"Not everybody," I said.

"You know that baby of yours has her father's eyes. They're as still as the creek Percy and me used to fish in. But everything else in her face is restless like yours. If we'd grown up together as girls, we probably wouldn't have had any more to say to each other than we do now. But I never thought it was important for you to have my approval. What mattered was that you knew that I accepted you for yourself, even if I didn't always care for the person you were trying to be. Now you've got the family you say Percy and me couldn't give you. I hope it turns out to be what you wanted. But knowing you, it probably won't."

"Why do you say that?"

"I've been lucky," she said. "For better and worse, I've gotten what I wanted out of life. And the better part of it was with Percy. Not many can say that. But things may turn out even better for you, since you seem to enjoy it more when you don't get what you want. And there're probably more people willing to help you fail than succeed. But that's the way you like it. You just got everybody fooled, including yourself."

There was no malice in Miss Mattie's voice. And her observations were completely free of judgment. But I refused to believe I'd allowed myself to become so twisted by the resistance to change in America that I now embraced opposition like a loved one. However, when I compared the indignities of my daily life to the parts that gave me satisfaction, the disparity was startling.

•••••

When I was completely focused on Tasha, I didn't think about my problems. She would make sounds and I answered back to what I thought she was trying to express. Sometimes Tasha made no sounds at all and listened to whatever I said with what looked like genuine interest. Miss Mattie was right about her face; it was a non-stop motion picture of every human feeling. And Tasha's eyes were serenity surrounded by the commotion in the rest of her face. I wondered how the combination of Raymond's need to be still within the swirl of events and my desire to rumble with the world would play out in Tasha.

In spite of Raymond's natural calm, he got very animated when it came to Tasha. He was willing to take her with him just about anywhere—whether it was shopping or to his classes. And if I was under the pressure of a deadline for a piece I was writing or wanted to get together with Khadijah or Naomi, he was glad to adjust his schedule to accommodate mine. Since Raymond's falling out with Frank, he spent all of his time, when not teaching, with Tasha and me.

I'd been trying to get to see Naomi for weeks without any success. As usual, she was overwhelmed by motions and briefs from her numerous court cases. However, we finally arranged to have dinner one evening.

"You look great!" I said. "Does that mean you and Gerald have gotten back together?"

"No. And it doesn't look as though we will."

"How do you feel about that?"

"Relieved."

"Why?"

"It was coming for a while. Refusing to be the fourth side of a sexual rectangle just made it happen sooner."

"Have you seen him since he moved in with Frank and Crystal?" I asked.

"No. But we've talked over the phone."

"How did that go?"

"It was okay, under the circumstances. But Gerald's furious with me. He thinks I betrayed him by agreeing to something I didn't intend to do. And then when the three of them went ahead anyway, he said I used that as an excuse to make him the heavy so it would be easier for me to leave our marriage."

"Do you think he's right about any of it?"

"Maybe."

"It's good you two are talking. That's probably the only way you're going to find out what actually happened."

"That's what I've been trying to do. But Gerald only wants to talk about blaming me. And that may make it easier for him to get out of our marriage."

I didn't say anything.

"What's wrong?" she asked. "You find my version more difficult to believe than his?"

"No. That's not it. I was just thinking about Miss Mattie and Mister Percy. There was something very special between them.

Whatever it was, I've spent most of my life trying to get them to give me some of it. But it doesn't look like that's going to happen."

Naomi reached across the table and touched my hand.

"They gave you what they had, Muriel. Maybe what you wanted from them was something they could only give each other."

"I guess it was just my luck to get raised by two people who were stingy with what they had to give except when it came to themselves."

"You know, my grandmother came here from Russia during the pogroms in 1905. She used to tell me Yiddish folktales and always started by saying *Amol iz geven*...Once upon a time, which is all the Yiddish I remember. One of my favorites was about a mother bird and her three young chicks. They had to cross a river so the mother put the first one under her wing and flew off. On the way across, she said: *Tell me child, when I'm old, will you carry me under your wing the way I'm carrying you now?* And the child said: *'Of course, how could you ask such a question.'* But the mother said: *You're lying!* And she let her child go and it fell into the river and drowned. She went back for the second one. And while flying across the river, she asked the same question and got the same answer. So she let her second child drop into the river and drown. On the last trip across the river, with her third child, the mother asked once again: *When I'm old, will you carry me under your wing the way I'm carrying you now?"* And the child said: *No, mother. How could I? By then I'll have children of my own to carry.* The mother bird said: *You are my dearest child. You're the one who tells the truth.* And she carried her child to the other side of the river."

Naomi folded her arms and smiled.

"Why are you telling me some horror story about mothers killing their babies?" I asked.

"It's not about that. It's about loving people enough to know when you can't carry them."

"I never wanted them to carry me. But I could've used some holding every once in a while."

"Well, now that you've got Tasha, you can make sure she gets that from you—and then make a mess of it just like most parents do."

"Did your folks make a mess of you?" I asked.

"That depends on what kind of mess you mean. Old World or New World? My grandparents on both sides of the family were from Odessa. They fled to America from that Old World; but in every other word they spoke to their children, the life of the Old World lived on. My parents were so stuffed with those stories that they made a point of trying to force into my mind everything that wasn't from the world that was drummed into them. So I was caught between the obsessions of my parents and grandparents. They were all in denial—my parents about the past, and my grandparents about the future. It was no surprise that I decided to become a lawyer."

"I would've liked to have known what it was like to grow up around people who wouldn't leave me alone."

"The police don't seem to leave you alone."

"Oh! That's very witty, Naomi. Maybe comedy is in your future."

"In my future! If all that's been going on in this country isn't comedy, I don't know what is?"

"I don't see many people laughing," I said.

"I think that's part of our problem."

"So what are you going to do about it?"

"I don't know. But I feel like I'm caught in another story my grandmother once told me. I'll make this the last one, I promise. Anyway, these dogs applied to a king for a decree that would forbid people from bothering them. Once it was signed, the dogs asked cats to hide it, since they knew places where no one would find it. Soon after that, dogcatchers began rounding up dogs. When they protested and mentioned the king's degree, the dogcatchers said: *Where is it?* The dogs then went to the cats and asked where they put the decree. The cats went to the eave of a roof but discovered that the decree had been chewed up by mice. The dogs were furious when they heard this and began chasing the cats who also became angry and started chasing the mice."

"You're going to have to break that one down for me," I said.

"My grandmother thought that story described human nature."

"Seems very cynical."

"Living through a pogrom will do that for you. But I've decided that I can longer represent people who've kept doing the terrible things that've been done to them or intend to. It all has to stop somewhere."

"So what will you do?" I asked.

"I don't know. Maybe find something to do that doesn't involve people who do evil to get ahead or to get even."

"You think that's going to take care of that itch you talked about last year?"

"Hopefully. At least until the next one comes along. And what about you?"

"I guess my itch is this feeling that I'm not done with Theo and Garrett."

Naomi raised her wineglass and I raised mine.

"To the itch," she said.

RAYMOND

1973

THE FIRST TIME I PUT A BASEBALL IN TASHA'S HAND, she tried to grasp it with her fingers and became flustered when she was unable to do it. However, she was appeased when I showed her that by pushing the ball across the floor, it was possible to manipulate it without having to be in complete control. Of course, Tasha would soon achieve this facility with human beings. In the mean time, she proved to be a great audience and willing pupil in my world of baseball fundamentals and trivia.

I demonstrated the way to grip a ball in the palm of the hand with the index and middle finger across the seam. I not only showed Tasha the flick of the wrist and grip required to throw a curve and knuckleball, but would take her to the park in a stroller so I could show her the dip the ball took when it was thrown properly. I was thrilled that Tasha seemed intrigued by all my enthusiastic baseball chatter and instruction. And gradually, I began to notice gestures she would make with her hands, imitating what I'd shown her.

What convinced me that Tasha had signed on as a full partner in my mania for baseball was during a Mets game at Shea Stadium. They were in the thick of a pennant race and had acquired the legendary Willie Mays in a trade from the Giants the year before. Mays was past forty and nearing the end of his career. It was painful to watch him botching plays in the outfield, swinging late, bailing out on pitches and popping up balls he used to crush. In the early 1960's, Mays was at his peak, and arguably, the best player in the game. And now, ten years later, I was watching him break down, just like the country seemed to be.

On this particular afternoon, Mays was playing centerfield. And every time a ball was hit to him, I would alert Tasha to watch. And on one ball skied to Mays, I said: "Look Tasha, there's another one hit to Willie!" I turned to her as she lifted her head, trying to pick up the flight of the ball. She frowned underneath the brim of her Mets cap and made a basket with her arms as though waiting to catch the ball just the way Willie did!

Willie Mays retired after the Mets lost the World Series to Oakland in October, and the Senate investigations into Watergate began. So that moment with Tasha at Shea Stadium was the peak of a year that didn't have much to recommend it—except for the Paris peace agreement and the withdrawal of the last combat troops from Vietnam. At least that's what I thought until a headline appeared across the front page of every newspaper that the son of one of the wealthiest families in America had been kidnapped by Maggie's Farmers.

M U R I E L

1973

AMERICA WAS FORCED TO ADMIT that it couldn't win the war in Vietnam in 1973. It was also the year I realized I couldn't win the war I was waging with the world over the lion's share of Tasha's affections. I knew there was a timeline on how long she would covet me above everyone and everything. But I didn't expect her undivided attention on me to shift as soon or in the way it did.

Tasha started walking on her own shortly after she was a year old. And even after she was on solid food, I kept breastfeeding her, more as a pacifier than for nourishment. Of course, I enjoyed the physical sensations, but I was thrilled even more by how quickly I was able to quell any anxiety or discomfort Tasha was feeling, just by allowing her to take my nipple into her mouth. She might be completely absorbed in playing on the floor, and suddenly lose interest; then she would crawl or walk over to me and start working her way under whatever top I was wearing. We were so, emotionally, bound together that I could usually anticipate when she was coming for my breast. So when I noticed Tasha stop what she was doing to come over to me on the couch, I began pulling my shirt out. She climbed onto the couch and I held my breast for her. I closed my eyes as Tasha's mouth bathed my nipple but felt a twinge of pain when she pulled on it a little too hard.

"Not so hard, honey," I said, opening my eyes. "That hurts."

Tasha's right leg was stretched out, trying touch something in the pile of toys at the end of the couch. She let go of me and crawled toward what had caught her eye. Tasha's reached out and grabbed a baseball, whose shape and weight seemed to interest her a great deal. She then tossed the ball to the floor and chased after it as it rolled away.

I couldn't believe it! Tasha never left my breast for anything until she had her fill. And now my breast had been rejected in favor of a baseball. The fear that I might be losing this connection with Tasha sooner than I wanted sent chills rushing over me. But from Tasha's point of view, it all made sense. Unlike my breast, a baseball was portable and she could keep it with her at all times. I tried being angry with Raymond but quickly came to my senses. I was as engaged with Tasha as Raymond was. But Tasha's connection to me was primarily through my body; so that was the focus of her fascination. Since Raymond couldn't match my physical intimacy with Tasha, he created his own. How could I blame him for that? But if Tasha was losing interest in the parts of my body I offered her, what else did I possess that would command her attention?

I didn't have to wait very long for an answer.

A day or so after pushing me aside for a baseball, Tasha tripped over one of her toys and fell on her face. She didn't cry but looked angrily at the rubber duck and then the floor for making her fall. She pounded on the head of the duck with her fist, which let out a squeak. Then she picked up a rubber hammer and retaliated against the floor. When the floor didn't give any indication that it felt her wrath, she looked up at me with great disappointment. I was stunned by how quickly Tasha struck back at what she thought was responsible for hurting her. I didn't want to believe that such a reaction could be learned so early in her young life.

The expression on my face must have frightened her, because it was only then that she broke the silence in the room with her screams. Before I could do anything, she ran toward me, burying herself in my lap. As I spoke soothing words to calm her, I realized Tasha had run to me, not because of hurt or anger from the fall, but from fear that she had wandered into this unfamiliar place that spelled out danger in my eyes. Obviously, Tasha didn't know the word, but I had introduced her to the feeling. The important thing for me was that she rushed back to my body in the same way I'd always gravitated toward people who put themselves in physical danger. But who did Tasha think was in danger—herself or me?

It didn't matter because I now knew what would bind us together forever. As Tasha's body continued to heave from sobbing, my own eyes began to swell with tears. In that moment, we were accepting the possibility that serious harm could come to either one of us without warning—something I'd never had a chance to share with my parents.

I was overwhelmed with despair over how danger, on any given day, might very easily stamp down with deadly force on Tasha and myself. I hadn't known my parents long enough to see them hurt in ways that didn't result in death. So I would relish attending to Tasha's every minor bump and bruise on her body and heart. If Raymond was better at making her happy, I would do whatever I could to take care of her hurts. But if I wanted the satisfaction of having Tasha run to me whenever she was in harm's way, I had to allow her to flirt with dangers Raymond didn't want her anywhere near.

•••••

When I read the news that Maggie's Farmers had kidnapped Quentin Smithfield, heir to a family who made its fortune growing tobacco, I wondered why Theo had departed from his plan by making this young college student the first *target of opportunity*. My question was answered a few days later by a videotape of Smithfield shown on the TV news. After saying he hadn't been harmed and was being treated as well as could be expected under the circumstances, Smithfield outlined, in his own words, Maggie's Farmers' demands.

Within seventy-two hours of the airing of the tape, a group of ten men and women with impeccable humanitarian credentials, chosen from a list provided by Maggie's Farmers, must hold a press conference, announcing their willingness to serve as trustees of a fund created by contributions from the very wealthy, such as Smithfield Tobacco, for the benefit of the poor. Evidence would have to be given at the press conference that the trust fund had actually been set up. Once these demands were met to the satisfaction of Maggie's Farmers, Quentin Smithfield would be released within twenty-four hours. However, if any attempts were made to prevent the trustees from using the funds as they deemed necessary, the outcome for the next *target of opportunity* from the wealthy, would prove fatal.

As I listened to Smithfield, it was apparent that he'd been terribly shaken by his ordeal. However, I was impressed by how well he was holding himself together. And his voice, while it wavered occasionally, never gave any hint of what he felt about what he was being forced to say. I could feel the strong pull Smithfield had on me. It was still about danger and my need to get closer to people on every side of it.

•••••

The event to commemorate the withdrawal of the remaining U.S. troops in Vietnam had been put off until late April when the cold sting of winter was finally soothed by the late arrival of spring. The 'Day of Reconciliation', as it was called, was pulled together by an assortment of veterans and peace groups. People began to arrive at the entrance of Central Park that led to the Great Lawn shortly after daybreak on Sunday morning. By noon, a huge crowd stretched out over the entire field. There were couples with young children in strollers, carried on their shoulders and backs and walking hand in hand. The air was weighty with the smell of reefer as clusters of people passed joints around in plain sight of the police who seemed not to take any notice. Men and women whose hair was streaked with gray or completely white mingled easily among the mix of different ages and races. They all seemed to have grown weary, at least for one day, of their efforts not to get along.

The veterans in the crowd were unmistakable. They had the look of having grown up and gotten old at the same time. They came in uniform and combat fatigues. Some wore the standard-issue civilian uniform of business suit and tie. Others showed up dressed in anything from khaki to down and out grungy. There were as many heads and faces that were razored close to the bone as there were those covered by a tempest of grizzled hair.

But what they had in common was in their eyes: a slow leak from some incoming memory that ached every time they blinked. Those who had been in the war recognized the look immediately. And the words that followed were usually:

"Where'd you serve?"

"In Danang!"

"What branch?"

"Marines, Ninth Regiment! What about you?"

"Army, Twenty-fifth Infantry Division! Mostly in Chu Lai."

"When'd you get back in the World?

"'71!"

"Same here!"

The veterans nodded to each other, moving through the crowd as they spotted *another piece of themselves in someone else's eyes. The Day of Reconciliation had no planned agenda or speakers to address the crowd. The unspoken hope was that each person would make a small gesture toward closing the wound the war had opened in the country. In several sections of the Great Lawn, melodies, finger-picked on 12-stringed guitars and rhythms glad-handed on conga drums, pulled all who were present into one pulse. The huge gathering of people in Central Park listened to the key in which each person spoke; and there was the hope that the harmony of the moment would begin to heal everyone, no matter how they found their way into and out of the war—and back to the World.*

RAYMOND

1973

ON THE MORNING OF THE DAY OF RECONCILIATION, there were news reports that Quentin Smithfield had been released unharmed by Maggie's Farmers. He was found wandering around blindfolded on an isolated road not far from Princeton, New Jersey. I didn't have a good feeling about the two events occurring so close together. I suggested to Muriel that we not take Tasha with us to the gathering in Central Park. I'd been to enough baseball games as a child to know people can turn bizarre and dangerous in a crowd and was worried about Tasha feeling overwhelmed by so many adults looming over her. But Muriel said my worries were unwarranted.

We took the bus and, after getting off, quickly merged with the droves of people walking toward the park. I looked at Tasha who was being carried piggyback style by Muriel. She seemed content and, as always, interested in everything around her. Naomi had agreed to meet us and was leaning against the stone abutment a half a block up from the entrance. Since the day we ran into each other in front of Frank's apartment building, my regard for her had grown. We hadn't become close friends, but I appreciated the way she related to Tasha. She talked directly to her, never at her. And Naomi didn't engage in any over-the-top giddiness at the mere sight of Tasha, which kids see right through.

"I guess you've heard about Maggie's Farmers," Naomi said.

"Yeah," Muriel said. "Do you think corporations will go along with this trust fund idea now that Smithfield has been released?"

"I don't know. They might, if they believe Theo will start picking off their family members. Then again, they might not bend to intimidation, which is not all that different from what they've done to become rich and powerful. But let's not dwell on that. This is supposed to be a festive occasion. But you wouldn't know it, looking at the two of you."

"I'm glad the government has finally come around to what we said it should've done years ago," Muriel said. "I just wish this had been done sooner, so all the people who died, Vietnamese and American, would be able to celebrate today along with us."

"You'll get no argument from me on that," Naomi said. "It's always been easier to make a mess than to get out of one."

"Unfortunately, that's usually the case," I said.

"So, professor! What's your prognosis on what we'll do now that we don't have the war to obsess about?"

Naomi's voice sounded run-ragged. And I wasn't exactly sure what she meant, Vietnam or our other battles.

"I don't know," I said. "We may be putting Vietnam out of sight but I'm not sure how successful we'll be in getting it out of our minds."

As we walked closer to the Great Lawn, I looked around at everything. It was a carnival atmosphere with concession stands, jugglers, acrobats, musicians and puppeteers. Actors gave recitations from Shakespeare; activists handed out leaflets and just about everyone else engaged in the lively give and take of conversation.

"I heard that our former favorite people are breaking up their *ménage à trois* and leaving New York," Naomi said quietly.

I didn't say anything and tried to keep my satisfaction from showing.

"Did Frank and Crystal split up?" Muriel asked.

"No. They're heading out to New Mexico."

"What about Gerald?"

"He's going back home to Baltimore."

"When are Frank and Crystal leaving?" I asked.

"Soon, I guess," Naomi said.

"You know why they're leaving?"

"You'll have to ask them yourself. *Why* is a question I've stopped asking."

"That's the one question I can't stop asking," Muriel said.

"I wonder which of us is worse off," Naomi said.

As we stopped to buy hamburgers and sodas at a concession stand, a conversation between some veterans and a few of the people hawking radical newspapers caught my attention.

"Maggie's Farmers are fighting the war the government really ought to be involved in," a man said with a stack of newspapers under his arm.

"What kind of a war is that?" one of the vets asked.

"One where opportunities are redistributed to people without them."

"You really think that's going to happen by threatening and kidnapping people?"

"Our government won't ever see the light until they fear losing something even more precious than their money."

"If you ask me," another vet said, "it's not just the rich and the government who're slow to see the light. These Maggie's Farmers got some eyesight problems too. When they talk about helping people, there's no mention of us."

"They're starting at the bottom."

"That's where a lot of us are."

"Yeah, but your bottom may be the ceiling for somebody living in Appalachia. Can't you see that?"

This did not look good. I turned to Muriel and Naomi. "I think we should move away from this scene."

"In a minute," Muriel said. "This could turn into something I can use in my *Out In Left Field* column about what happened today."

The vet moved to within a few inches of the other man, who didn't give any ground.

"Let me ask you this, asshole. If I knocked you the fuck down and dared you to get up, would you be thinking about how much better your situation is than somebody in Appalachia?"

"That's an example of the false consciousness that sent you to Vietnam and kept me from going."

The two men started throwing punches and were immediately swallowed up among friends and foes who tried to separate them or land some blows of their own. The people closest to the fighting, like us, grabbed their children and belongings, as though rushing for cover in a storm. Tasha was whimpering and her arms were locked around Muriel's neck. Screams cut the air all around us. And we were swept up in a reckless dance with hordes of people trying to get out of the park. Screams behind us began to stab closer. I turned around and there were swarms of teenagers bearing down on us, only slowing down to snatch handbags.

One kid had singled us out. I let Muriel, Tasha and Naomi get ahead of me and turned to face him. He stopped running and seemed startled that I was in his way.

"What the fuck you doing?"

"That's my wife and daughter you're chasing."

"I'm not chasing nobody."

"Then go another way."

He opened his mouth slightly but no words came. His eyes locked onto me. My hands shook as though afflicted with palsy. A smile curved with disdain on his mouth and he shrugged.

"Forget you, man!" he said and ran off in another direction.

When I finally got to the sidewalk on Central Park West, I had no sense of having come out of the park under my own power. I was jarred out of my haze by the police who were running past me into the park. Looking around to get my bearings, I figured Muriel and Naomi wouldn't have gone too far once they realized I wasn't with them. I turned down a side street, a block from the park entrance, and stopped cold in my tracks. Muriel, Tasha and Naomi were standing mid-way down the block with their backs to me. Blocking their path was a young black man. One hand was covering his face, while the other pointed toward them.

I ran toward them screaming. "Get away from them!"

The man turned and ran off.

When I reached them, I grabbed hold of Muriel and Tasha.

"Are you all right?"

"We'll live," Muriel said.

"How about you?" I said, looking at Naomi.

"I'm all right," she said, but her words seemed at odds with her shocked face.

I bent down to Tasha, who had wrapped herself around Muriel's leg.

"How's my little girl?"

"Mommy let the man see her needle."

I looked up at Muriel.

"What needle?"

"This," she said, holding out a darning needle in her right hand.

"Didn't you give him all your money?"

"Yeah, but I only had a couple of dollars and some tokens and Naomi had less than that. He said he didn't believe us and would hurt Tasha unless we came up with more money. He reached for her and I went for his face with my nails. I pulled this out of my bag, when he said he was going to do something much worse to us than the scratches I made on his face. Fortunately for him, you got here just in time."

"What do you mean? Fortunately for him?"

"Just that you saved his life."

Sweat began to crawl, spider-like, down my spine. "How did I do that?"

"When he heard your voice, I could see he was relieved. I told him right before you got here that he could forget about living, if he made another move toward me or my child."

"You're fuckin' unbelievable, Muriel! First, you refuse to leave the park when we could've avoided all this trouble. Then you bait this kid, hoping he'll back down. But you put Tasha in danger!"

"You don't understand, Raymond. I wasn't counting on him backing down. I was counting on killing him. Even if he killed me, he had no chance of hurting Tasha."

I looked down at Tasha, still fused to Muriel's leg.

"Tasha? Do you want Daddy to give you a piggy-back ride?"

"No Daddy. I want Mommy to give me one."

We walked in silence to the bus stop where Naomi left us to get into a cab she'd hailed.

"I'm going to take a walk," I said. "I'll be home a little later."

"Why don't you ride home on the bus with us and then take your walk?"

"You'll be all right," I said, kissing Tasha on the cheek. "You're like Theo. You're a one-woman revolution."

MURIEL

1973

I WAS TERRIFIED until he actually threatened us.

"Bitch! If you don't gimme something I can get some money for, I'm gonna take your fuckin' kid!"

He didn't have a gun but his words were the same as having one. But instead of the shock I felt when the cops burst in on Walter and me with shotguns, I was sweaty with desire to crush the life out of his body. I never gave a thought to what he might do to me.

Instead, my mind was focused on what I knew I was going to do to him. It was my turn to do what the police had done. I could tell he wanted no part of me, but tried to talk himself into the nerve he didn't have.

"What you think you gonna do with that? I ought a take that shit 'way from you and jam it up your pussy!"

"Shut the fuck up and come on, if you wanna die," I hissed. "Cause I'm gonna make you dead, so help me!"

Raymond's distant voice added to my adrenaline rush.

"Your lucky day, you cunt-face bitch!"

After this, the guy ran off.

If I had to say what I felt in the seconds it took for Raymond to reach us, it was relief and disappointment.

RAYMOND

1973

I THOUGHT ABOUT IT FOR A FEW DAYS before deciding to go see Frank. I rang the bell to the apartment and heard the peephole cover open.

"Frank and Crystal aren't here," a voice said, which sounded like Gerald's.

"I'd like to wait, if that's okay."

There was the sound of locks being unbolted before the door opened. I hadn't seen Gerald since the day Muriel and I were married. He didn't seem surprised or bothered by my unexpected visit.

"They said they had to do some things but I'm not sure how long they'll be gone."

"I'm in no hurry," I said, walking into the living room filled with boxes of books, household items, piles of clothing and furniture that had been pushed against the walls. I found a box to sit on in the middle of the clutter as Gerald began putting oversized art books into boxes.

"Hear you're moving to Baltimore," I said.

"I hope this small talk you're about to launch into isn't for my benefit, cause I really don't need it."

"I was just curious, that's all. We've never really gotten to know each other. And this could be the last time we speak."

"I don't think either one of us will be worse off because we didn't become friends."

"Are you still holding what I said to you a few years ago against me?"

"No. Are you?"

"Am I what?" I asked.

"Holding what you said against me?"

"Of course not!"

"Glad we got that settled."

"Is something, wrong?" I asked.

"Look man, I know you and Frank had a falling out. But if you want to mend fences, talk to him. Don't practice on me."

I didn't say anything right away. It looked as though our last contact with each other would end the way it had that night in the bar.

"Why are you leaving New York?" I asked.

He eyed me warily before he spoke, as if to say *You better not be jerking me around!*

"I used to see New York as a place that had so much to feast on. Now it looks like someone who's eating himself alive. I've become a living example of my painting of the Hindu god, Kirtimukha, who eats his own head to rid himself of his insatiable appetite."

"So you think leaving New York will prevent that from happening?"

"I don't know. But at this point, I'm tempted to do almost anything."

He spread his arms apart, as though to include the apartment in what he was saying.

"I need to go some place where I can get detoxed," he said.

"So you're going to Baltimore?"

"That's right. You know, LeRoi Jones, who now calls himself Imamu Baraka, has this poem where he realizes that while his mind is the sky, his ass ain't."

I shook my head. "What about Naomi? You think you might get back together?"

"Like living with Frank and Crystal, she's in that part of my life when my mind was in the sky."

"But you were together for ten years. It couldn't have all been fantasy."

"Enough of it was so that now I can see it for what it really was."

"And what was that?" I asked.

"A betrayal of myself."

"You mean because she's white?"

"See how simple that was for you? I wish I'd figured it out that easily. I could've saved Naomi and myself a lot of grief."

"I don't think you really believe that."

"Why not? It's people like you and Muriel who finally convinced me it was true."

"Muriel? What did she do?"

"Basically, the same thing you did."

"I thought you said you'd gotten over it."

"I never got over it. I got through it. But I don't blame you any-more because I thought the same thing when I saw interracial couples in the street. Of course, I didn't include myself in those judgments because I believed Naomi and I were above and beyond all that. So you, Muriel and all those other blacks who've hammered away at me all these years can take some of the credit for bringing me down to earth and back home again!"

"You don't sound too happy about it."

"I'm not. But that'll change once I get back to Baltimore and start a regimen to remove all my doubts and hostility against black folks like you and Muriel."

"I can understand you wanting to get rid of hostility, but removing doubt from your life isn't something I'd think you'd want to do. Especially being an artist."

"I don't know what I am anymore. But the only way I'm going to find out is by abstaining from everything I used to think was important. And whatever's left over from what I strip away will be raw material for a new me that won't be burdened by confusion or uncertainty."

When Gerald put the last of the books in a box, he looked around to see if there was anything left undone.

"I'm going to split," he said. "You're welcome to hang out here, if you want."

He hesitated at the door.

"May I ask you a question?"

"Go ahead," I said.

"Why did you come here?"

"Frank and I go back a long way. I didn't want him to leave without, at least, trying to talk about what happened between us."

"Frank has changed a bit since you've seen him."

"In what way?"

"You may find him more interested in people as *subjects for study* rather than as friends. But as someone who treated me like a subject, you may find that more to your liking. I know that sounds hostile, but I still have a ways to go before I evolve into a new self. Whoever the fuck that is!"

After Gerald left, I must have dozed off because a key turning the lock awakened me. Frank and Crystal didn't seem surprised to find me in the apartment.

"What's going on?" Frank said. The jittery edge his voice always had was gone and he'd lost weight.

"Not much," I said. "Gerald let me in. Just thought I'd drop by and see you both before you left."

"How are you, Raymond?" Crystal said with her usual wide-eyed openness.

"I'm okay. When are you leaving?"

"The day after tomorrow," Frank said.

"Naomi said you were going to New Mexico."

"We want to spend some time there. But Mexico is where we're heading."

"Why's that?"

"We've gotten turned onto some books about Indian shamans in Mexico who use jimson weed, peyote and mushrooms to take themselves out of the world, so they can live in it more fully."

"You mean by getting high."

"Yeah, but it's not about escape but getting closer to ourselves by discovering how little we actually see of what's going on around and inside us. But before that can happen, the world has to be brought to a halt."

"Is that where the peyote and mushrooms come in?"

"That's just the beginning. The next step is to let go of everything we think we know and open up to the world the way an infant does. Of course, Crystal can do that without mushrooms. She's as porous as running water and allows whatever comes her way to pass through. I just hope I can evolve to where she is before too long."

I looked over at Crystal who was sitting on the floor with her eyes closed, smiling and murmuring something I couldn't hear.

"What you're saying," I said. "is the opposite of what Gerald told me he was going through. I see why he's not going with you and Crystal."

"Gerald needs to feel that he and the people in his life are present and accounted for at all times," Frank said. "But there's no way I can be like that anymore."

"Do you feel that way too, Crystal?" I asked.

She opened her eyes and looked up at me.

"I do," she said. "And even though Gerald never talked to me the way he did with Frank, I knew he wanted everything to be solid as a rock. But Frank and me want to become like...like fog."

"In that case, I think I need to get a few things said before you two vaporize."

"That's not necessary," Frank said. "I'm beyond all that now."

"But I'm not!"

"Raymond! I don't want to go over ancient history. I've already let go of it."

"If you've let go of what happened, then you've also let go of me. Is that it?"

"What I've let go of is the belief that I really know you or myself."

"So where does that leave us?"

"I can't speak for you, but I hope to be in a better place than I was for all those years when I thought I knew something."

"Did you feel that way about Vietnam?" I asked.

"I've never met anybody who fought in the War who was sure of anything about it, except wanting to get home in one piece without being zip-locked in a body bag. Knowing what it was all about was usually reserved for those who only talked about the war, whether they were for or against it. While I was in the 'Nam, I never learned as much about that country as I did about America, which was the one place I thought I knew. All I want to do now is chase what I don't know while remaining a mystery to myself."

"That doesn't leave much room for our friendship." I said.

"Probably not. But it does leave me with some time and enough room to learn how to be friendly. Maybe by then, I might be a better friend."

Frank seemed to have entered some ethereal region in his head with the clever maneuvering of words. At least when we used to argue and got upset with each other, the vital life signs between us were present and very much alive. Now there was barely a pulse. I stood up. Frank stopped sealing a box with masking tape and

Crystal quit her murmuring.

"I remember reading somewhere," I said, "that history is made up of events that people agree actually took place. But what is it called when you live with and among people who can't agree on anything that's happened to them? That's where someone like me comes along to do some housekeeping so the world will look more presentable when guests arrive. I'm like you, Frank. I feel I don't know much of anything either. But what I do know is that my best friend is leaving to find himself by erasing every trace of what we were before. This is some addition by subtraction bullshit and I feel like you're about to cancel me out."

I searched their faces for any sign that what I'd said had some effect, but they seemed to be glowing with anticipation for a journey they couldn't wait to begin.

"I hope you both find what you're looking for. But I guess you'll be satisfied just being able to look for it. I know you'll appreciate my leaving without saying anything else. Because you're already gone."

MURIEL

1973

OVER THE NEXT SEVERAL WEEKS, whenever the three of us were together, Raymond was poised to step in and stop me before I went too far—if I crossed a street in the middle of the block, scolded someone for their bad behavior or objected too strongly during a parent's meeting at Tasha's preschool. I found myself acting out just to watch him try to stop me.

Given the difficulties Raymond and I were having, I tried to keep in touch with my two closest friends. Naomi had left her law firm and was busy trying to figure out what she was going to do with her life. And Khadijah had found fulfillment with midwifery and Imani. I was finally able to make a date with Khadijah to have dinner.

Since Khadijah was a vegetarian, we met at one of the macrobiotic restaurants that had opened up in the East Village. Khadijah ordered a drink made from herbs and plant roots and said it was not only nutritious but would cleanse the system out. Like an enema. I ordered a chamomile tea.

"You don't know what you're missing," she said, taking a sip of her drink.

"I know exactly what I'm missing."

"You don't mind creating disturbances but you don't like being on the receiving end."

"Not if I can help it."

"Well, I hope you learned your lesson after that business in Central Park."

"I have. From now on I'm carrying a can of mace with me," I said.

"That's not exactly what I meant."

"Then what are you saying?"

"I'm saying you need to stop putting yourself in situations where a crowd can easily turn into a mob."

"I go where the stories are."

"If you're not more careful, you're gonna end up being the story."

"You sound like Raymond."

"It's a sound you need to listen to."

"He wants me to walk around on tiptoes, so I won't disturb anybody. I can't do that."

"Then be more cautious. Look at what a lot of your friends are doing. Naomi has given up defending people who end up buried in prison or in the ground. Gerald, runs home to Baltimore after going off the deep end in a *ménage à trois* with Frank and Crystal. And they're off to New Mexico in search of a spiritual chef and a diet of peyote and mushrooms. Don't you find it interesting that all these folks have decided to put some distance between themselves and their pain? And there're a lot more who're doing the same thing."

"I don't care about what a lot of people are doing. I just want the friends I have left near me."

"That's about to change," Khadijah said.

"What are you talking about?"

"Imani and I are moving to a commune near Boston."

"You've gotta be kidding."

"Muriel, you know me well enough to know I never deliberately try to be funny."

"But why?"

"We want to slow our lives down and live in a city that doesn't have the extremes of New York."

"Do you know who you'll be living with?"

"Imani knows some of them from years ago when she lived in Boston."

"And they don't have any problems with you and Imani being together?"

The health drink almost spewed out of Khadijah's mouth.

"You can be incredibly naive at times," she said, laughing. "You scream at the world for not being what it should be, but don't have a clue that it's changing right in front of you."

"I'm not following," I said.

"Imani and I won't have to worry about being accepted because everyone there is just like us."

"You mean black?"

"No."

"Oh! I see."

"I never know exactly what you mean when you say that," she said.

"All I'm saying, Khadijah, is that I understand. You and Imani will be living with lesbians."

"Which we are, as well."

"That's what I said!"

"Well, that's not quite what you said. But I won't press the point."

"So is this a commune for lesbians only?" I asked.

"It seems to have worked out that way."

"So I wouldn't be welcome?"

"Of course you would, as long as you didn't come with a man."

"Does that include male children?" I asked.

"Yes. But that wouldn't be something you'd have to worry about."

"You dislike men that much?"

"Those are the rules of the commune. They have nothing to do with my feelings toward men," she said.

"But you're willing to live under those conditions."

"That's right. Just like we did in Push Comes to Shove, when we didn't allow whites to become members."

"But we made that decision, not someone else," I said.

"I don't know about that. I think the times we were living in made the decision for us."

"And you think cutting yourself off from men is necessary?"

"I just enjoy the company of women more than I do men."

"Like you used to enjoy the company of blacks more than whites," I said.

"As I recall, so did you, my forgetful soul sister."

"I haven't forgotten," I said. "I'm just wondering how far we can go in this desire to keep reducing the number of people we want in our lives."

"Oh! In that area, you're much more advanced than I am."

"What's that supposed to mean?" I asked.

"Well, Raymond, Tasha and Theo may be the only people you feel really connected to."

"With Theo it's political, not personal."

"Same difference," Khadijah said.

"No it's not. And you left yourself off the list of people you say I feel close to."

"Come up and visit me and I might change my mind about that."

"But I can't bring Raymond?"

Khadijah gave me that look of someone who was reaching the limit of her patience.

"He's not here with us now is he?"

RAYMOND

1973

WHEN I WAS IN GRADUATE SCHOOL, I read Tolstoy's *War and Peace* and was fascinated by his lengthy meditations on the self-deceptions of Napoleon, Emperor Alexander and Louis XIV, who believed they could bend events to their will with their deep understanding and intellect. In Tolstoy's view, the more inflated the ambition to steer events in a particular direction, the further away one moved from that destination.

Although, Theo and Muriel would never have considered themselves aligned with the likes of Napoleon and Louis XIV, they were similar in their need to wrestle events into submission. Many, including Tolstoy, have said the same about historians. It's unlikely that any of us can fully protect ourselves from the consequences of events, even those that are within our grasp. Theo must've known that he'd was going to be killed before too long. If he was lucky, he might have something to say about how it would be done. As far as Muriel and I were concerned, we assumed that I'd always stop her before things got out of hand.

·····

Maggie's Farmers had read Marx and believed they'd found a way to use their labor and never feel alienated from it. They would work up a sweat for the sole purpose of making the rich sweat too. The kidnapping of the heir to the Smithfield tobacco fortune forced many of the wealthiest people in America to put their money to work for the poor, whose labor helped make those fortunes in the first place.

Once Smithfield was released, Maggie's Farmers faced the problem of what to do next. They discussed ways to monitor whether the trustees could actually use the money set aside for the benefit of the poor. But these conversations lacked the enthusiasm of planning the kidnapping and quickly bogged down in tedious details. Theo warned everyone that they were in jeopardy of losing their revolutionary zeal, becoming no more than a bunch of auditors. The rich in America had already been revealed as greedy and selfish. So there was no point in carrying out an investigation to find out whether corporations would abide by promises they had no intention of keeping.

Theo insisted that the job of Maggie's Farmers was not to help reform the system but to remove it. When someone asked how they would go about removing something vile from the world as if it were garbage, Theo said the answer was obvious once you understood the difference between sanitation and demolition.

Up until that moment, Maggie's Farmers were beginning to wonder whether the excitement of the kidnapping would ever return. They spent much of the time watching television, smoking dope, having sex, and waiting for money from supporters—and instructions about when to move to the next safehouse. Just when cabin fever had Maggie's Farmers sniping at each other, Theo got them thinking about the next place in the system where they would swing their wrecking ball.

Theo had never been comfortable with idea of relying on others for money. It wasn't stealing money that bothered him, but waiting for it— money that could be cut off whenever their benefactors lost interest in them, as they probably would. It made sense that Maggie's Farmers should rob banks, since that's where the Maggies of the world kept their ill-gotten gains safe.

They cased a bank in a Northeastern city whose size was large enough to get into without drawing too much attention, but small enough to get out of without getting trapped in the congestion of urban traffic. Theo made a point of choosing only those banks with affiliations to the corporations named as contributors to the trust fund. They rehearsed every aspect of the robbery: the location of the getaway car, entering the bank, the ski masks and disguises, how to let the bank employees and customers know they meant business, and announcing that Maggie's Farmers were responsible for the robbery.

The first heist went off without a hitch. And Maggie's Farmers talked at great length afterwards about how each of them had played their roles and how their performances could be improved. They couldn't wait to see the videotape of the robbery on television, which had been filmed by surveillance cameras in the bank. Watching themselves on television news broadcasts gave proof that their actions mattered in the world beyond the *isolated safehouses where they schemed and plotted.*

In the days following nationwide television coverage of the robbery, Maggie's Farmers began discussing what they believed would be their most significant political act. There would be no more demands for change. Their rhetoric left them no choice but to make war against all those who were the cornerstones that held the system together. The only question was who would be the first casualty in their demolition effort? There were any number of likely candidates. But the person chosen had to be a recognizable figure whose abuse of power showed a glaring disrespect for the great majority of humanity.

After considering and eliminating many names of individuals, Theo remembered the school building without windows in Harlem. It was built by an architecture firm called Atlas Unlimited and headed by the architect, Charles Sinclair, whose personality was as flamboyant as his buildings. He gained his reputation after World War II, designing homes with bomb shelters. All of his designs were based on the general principle that the form of a building should follow its function. Of course, function meant whatever Sinclair envisioned. He revered Frank Lloyd Wright and, like him, wanted people to look at a building and know immediately that it was one of his.

When the protest over the school without windows peaked after the demonstrations by Push Comes to Shove, Sinclair was not timid about instructing people on the unimpeachable logic that went into his selection of the particular design. The light coming through windows would have been, in Sinclair's view, a distraction from the learning environment he created inside the building, which had a layout similar to a park. By keeping natural light out, teachers would have to be more resourceful in using the blend of books, space and objects made from and by nature to turn the light on within each child.

Theo had to admit that Sinclair cut a very impressive figure, in the debonair mold of a late middle-aged Cary Grant. He also exuded a confident ease and arrogance when he dismissed all of his detractors, especially Push Comes to Shove whom he characterized as, at the very least, vandals and, at the worst, desecraters of a school, a sacred place. Theo remembered smiling to himself when Sinclair used the term 'sacred' to describe the school. He didn't believe Sinclair's use of the word had anything to do with children—just any building he designed. Theo could barely contain his anger as he watched Sinclair's news conference. The television cameras had fallen in love with his image. And Theo despised and envied him.

The other members of Maggie's Farmers questioned the selection of someone who was not positioned in the upper echelons of corporate or government power. They also wondered whether Theo's reasons for choosing Sinclair as the first 'target of opportunity' to be killed was more personal than politically motivated. Theo argued that people would respond more favorably to an execution for a specific crime than a random murder for symbolic reasons. That had been the mistake of groups like By Any Means Necessary, when they killed policemen at random rather than only going after those cops responsible for murdering blacks.

Charles Sinclair lived in a suburb of Chicago and was a force in the city's social and cultural life. Maggie's Farmers left the Northeast separately and on different days, traveling by bus and train to get to Chicago. They were each given the name of a person to contact, who provided them with a place to stay. Once they were settled, they spent weeks tracking Sinclair's movements, particularly the many social events he attended. Finally, Maggie's Farmers decided on an evening when Sinclair would attend the opening of an art exhibition.

The plan for the murder of Sinclair was inspired by Theo's study of the game of field hockey, invented by North American Indians, known as lacrosse. Theo had read an 18th-century account of the game played between the Ojibwa and the Ozaagii, in front of a British fort near Lake Michigan. The soldiers opened the fort's gates to watch the savages banging one another around. At a point when the game had reached its peak, a player hurled the ball through the entrance of the fort. The Indians ran into the fort to retrieve the ball and the game turned into a brutal assault on the fort. Most of the soldiers were killed.

Maggie's Farmers gathered on the street, in front of the museum steps, shortly before people started arriving for the opening. It was a balmy autumn day in late afternoon. The sidewalk was crowded with street vendors and people. Maggie's Farmers staked out a piece of the sidewalk for themselves. They had learned some of the fundamentals of the game, especially how to handle the long sticks with the oversized baseball mitt-shaped nets attached to the end. Three put on rubber masks and faced three others. They moved in lines and circles around an imaginary goal. Without speaking, they used their sticks to gain control of the lacrosse ball and body checked each other in slow motion. People stopped to watch as limousines began pulling up in front of the museum. Chicago's royalty made their way up the steps. A few stopped to look at the intriguing spectacle, which they assumed was some kind of performance art.

Theo spotted Sinclair getting out of one of the limousines. He lingered briefly on the first few steps, watching the performance for a moment before heading up to the museum entrance. Soon after Sinclair's arrival, Maggie's Farmers stopped their mimed game and lined up in ascending order on the steps in two rows in the shape of the letter 'A'. They stood without moving or speaking, holding their long sticks across their chests like sentries.

They still held that position a few hours later as people began leaving the museum. It was dark and the people and vendors were gone. Maggie's Farmers broke out of their statue poses and moved down the museum steps to the sidewalk. Once again, they formed a circle and moved in slow motion. Sinclair left the building with several people. When Theo gave the signal, they raised the long sticks above their heads and began knocking them together. Theo kept Sinclair in view and widened their circular orbit to get closer to him. When Maggie's Farmers were within a few feet of Sinclair and his entourage, they formed a circle around them.

Sinclair seemed amused. Suddenly, the circle around him broke and the others moved back. Theo launched a lacrosse ball skyward. Everyone looked up to follow its flight. As Sinclair watched, distracted, a line of masked players touched him slightly as they jogged by, Theo last among them. As he brushed against Sinclair, he startled at the popping sounds, as if recoiling from a camera flash. Sinclair reached out to grab hold of someone to steady himself, then fell to his knees. Someone screamed and Sinclair felt his insides go up in flames.

The Maggie's Farmers ran in different directions and disappeared in the night. Those who eluded the police were spirited out of the city by their Chicago supporters and reunited with the rest of Maggie's Farmers *in the Black Hills of South Dakota: the setting for Theo's next, most significant dream.*

THEO

1973

Dear Naomi Golden:

After kidnapping Smithfield and the bank robberies, we had no other choice but to identify a target of opportunity who we'd be willing to kill. I never forgot watching Charles Sinclair on television, dismissing Push Comes to Shove. He said we weren't interested in bringing attention to the plight of the children in schools, but only to ourselves. I remember rocking to calm myself while we watched Sinclair's news conference.

I read as much as I could about people who had convinced themselves that violence was a necessary evil in the effort to bring about revolution. After a lot of study, I told myself that while an act of violence would probably not lead to a revolution, it could make me a revolutionary. And there was no better place to direct my violence at than Charles Sinclair. In his own way, he was what I really wanted to be: a man absolutely committed to the world he imagined in his head, who then went out and made the world conform to his idea of it. At least until he changed his mind.

It was my study of the Lakota Indian, Crazy Horse and lacrosse that led to my dream of how I would kill Sinclair on the steps of the Art Institute of Chicago. Dreaming allowed Crazy Horse to take himself to places beyond the land he knew would eventually be taken from him. Once he dreamed he was standing high above the ground, watching an eagle flying overhead. Suddenly, the eagle fell and crashed to the ground at his feet. When Crazy Horse looked down at the body, he realized it was his own.

I needed dreams to take me away from the life I was losing, and make room for the next. In my version of Crazy Horse's dream, I was made out of sand. But whenever I moved, I fell apart. Then I saw someone who looked like me not too far away. I ran toward him, hoping to get to this other self before my body of sand fell apart. Each time I had the dream, there was less and less of me left.

This dream told me I was running out of time. I didn't share it with the other members of Maggie's Farmers. But I knew we had to have a destination. I remember reading somewhere that the mark of a true revolutionary wasn't his willingness to kill but his readiness to die. And there was no better place for our last stand than the Black Hills in South Dakota, the sacred ground of the Lakota. This information was kept secret from everyone until they were picked up by the underground network and moved safely out of Chicago. When we all got to the Black Hills, we started to rehearse for our final performance.

I'd worked all this out weeks before we surrounded Charles Sinclair on the steps of the Art Institute of Chicago. Once the plan was done, I started getting myself ready to be an assassin. A book that really helped me out was one called *Man's Fate*, where this Chinese revolutionary had to stab somebody through a mosquito net. The thing that freaked him out more than killing this guy was having to touch him. I knew that for me to kill Sinclair, I had to touch him. But before I shot Sinclair, everyone of Maggie's Farmers brushed against him. The Lakota called it counting coup, which meant getting close enough to the enemy to touch as many of them as possible before retreating.

I remember watching the lacrosse ball streaking up in the air. Just as I touched Sinclair, I felt my finger pull against hard steel that finally gave way. I never heard the sound of the gun, but saw Sinclair's body twitch like someone being stung. By the time I got to the car waiting for me, I didn't know that the gun was still in my hand. When the driver pointed this out to me, I couldn't put it down. I kept seeing Sinclair's body react to every pull of the trigger. And I had this strange feeling of wanting my body to go through what I'd done to him.

I knew then that I'd completed my role as an assassin. I was ready to take on a new part of someone who would be killed. And I would make sure Garrett got a front-row seat.

Crazy Horse had George Armstrong Custer. I had Detective Garrett. Of all the stories I read about Crazy Horse and Custer, the most memorable was the one where Custer broke a horn off from the skull of a dead buffalo and found a piece of paper inside that had something written on it in a language no one could read. After they both were dead, people said it was a message from Crazy Horse, telling Custer that the Great Mystery would eventually bring them together on the field of battle.

This was how it was between Garrett and me. We needed each other like the ax needs the tree. The problem was that he believed he was the only one who could be the ax. Garrett also thought he should get all the credit for dreaming me up. And I was willing to give it to him, up to a point. But Garrett never wanted to admit that I outran his dream and had him trying to catch up with mine. If I made myself into a tree for his ax to taste, I could also be an ax, a termite, an owl or a tumbleweed.

It wasn't clear to me whether the other members of Maggie's Farmers were ready for what was next. They had proven their willingness to fight in order not to work on Maggie's Farm anymore. But were they ready to perform the final act of dying? Was I?

MURIEL

1973

WHEN THE STORY HIT THE NEWSPAPERS that Charles Sinclair had been shot and killed on the steps of the Chicago Art Institute, I didn't need to wait long to find out who was responsible for the act. Maggie's Farmers wasted no time in taking credit. Then I waited for Detective Garrett to surface. When he called, he asked me to come talk with him at the precinct in central Harlem. He'd always just show up when he wanted to see me. So I was put on my guard when he asked me to come to his home court.

I hadn't been to my old Harlem neighborhood, where Walter, Khadijah, Theo and I lived years ago. The vitality and promise that the 1960's brought to almost every block was gone. People in the street seemed to have had the wind knocked out of them and were taking it slow to catch their breath. The bunker-shaped police precinct, built of dingy gray concrete, was even more ominous than I remembered.

The desk sergeant told me to have a seat while he put in a call to Garrett. When I saw him coming down the last few steps to the main floor, he was much heavier than the last time I saw him. With his jacket off, Garrett's belly bulged, balloon-like, beneath his shirt.

His gut left no trace of a waistline and rested like a huge boulder on his hips. He wore suspenders that seemed to keep him balanced so the weight of his upper body wouldn't topple off of his legs.

"This way, Muriel." Garrett barely looked in my direction as he led me to one of the interrogation rooms. He waved with one hand for me to take a seat.

"Looks like our friend has surfaced again," he said.

"That doesn't surprise me. But I'm surprised you didn't keep your promise to never get in touch with me again."

"All promises are off, now that Theo's on the F.B.I.'s Ten Most Wanted list."

"You brought me here to tell me that?"

"Not exactly. Why don't you take a look at this," he said, handing me a piece of paper covered with letters cut from a magazine.

> *Garrett:*
>
> *You are cordially invited to attend the final dream of Maggie's Farmers, performed in a place too sacred to be named, and at a time no sooner than it takes to make the world twice. Hope to see you in my dream, just before I leave it.*
> *Tasunke Witc*

"Is this supposed to mean something to me?" I asked.

"It means Theo needs me as much as ever. Just like all you would-be revolutionaries need the very people you say you want to get rid of. You don't really want change. You want people around who'll try to stop you. If you didn't have that, you wouldn't know what to do with yourselves."

"And what about you, Garrett? Do you know what to do with yourself?"

"I'm doing it. I'm with the folks on top, not on my back looking up, like you and Theo."

"Can I go now," I said, standing up.

"Not...just...yet," he said, with a deliberate calm that frightened me more than if he had shouted. But I wasn't about to sit down.

"So what do you think Theo's saying?" he asked.

"How do you know he wrote it?"

"He signed the letter, using Crazy Horse's name in Lakota. He's been a Crazy Horse freak ever since I gave him a biography to read."

"Well, whoever Theo's trying to be this week, I have no idea what he's saying."

"You didn't read it carefully enough. The place too sacred to name is the Black Hills. And he'll be there in twelve days, which is twice as long as it took God to make the world."

"How do you expect to find him? The Black Hills take up a bit more room than Mount Morris Park."

"By using Crazy Horse's name at the end of the letter, Theo's telling me that he'll be at Thunderhead Mountain, where a statue of Crazy Horse is being carved out of the rock."

"I still don't understand why you're telling me all this," I said.

"I figured you'd want to know about Theo's last stand. In a perverse sort of way, I see the three of us as kind of a family."

"You could be right," I said. "Maybe you and Theo have been my home away from home."

"Before you get too clever, just remember, I know you want to be in the Black Hills in twelve days."

"Oh? What makes you think that?"

Garrett reached into his shirt pocket, took something out and handed it to me.

"This press pass will let you be on the scene when we put Maggie's Farmers in prison, or underneath the ground."

RAYMOND

1973

MURIEL WAS WAITING FOR ME when I came out of my class.

"We need to talk," she said, and stalked off down the hall. We ended up in Washington Square Park with Muriel stamping around, too angry to sit down.

"Garrett won't leave me the fuck alone. He keeps trying to paint me with the same brush that he and Theo use on each other."

"He knows what's going on between him and Theo has nothing to do with you," I said. "He would use anybody to justify whatever they're doing together. Fortunately, it's about to end and you won't have to be there to see it."

She looked at me in disbelief. "What do you mean?"

"Just what I said. There's no reason for you to go, is there?"

"Of course there is!"

"I don't understand. Didn't you just say you were tired of being drawn into their shit?"

"Yeah! But that's because they want me to think I'm like them. I'm not. But I still need to go to the Black Hills to see it through to the end."

"You really think it's going to end there?" I asked. "It won't. What happened to you in that room with Walter was horrible. That's something you'll never get over. So why don't you just stop playing these dangerous games?"

"I'm going," she said.

"How long are Tasha and I supposed to wait before you've had enough of this bullshit?"

"Don't worry about Tasha. She knows I'll protect her."

"Right! Only after you've put her in danger!"

"At least I'm going to let her get close enough to the world so she'll know how much it can hurt her. Who else is going to do that? Not you, always the spectator."

We walked home without talking, which was probably wise. As we headed west on Greenwich Avenue, toward 8th Avenue, a black man and a white woman, walking hand-in-hand, approached us from the opposite end of the block. The man passed what appeared to be a joint to the woman. They didn't look like they were living very high on the hog and were having trouble navigating the sidewalk. When we walked closer to them, the woman cut her eyes at Muriel.

"What the fuck you looking at?" the woman said.

"Don't worry about it!" Muriel shot back. "You just need to keep sucking your nigger's dick!"

We all stopped, momentarily frozen in time.

"You hear what that bitch said to me?" the woman said to the man.

"Why don't you come on over here," Muriel said. "So I can smack the stink out your mouth!"

I couldn't believe what I was hearing.

The guy squinted at us. "Hey man! Why she wanna say some shit like that?"

"You got a problem with what I said, then deal with me, muthafucka!"

Muriel tried to rush at them. I grabbed her and she swung her arm around, hitting me with a glancing blow on the side of my face. She stopped in her tracks, as much in shock at what had just happened as I was.

"Do you have any fucking idea what you're doing anymore?" I asked, after we got home.

"Yeah! Everything you won't do."

"You're talking about yourself, not me. You like the idea of waging a war. But I can't let you bring your war into my life and Tasha's anymore. If you go out to the Black Hills, you better join Maggie's Farmers because there won't be a place for you here when you get back."

"I have to do this, Raymond."

"Then do it. But remember, with all the things you say I won't do, this is one thing I will do."

Muriel went into the bedroom and we didn't speak for hours.

MURIEL

1973-1975

NAOMI SAID I COULD STAY WITH HER for as long as I needed to. Since she took a leave of absence from her law firm, she'd been spending her time going to museums, plays, movies and concerts. I was pleased when she offered to drive out with me to the Black Hills.

A few days before we left I told Tasha that her daddy and I were not going to live together for a while. I'd given a lot of thought to the question I knew she would ask. I said that when adults didn't get along they had to spend some quiet time by themselves, the same way kids did. I was in tears by the time I got to the part where I said I wasn't leaving her but just living somewhere else. She asked me why I was crying. I told her that I loved her and that grown-ups sometimes cry when they're happy.

Tasha stepped away from me and didn't say another word, no matter how much I tried to coax her to talk. I couldn't blame her. The only thing that talking to me had brought her was confusion. I'd frightened Tasha with upsetting information that she probably didn't want to believe. How could she believe I'd keep my promise to protect her from this world when every word I said scared her?

Naomi and I left in my rental car, beginning our journey in New Jersey before heading west through the pine forests and Pocono Mountains of Pennsylvania. Crossing the state line into Ohio, the skyline dropped to ground level. And after hours of driving over the tabletop landscape of Ohio farm country, I felt as though I was in a drug-induced trance.

We stopped at a motel on the first night. While driving, Naomi talked quite a bit about her effort to reinvent herself. Into what, she didn't know. She'd gotten her hair cropped close to the scalp like an army recruit's.

"It's going to take me a while to get used to your hair like that," I said, sitting across from her in the motel restaurant.

"Stay tuned! This may turn out to be the easiest thing about me to get used to."

"What do you have in mind?" I asked.

"I really don't know."

"How long do you think it's going to take for you to find out?"

"The firm has given me a year off. So I'll see where I'm at by then."

"So it's over between you and Gerald."

"Yeah. I think we've done pretty much all we're going to do together in this life."

"How're you taking care of your needs?" I asked.

"I'm trying to find out what they are."

"I mean skin hunger."

"Don't worry! I'm taking care of it."

"With whom?"

"Myself!"

"You're not going to tell me that you no longer have any interest in men?"

"I'm not going to say that. But men have never been my only interest."

"You know what I'm talking about," I said.

"Let's just say, I'll follow my instincts."

"That's what I'm trying to do. But Raymond doesn't trust mine anymore."

"Do you trust them?"

"I'm not sure anymore."

"Like right now?" she asked.

I nodded my head.

"You think you'll be able to straighten things out with Raymond when you get back?"

"I don't know if we can. When I hit him, it confirmed what he's always believed—that human beings can't help doing bad shit to each other. I don't know if he can ever forgive me for not making him believe otherwise."

"Maybe you can get him to try."

"I don't know if I want to. He didn't do such a good job of looking after me either."

"All right, so you let each other down. You think that's reason enough to end it all!"

"Why not? You ended it with Gerald because of an itch!"

"I think I'll shut up now," she said.

•••••

Naomi and I had a room with a single bed. I hadn't given it any thought until she made that remark about discovering what her needs were by following her instincts. When we finally got into bed, I was a bit uptight. I tried to be completely still. But trying not to move made me even more uncomfortable.

"Muriel, you okay?"

"What do you mean?"

"You don't mind us sleeping in the same bed, do you?"

"Of course not. It's just that sleeping with the same person for so long makes being in a bed with someone else feel strange."

"Then I should have even more reason to be uncomfortable than you do. But maybe it's being in a bed with another woman that's really bothering you."

"I wasn't thinking about that," I said.

"If you say so."

"Naomi! What makes you think you can read my mind?"

"I never said I could. But maybe I got lucky."

I was furious with her; but it burned itself out, along with my uneasiness.

•••••

Muriel and Naomi continued their journey west through Ohio, Indiana, Illinois, Wisconsin and Minnesota. When they crossed into South Dakota, the land on either side of the highway undulated like an ocean of earth. This gave way to the Badlands with its more rugged, clench-fisted terrain, knuckled at the top. As we drove higher, the landscape was blanketed by pine trees and the horizon vanished, leaving only the skylight above. Near the mountain summits, the trees gave way to cathedral-like spires of granite. These were the Black Hills, a place the Indians believed brought together the pulse and breath of everything living.

Theo and five other members of Maggie's Farmers had succeeded in escaping from Chicago. Others failed to show up at their rendezvous point. Those who were left were camped out among the thickly clustered pine forests near the bottom of the Black Hills.

Theo never told his comrades about his communication with Detective Garrett. He worried about more defections if the others knew that Garrett was part of the commitment they'd made to a revolutionary death. In Theo's most recent dream, the sun had turned against Maggie's

Farmers, shooting flames directly at them. But they were able to ward off the hellfire by forming a circle and reflecting the sun that was trying to burn them to ash.

Detective Garrett arrived in the Black Hills with a dozen federal agents. He contacted the state authorities in Rapid City, but told them he was only there to follow up a few leads on Maggie's Farmers. Garrett studied Thunderhead Mountain carefully and decided to position his men on the eastern side of the mountain so their backs would be to the sun when it rose in the morning. This was also the only side where the ground was not smothered by pine trees, which were pressed in close to the rock facing. Here the land had very few trees on it, or anything else except buffalo grass. Garrett was counting on Maggie's Farmers to show themselves on the same side of the mountain.

The next morning was the thirteenth day since Garrett received Theo's note. Six figures were spotted at the edge of the treeline several hundred yards in front of the mountain. Garrett signaled his sharpshooters to get into position. He looked at his watch and then up at the sun. It was a little after 10:00 A.M. and the sun had cleared the mountain behind him, brightening the area where the six had gathered. Garrett raised the bullhorn.

"Theo! This is Garrett. Your directions were very helpful. Now I'd like to give you a few. I brought some visitors with me who have all of you in sight. And they'll be helping me escort you and your farmers back to New York. I'm sorry, but this show of yours is closing before it opens. You've got ten minutes to strip naked, throw your weapons next to your clothes and walk toward us."

Muriel stood a few feet behind Garrett as he spoke. She was the only journalist present. Garrett had refused to allow Naomi to accompany her, so she waited at the motel in Custer.

From a distance, it looked as though Maggie's Farmers were complying with Garrett's instructions. He monitored their progress through binoculars and wondered what they were talking about.

"What did he mean when he said: 'Your directions were helpful'?" a woman asked.

"It's the old, tired ploy: divide them before you conquer them," Theo said.

"I'd still like to know how they found us," a man said.

"Have you forgotten that four of us never got here? I think that explains why they were here waiting for us. But that shouldn't matter, since everything, from the position of the sun to where we are, follows what I saw in my dream."

"I thought we'd be the ones to decide when it was time for them to know what we were going to do, not the other way around."

"I don't think it matters that much," Theo said. "We've rehearsed the dream enough to bring it to life. And today, just like it was in the dream, we have the attention of the enforcers of the powerful, who believe they are separate from us and untouched by the consequences of what they've made the world into. We want a world we'll never see. But at least we'll see the death we've chosen. So are we ready to close the distance between ourselves and those who've abused their power and touch them with our last breath?"

Everyone nodded. When they were naked, Theo handed out mirrors attached to headbands. They put them around their heads with the mirrors at the back. Making a circle, they began to run slowly around Theo. Two of Maggie's Farmers mimed the movement of hitting a lacrosse ball toward Theo with imaginary sticks; the other three made poking gestures with their arms, imitating the way players defending their goal tried to stop opponents from getting off any shots at the net. As Maggie's Farmers continued to move around Theo, they also began making a circle around the edge of the field. This caused the mirrors at the back of their heads to reflect the sun back into the eyes of Garrett and his men, standing close to Thunderhead Mountain.

"What the fuck are they doing?" Garrett said, looking through his binoculars. He raised the bullhorn to his mouth again.

"I told you to separate and walk in this direction. Not dance!"

Garrett and the federal agents shielded their eyes. The six figures looked like sunspots.

"Do you want us to fire?" one of the shooters asked.

"Not yet!" Garrett said.

Suddenly, Maggie's Farmers linked hands, locking Theo inside the circle. They swirled around Theo faster and faster until their linked hands came apart. Slowing just long enough to pull the mirrors on their

headbands around to the front, they started running in the staggered formation. They ran around a curve that led to the area where Garrett and
the others were standing. But the agents saw nothing but blinding flashes
of light in their sights.

"I'm ordering you to stop!" Garrett said through the bullhorn.

He turned to the shooters who seemed uncertain of where to aim.

"Take them out!" he said,

"No! Don't!" Muriel ran toward the Maggie's Farmers but Garrett
grabbed her from behind.

"Where do you think you're going," he said, tightening his grip
around her neck as she struggled to get free.

"I invited you out here to cover this story, not to be the story. Just
relax and watch the show."

The first few shots rumbled through the upper reaches of the Black
Hills. More shots rang out and Theo saw the first of Maggie's Farmers
tumble and sprawl on the ground, then another. Furthest from the edge
of the field, Theo was shielded by the four remaining runners. Slowing
down, two of Maggie's Farmers split off from the rest and ran in a zigzag
toward Garrett. The sun's glare, ricocheting off the headband mirrors,
made it impossible for them to get off a clear shot at anyone. The agents
fired wildly. Theo ran behind two other naked people in a direct line
toward Garrett. Screams filled the air. It wasn't clear whether they were
coming from Garrett's men or Maggie's Farmers.

The man and the woman running ahead of Theo were hit and
thrown a few feet in the air, wounded and jubilant, before falling to the
ground. Theo was only two body lengths from Garrett, who still held
Muriel in front of him. He pushed Muriel to the ground, drew the gun
from his shoulder holster and took aim. Theo turned from glittering
flame to flesh and launched himself into the air. Garrett fired and was
sprayed in the face by the blood that spewed from Theo's neck. Muriel
watched Garrett's huge body fall backwards with Theo on top of him.
Theo convulsed once and didn't move again. Agents ran over to pull
Theo off of Garrett. They bent down to see if Garrett was all right.

"I think he's dead!" Muriel heard one of them say.

"Was he shot?" another asked.

"Doesn't look like it."

The wind shifted restlessly and made small talk with the pine trees of the Black Hills. The six bodies of those who once called themselves Maggie's Farmers were scattered about the field in a broken circle. While they awaited the arrival of the local police, Garrett's men sat on the ground in a stupor, the grip of death all around them.

Muriel walked over to the bodies to look for Cynthia, the woman who had driven the van that took her to Theo. She remembered one of the last things Cynthia said was that Theo knew how to get America to pay attention to what it didn't want to see. She may have been right—the sickening sight of the gunshot wounds in the heads of many of the bodies stopped Muriel in her tracks. Averting her eyes from Theo's body, Muriel walked over to the spot where Garrett still lay on his back. His face was splashed with Theo's blood and frozen in wide-eyed surprise.

Theo had been true to his word and succeeded in drawing Garrett into his dream and keeping him there. Muriel believed there were two possible explanations for what appeared to be Garrett's fatal heart attack. The first was that if you killed someone while a captive in their dream, it seemed likely that you would suffer the same fate.

The other explanation was that Garrett went into full arrest when he found himself where he was so intent on keeping others—on their backs, looking up at the world.

MURIEL

1973-1975

THE FEDS HAD A LOT OF EXPLAINING TO DO when the government's handling of the confrontation with Maggie's Farmers hit the news several hours later. As the story unfolded, questions were raised about the killing of six unarmed, naked people, Detective Garrett's death of an apparent heart attack and my presence as the only journalist.

My only comment was that I'd been given permission by Garrett to cover what was supposed to be the peaceful surrender of Maggie's Farmers. This excuse made me sound as devious as I always accused the government of being when it altered or omitted information so its actions would be viewed in a more favorable light. But I wasn't about to reveal the contents of Theo's note to Garrett, which would've implicated me in the plan of Maggie's Farmers to manipulate the government in making martyrs of them. Theo had also written two letters to Naomi which were found among his personal effects and subsequently published in *The New York Times*.

In the article I wrote for *Out In Left Field* a few weeks after I returned from the Black Hills, I took issue with the agents for not finding a less deadly way of taking Maggie's Farmers into custody. Not surprisingly, I was condemned by radicals for collaborating with the government in the execution-style murder of six revolutionaries. This didn't bother me nearly as much as knowing that the radical movement, which had defined and challenged me, was lying in ruins.

Moving in with Naomi was almost like living alone. She traveled a lot and flew out to New Mexico to visit Frank and Crystal a week after we returned to New York. Raymond and I worked out a schedule that allowed us to divide our time with Tasha equally. But we avoided discussing how much or how little of our time we wanted to spend with each other.

RAYMOND

1973-1975

I MARK THE END OF THE SIXTIES with the swift decline of the New York Mets after their loss to Oakland in the 1973 World Series. They had slogged their way through the abysmal early years, beginning in 1962, to an improbable World Championship in 1969. They came close again four years later. But what had been amazing about those teams, and the times in which they played, was short-lived. I never lost my interest in either one. For the rest of the 1970's, I watched the Mets the way I studied history—for the subtleties and nuances of the event rather than just the outcome.

The result of any contest was always less important to me than it was for Muriel and other radicals. Our generation often reminded me of Tom Seaver, a young, immensely talented and driven power pitcher for the Mets, who arrived in 1967 with a 90-mile-an-hour fastball. But by 1974, Tom Terrific realized that success and longevity in the major leagues required more than speed. He added curves, change-ups and sliders to his repertoire and became a great pitcher on mediocre to terrible Mets teams. Unlike Seaver, many leftist radicals found it difficult to do anything at more than one speed, even after it was apparent that the opposition wasn't going to be blown away by sheer velocity.

I made these comparisons between baseball and the radical movements of the Sixties in many of my American history courses. My students were amused but not persuaded by my arguments. I took classes to several Mets games at Shea Stadium, hoping to illustrate my point.

During an afternoon game with the San Francisco Giants, Seaver pitched and was masterful for seven innings, freezing hitters with nasty breaking pitches that started out around their eyes before dropping over the plate at the knees—which set them up for late swings at the heat from high fastballs. In the top of the eighth the first batter got on by hitting a pitch off home plate that didn't come down soon enough from its high bounce for the third basemen to throw the runner out. A Seaver fastball shattered the bat of the next hitter, who popped the ball up just out of reach of the second basemen and right fielder. A classic duel followed with Seaver making great pitches to Gary Matthews, a dangerous hitter, who barely missed being called out on strikes after fouling off several pitches. On Seaver's eleventh pitch, he threw a fastball, not quite chest high, that Matthews launched over the center field fence for a three-run homer.

In the discussion we had in class the next day, my students saw no point in examining anything about Seaver's performance other than the fact that he was responsible for the Mets being on the short-end of a 3-2 loss to the Giants.

"What about the other one hundred four pitches he threw before the home run?" I asked.

"What about them?" a student asked with some irritation.

"Well, didn't you enjoy the guessing game between Seaver and

Matthews before each pitch?"

"No offense, Professor Bonner," someone else said, "but most people don't go to baseball games to watch players think. They just want to see their team win."

"Do you think that holds true in movements for political change?"

"Of course! Why go through all that struggle if you're not going to win."

"What does it mean to win?"

"To get what you want!"

"And suppose you don't get it? Then what?"

"You keep at it until you do!"

"But what if, like Tom Seaver's confrontation with Gary Matthews, you still can't get what you want, no matter how many times you try?"

"Well, you don't do what he did and throw a pitch right over the plate for the batter to hit out of the park."

"I don't think Seaver wanted to do that either," I said.

"If Seaver had hit Matthews with the pitch, then he wouldn't have gotten hit himself!"

The class burst into laughter.

"Would that have been justified?" I asked.

"As long as Matthews wasn't hurt, it would've been."

"But like the pitch Seaver threw that the batter hit for a home run, you can't always be sure the ball is going to go where you want it to go."

"Then he should've just walked him."

"No!" another student countered. "That would mean Seaver was afraid to challenge Matthews and was admitting he couldn't get him out. Hitting him deliberately would've let Matthews know that Seaver wasn't going to give in and wasn't going to be intimidated either."

"That's very interesting," I said. "And it's a good lead-in to what we've been reading about groups who resort to violence to get what they want. Remember the 1909 steelworkers strike in McKees Rocks, Pennsylvania? The Industrial Workers of the World, who led the strike of six thousand workers, were often accused of initiating violence. But they said they only fought back when attacked. But in the confrontation with state troopers, the I.W.W. announced they would kill a trooper for every worker that was killed. A gun battle followed and four workers and three troopers were killed. Now we know that local and state police were notorious for vicious attacks on striking workers without provocation, like those against women and children during the mill workers strike in Lawrence, Massachusetts in 1912. But do you think the I.W.W. might have contributed to the violence during the steelworkers strike by the provocative language they used?"

"Professor Bonner? Are you comparing what the workers did in defense of their lives to what the police did?"

"I'm asking a question."

"Yeah, but the question seems to imply that you're holding the I.W.W. responsible for the violence the steelworkers suffered at the hands of the police."

"Let me put it this way," I said. "Tom Seaver threw a pitch that Gary Matthews hit out of the ballpark. Matthews couldn't have hit the home run unless Seaver threw the ball in a spot that allowed him to get the fat part of the bat on it. You said yourselves that Seaver was responsible for the Mets losing the game. It goes without saying that if Seaver had struck Matthews out, he would've been responsible for the Mets winning. My question is if the I.W.W. took some of the credit for the success of the strike, do they also share in the responsibility for arousing the passions of the workers and the police which led to several people losing their lives?"

"But you're blaming the victims!"

"If they were only victims, would they have won the strike?" I asked."

"You know, Professor Bonner, Huey Newton once said that *Power is the ability to define a phenomenon and make it act in a desired manner.* And I think the police were able to make those steelworkers act in a desired manner much more than the other way around."

"I'm not disagreeing with you," I said. "All I'm saying is that the I.W.W organizers got the striking workers to use their limited power and that implicated them in whatever resulted from what the workers did."

"What about the people who didn't want to be involved in the strike," a woman asked, "but watched others take risks? Were they implicated in the consequences of their inaction?"

"Absolutely," I said, appreciating her not so veiled accusation, aimed at me, always the observer. "But the thing to keep in mind is that the consequences from what people do or fail to do are never the same."

"So Professor Bonner, who was more to blame for the violence during the steelworkers strike? The police who were supposed to keep the peace, the people who did nothing or those who believed that in order to fix something, you sometimes have to break more than what's broken already?"

"I guess the short answer is the police," I said. "But since we've been discussing disenfranchised groups who resort to violence, I'm intrigued by what you said about breaking things that aren't broken while trying to fix things that are."

"If you're in the position those steelworkers were in," she said, "I don't think there's any way to avoid breaking more than the thing you're trying to fix."

"Maybe you're right. Of course that means what they end up breaking includes themselves."

This remark created a stir in the room, as several hands went up at once.

"So what should they have done differently?" another student asked.

"I don't know. But I'm interested in what I.W.W. actually did do and the consequences of their actions."

"What about the consequences of your actions, Professor Bonner?"

"What do you mean?"

"It seems like the way you look at things only leads to paralysis!"

"In what way?"

"Instead of paying more attention to what needs to be fixed, you seem obsessed with what gets broken in the process."

"Historians have to be concerned with both."

"People who want to make history, rather than watch it go by, don't have that luxury."

"I think if people study history, they're more likely to make history that doesn't turn into disaster. That's why Tom Seaver is becoming a more complete pitcher in a year when the Mets, as a team, are closer to being terrible than terrific. He has obviously studied his early years as a young pitcher with raw talent and is learning how to be a winning pitcher even while losing."

"What does that have to do with making history?"

Fortunately, the class period ended before I had to come up with an answer to that question. My Tom Seaver and baseball metaphors probably didn't have much to do with history and even less to do with what was really bothering me. I've always understood this about Muriel—if she couldn't fix what was broken, she would break something else. Unlike her, I believed we were broken at birth by the history that made us. Her failure was to stop arguing with me, as she promised she would—especially when I needed to believe rage wouldn't put us in a fix we could never get out of.

MURIEL

1973-1975

AFTER I CAME BACK FROM THE BLACK HILLS nothing seemed to interest me enough to write about it. Since Naomi was away, I spent a lot of time alone with Tasha. One day when we were in the park, she got on a swing and asked me to push her. I began pushing and Tasha squealed as the swing carried her higher and higher. She had just turned four and couldn't wait for me to take the training wheels off her bicycle. And she never missed an opportunity to get me to do something to scare her.

Nothing made Tasha happier than being swung through the air by her wrists, losing her balance while ice skating, climbing a tree and not knowing how to get down, having me hide and surprise her by saying, *BOO!*, listening to the ominous cellos, signaling the coming of the wolf in the cartoon version of 'Peter and the Wolf', and having me read to her in the dark with a flashlight. Her favorite stories were "The Gashlycrumb Tinies" and "The Wuggly Ump" by Edward Gorey. I taught her the alphabet, with stories about the horrible fate of twenty-six children being bludgeoned, drowned, frozen, poisoned and trampled.

It didn't take Tasha long to learn that I was much better than Raymond as a guide to her own fears. I was happy that she wanted me to be her companion on rides through her version of the Coney Island Tunnel of Horrors. Raymond preferred to divert Tasha's attention away from the world's dangers.

•••••

When Naomi returned from her trip to the Southwest, she had many stories to tell about Frank and Crystal. They had met others who were searching for a way of life that would put them in a permanent condition of feeling unnecessary.

"What does that mean?" I asked.

"They've come under the influence of a man who calls himself Coyote. He shows them how the routines governing their lives give us a false sense of what is necessary. Coyote helps them become more unnecessary."

"How does he do that?"

"By having them do exercises on how to be inaccessible without being oblivious to one's surroundings."

"You meet this...Coyote?"

"I went to one of the meditations in the desert with Crystal and Frank. He's a slight man and very unassuming when he speaks. His face is incredible—glows like finished mahogany. I guess he's a mix of every kind of person who's ever settled near the Mexican border. His eyes reminded me of what you said about Theo. They're piercing but impossible to read."

"How old is he?"

"Hard to say. He could be anywhere from forty to eighty."

"What are these exercises they do to become inaccessible?"

"I wasn't allowed to see any and Frank and Crystal wouldn't discuss it."

"How are they doing?"

"They seem to be moving further apart."

"Do they talk?" I asked.

"They talked to me but not that much with each other. They seemed to communicate through body language and eye contact."

"Is Crystal as strange as ever?"

"Pretty much. But she's just being Crystal. I did get the feeling that human beings have slipped in Crystal's estimation of what is necessary. She spends more time with animals, vegetables and minerals."

"What do you make of it all?" I asked.

"They're searching, like we all are."

"So did you come back with any ideas about where your search is headed?"

"I want to keep doing what I've been doing. I've stayed put for so long, moving around is what I need to do."

"How are you going to do that without giving up your day job?"

"When I left New Mexico, I got a flight to California to visit friends in Berkeley. I heard about this private foundation that's exploring the feasibility of applying socialist solutions in an American context. It's going to fund people from various professions to travel to countries that are trying to build democratic socialism. They want to promote economic justice without violence. You spend a year each in Jamaica and Tanzania. I got one of the eight positions."

"I guess it's safe to say that you accepted?"

"I did. But I took a few days before deciding."

"What made up your mind?"

"I was hanging out with friends in the Bay area and realized I'd gotten tired of hearing myself talk about how fucked up everything is. It's always us against them. And whether the us is—women, gays, blacks, Indians, Chicanos or Asians—we all know that the more we turn up the volume, the less likely it is that we'll hear what anyone else has to say. I used that as a defense strategy in most of my cases for years. Deny all accusations and blame anyone who happens to be available. I know that's what I had to do for my clients. But that didn't make me despise them or myself any less."

"Am I included in that company?" I asked.

"No, you were a refreshing surprise. You didn't peddle a political line of bullshit to justify everything you did. And I hate to admit it, but neither did Khadijah."

I was grateful to Naomi for saying that, especially with all the charges of opportunism against me. But somehow I couldn't allow her goodwill to go unpunished.

"You know, Naomi, I was just wondering how you justify being part of a project that's going to spend millions of dollars demonstrating what countries like Jamaica and Tanzania already know—that superpowers like the U.S. have a lot to do with why democratic socialism hasn't been successful anywhere."

"That doesn't mean you don't keep looking for ways, besides violence, to make it work."

"How can you hope to create socialism, when the people paying you to study it have the most to lose if you succeed?"

"I'm not that ambitious, Muriel. I think there's more to be learned from what people have tried to do and failed than in what they're succeeding at."

"Then you've failed already," I said. "If you don't address the contradictions in working for people who are already compromised, what can you really hope to accomplish? I know. I've been in that situation more than I care to admit."

"I don't mind admitting that about myself," she said. "I accept my contradictions. I don't think we have any other choice. The only way to resolve them is to die."

•••••

Naomi made arrangements for me to sublet her apartment before she left for Tanzania. I admired her willingness to leave a familiar world of indictments, burdens of proof and verdicts and take a leap into newly independent nations, trying to remake themselves. Naomi was right. We were all searching, going our separate ways, while not being entirely clear about the direction. Years ago, in Mississippi, someone in the movement said the best way to get through moments of confusion and indecision was to stay in motion. But unlike Naomi, I had no animating idea of my own to keep me moving. I could only follow the fumes from the exhaust of someone else's search.

I decided to head out to the Southwest and visit Frank and Crystal. Raymond agreed to let Tasha go with me. In another year, when she'd be starting kindergarten, such a trip on the spur of the moment wouldn't be possible. Of course, what worried Raymond was the possibility that I might lose my temper and do something stupid to endanger Tasha.

RAYMOND

1973-1975

I NEVER BELIEVED Muriel knowingly put Tasha in danger. My concerns had more to do with her reflexes, which often operated without regard for her intentions. And it shouldn't have surprised me when Tasha began to exhibit the same tendencies. I signed her up on a tee ball team and watched in disbelief as she changed the rules to suit herself. Once Tasha discovered that the ball went further when it was in motion, she would take it off the tee and toss it in the air before swinging. Sometimes she ran out of the base paths and into the outfield to avoid being tagged out or grabbed the wrists of a kid who was about to tag her. And on one occasion, after popping the ball up on the infield, she screamed at a boy to watch out just as he was about to catch it. He was distracted just enough to drop the ball. I scolded Tasha severely about this unsportsmanlike behavior, reminding her that the Mets never played that way. She looked at me, completely befuddled.

"But Daddy, they lose all the time."

I cringed as I heard myself mouth the tired platitude about how you played being more important than winning or losing. Tasha beamed and nodded her head, as though she knew exactly what I meant.

"That's good, cause this is how I play!"

MURIEL

Summer, 1975

TASHA AND I took a flight to Albuquerque and I rented a car for the drive to Taos. Frank and Crystal didn't have a phone and could only be reached via a mail drop near the pueblo where they lived. I wrote telling them I was coming but never heard from them. Naomi had warned me about this. It was part of eliminating non-essential actions from their lives and becoming more unnecessary. The two-hour drive north began with the closed-fisted congestion of the city but soon stretched out into the open palm of the desert. Unlike the Black Hills, the surrounding mountains were set back quite a distance from the highway. The scrawny shrubs and other meager vegetation reminded me of a line from a movie where one of the characters remarked that the desert had no pity.

Tasha was fascinated by the landscape and peppered me with questions when she wasn't reading one of her books out loud. Time passed quickly and before I knew it, we were turning off the main highway. After a few miles, we entered a pueblo with several single-story adobe houses. I parked the car and walked with Tasha into what looked like a 7-Eleven. In my halting Spanish, I asked the man behind the counter if he knew anyone who fit the descriptions of Frank, Crystal and the Indian called Coyote.

The man spoke to several other men who were hanging out in the store. After a brief exchange, which I couldn't make out as Spanish, the man behind the counter pointed to one of the men who waved for us to go with him. I took Tasha's hand and we followed the man through narrow pathways winding between the adobe houses. Finally, he stopped in front of one, pointed at it and walked away before I could thank him. The door was slightly ajar and I knocked.

"*Quien es?*" a voice asked.

"*Un amiga, de Francisco y Crystal,*" I said.

There was a sound of someone moving. The door opened. Frank stood in front of us. He was clean-shaven and his shoulder-length hair was tied in a ponytail. He was much thinner and his swagger was gone; his upper body seemed lost in the smock he wore over his pants. Frank looked at me and Tasha as if it was the most natural thing for us to be standing in front of him. He pushed the door open all the way and let us into one room with a sink, a kitchen counter, a tattered floor rug and a mattress. I sat in the only chair, Tasha on my lap. Frank sat cross-legged in the middle of the room, lit by a shaft of sunlight. He still hadn't spoken.

"You got my letter?" I asked.

"Yes. But I never read it because it didn't seem right to read something that I wasn't going to answer."

"I was worried about coming all this way and not knowing whether you'd be here. But Naomi said it would be all right. It is isn't it?"

"That's what I'm working on."

"What's that?"

"The feeling of everything being all right."

"Where's Crystal?"

"She's up in a tree."

"What?"

"She no longer wanted to be part of the violence to the earth."

"Where did she go?"

"To the redwood forests up in northern California. She heard that some of the oldest trees were going to be cut down. You can fill in the rest."

"Does Crystal really believe they won't cut down those trees just because she's in one of them?"

"Whether that happens or not doesn't matter as much to her as living in the tree."

"When did she leave?"

"About a month ago."

"How did she intend to get up into one of those redwoods?"

"She didn't know. But that's the best way to find out how to do anything."

Tasha shifted in my lap and got down.

"Mommy, can I go outside and play?"

"Not yet, honey. I have to talk with Frank for a little while and I don't want you going outside and getting lost."

Frank was smiling at me.

"What's so funny?" I asked.

"Human beings, but me most of all. I've watched other people and then myself spend so much time trying to make sure I never lost my way. And now I've discovered that what I really needed was to get myself lost."

"And how did you make this discovery?"

"It began in Vietnam but I didn't know it until my spiritual guide, Coyote made me see the death I lived with everyday was a companion and not an adversary. When I was in the war, death was always a hair's breath away. I didn't want to die, so I did what I had to do to survive. And I brought that mentality back with me to the world. I found I couldn't function without the force and violence that were the source of the death, always so close in the 'Nam. I created my own bunkers and combat zones on the Lower East Side in order to fight my way out of them. I was in good company because groups like Push Comes to Shove were into the same thing. When I came home, I knew how to survive, but not how to live."

I nodded.

"When Raymond hit me and bloodied my nose, I went into the bathroom where I kept a .45 automatic. I looked at myself in the mirror and saw the fear pulsing in my face. I realized that, ever since I was a kid, violence or the threat of it always meant death was close. And the only way to meet the threat to my life was to escalate the violence. Going to Vietnam just confirmed what I thought life and death were about. I got down on the floor and wrapped my arms around the toilet. I knew if I came out of the bathroom, I would've killed Raymond."

"But you didn't."

"I could have. In that moment, I saw Raymond as the same as the Viet Cong. And if I believed my best friend was a threat to me, then everybody in the world was suspect. I knew I needed to live differently. So I started reading a lot of Eastern philosophy and found out that some of what was in those books was being practiced by shamans in the Southwest. Coyote has taught me to embrace the presence of death without fear and see it as part of the wonder of being alive. But first I have to escape the confines of my body and lose myself completely in the wide open spaces of own my mind."

I turned to see that Tasha had opened the door and was standing just outside it.

"Tasha, come back in here," I said.

"I see a doggy, Mommy."

"What did I say?"

Tasha lingered at the doorway a few seconds and then walked slowly over to me and got back on my lap.

"How's Raymond doing?" Frank asked.

"I guess he's okay. I don't know if Naomi told you but we're not together."

"You're lucky. Most people living with someone else aren't together either. They just don't know it."

"Look Mommy!" Tasha said. A man entered the house and was sitting in a darkened area of the room. I assumed it was Coyote since the bronze gloss to his face was just as Naomi had described it. And even without being directly in the light, the eyes peering at me seemed to be the size of almonds.

"This is Muriel and her daughter, Tasha," Frank said.

"Nice to meet you," I said.

He looked at us without responding.

"Which of the four worlds do you want to visit?" He spoke in English.

"Excuse me?" I said.

"The two-legged human animals have passed through four different worlds—the first was the world of shadows, the second was the world of forgetfulness, the third was pleasure and the fourth and present one is the world of discovery."

Coyote stood up and walked over to me. He held out the palm of his hand and there were four seeds in it.

"What are they?" I asked.

"Peyote."

"No thank you."

He walked over to Frank who took all four seeds and put them in his mouth and began to chew. Coyote returned to the spot where he'd been sitting.

"Have you come to get lost, like your friend?" Coyote asked.

"Why do you ask?"

"Because many people who want to experience the desert come here to lose themselves. They believe the truth of their lives can be found in the uncluttered landscape of light, darkness and earth."

"I'm not sure what I came for," I said. "I probably won't know until after I leave."

"You sound like you have your hands and feet in all four worlds."

I looked over at Frank but he seemed unaware of Coyote and me. Tasha was getting restless again. She got off my lap, sat on the floor and hugged my legs.

"What makes you say that?" I asked.

"Do you know what the coyote represents among Indian people?"

"No, I don't."

"The coyote is a teller of tales about all living creatures. It knows the importance of exaggerating to telling a good story, especially if it's being told to one person about someone else. Like the coyote tells the squirrel that the lynx clawed his brother, tells the lynx that a deer stomped on a mouse, tells the deer that a bear is lazy, tells the bear that a wolf bites her children, tells the wolf that a porcupine picks his nose, tells the porcupine that the prairie dog never takes a bath, tells the prairie dog that the mountain goat has fleas and tells the mountain goat that the squirrel spits."

Tasha giggled into my leg.

"Is that what you do?" I asked.

"I tell stories."

"But in your story, all the coyote does is gossip."

"Yes. But that's not the only kind of story I tell."

"Tell me another one," I said.

"What do you want to hear?"

"Why my hands and feet are in all four worlds."

Coyote reached for a ball of string that was on the floor. He pulled a pocketknife out of his pocket and cut four long strips of string from the ball.

"You want to play a game with me, Tasha?" he asked.

Tasha, who'd been dozing off earlier, was fully awake.

"Can I Mommy?"

"Go ahead."

She walked over to Coyote and sat down beside him.

"I want you to watch what I do very closely."

Tasha nodded her head, excitedly.

Coyote took an end of one of the strings, placed it on the floor and began making an irregular circular pattern with the rest of the string. He repeated this three more times with the other pieces.

"Now follow the direction of the string in each circle with your eyes, and tell me which piece of string is the longest."

Immediately, Tasha tried to trace the direction of the string direction with her finger.

"No. You can only use your eyes."

She frowned but followed Coyote's instructions. After a few minutes of intense concentration, Tasha pointed to one of the circles.

Coyote stretched the string out from end to end and measured it against the length of the other three.

"Well, it looks like you did it."

Tasha squealed with delight over her accomplishment. And without missing a beat, she began making new patterns with the four pieces of string.

"So what does that say about me being in the world of shadows, forgetfulness, pleasure and discovery?" I asked.

"I said I'd tell you a story. I didn't say I'd tell you what it means."

"Are you a shaman?" I asked.

"Who told you that?"

"My friend Naomi who visited Frank and Crystal a couple of months ago."

"She must have misunderstood me. I told her I was a storyteller, better known as a *sham-man*, not a shaman."

"Does that mean you're a liar?"

"I tell lies but I'm not a liar!"

"What's the difference?"

"A liar says something is true that he knows to be a lie. I tell stories, which I admit are lies, but I know to be true. It's deceit that makes someone a liar."

"So tell me a lie that you know to be true," I said.

Coyote smiled, almost showing his teeth.

"The four symbols I made on the floor for Tasha are maps, charting the journeys of the soul. She was able to pick out the longest one more easily than you or I would because children's imaginations follow twisting and turning paths, like the strings. But the time comes when they want to solve all the riddles of existence until every mystery is a straight line."

"But isn't that why people come to see you?" I asked.

"Most do. But I try to tell them that anything I say is suspect, that I'm unreliable. That's why I'm called Coyote. When they finally realize they're not going to get what they came for, they leave."

"And what do most come for?"

"Answers that make it easier to lie to themselves."

"And what about those who don't want answers?"

"Well, if they stay around long enough, like your friend, I have no choice but to point them toward the path of becoming a coyote."

I looked at Frank and his eyes were glazed over. Tasha had fallen asleep, but not before she had made each one of the four long strings into amazing circular patterns.

"Would you like some tea?" Coyote asked, getting to his feet. "Francisco always keeps some brewing in the kettle."

Coyote walked over to the kitchen counter, lifted the kettle from the hot plate and poured tea into one of the mugs sitting on the counter. I stood up, took the mug from him.

"Thank you," I said.

I walked to the opened door, blowing into the mug before taking a sip. It tasted like chamomile. Dusk had begun to darken the sky; and in the open spaces beyond the adobes, the wind picked up some sagebrush and spun it around wildly.

"Indians call them dust devils," Coyote said. "They're seen as an omen for the coming of some evil."

"Do you believe that?" I asked.

"I believe you shouldn't try to drive back to Albuquerque tonight."

I turned toward Frank and he had fallen asleep crosslegged. And Tasha looked so content as she slept, that it seemed a shame to wake her.

"I guess we'll stay," I said.

Coyote took a few blankets from a closet and sat back down. I gathered up the string that Tasha had shaped into circles and covered her with one of the blankets. I turned toward Coyote but he was gone. I went to the open door, venturing out a few feet and called out to him.

"Coyote!"

There was no answer except for the wind. I could barely make out the outlines of the adobes and the stars provided the only light in a sky blackened by night. Stepping back inside, I closed the door, sat down in the chair and finished my tea. Frank was sleeping so peacefully in the lotus position that I didn't bother waking him. I lay down beside Tasha and pulled a blanket over me.

It seemed as though only a few minutes had passed before the door creaked open and I heard what sounded like the foot patter of at least two people wearing slippers. I turned over toward the door and in the starlight spilling into the house, I saw two animals resembling dogs. They panted heavily and stretched their jaws into frightening yawns. One of them had pieces of metal hanging around its neck from a chain that jingled whenever the dog moved. I glanced at Tasha and Frank; they were still sound asleep. The two dogs lengthened their backs and crept slowly toward me. They drooled from their mouths and were only inches from my face when I saw what was jingling around the neck of one of them. They were military dog tags with the name Frank Livolsi engraved on them.

I screamed and scrambled to my feet. I felt the glare of sunlight in my eyes and heard Tasha crying.

"You scared me Mommy!"

"I'm sorry, honey," I said, hugging her. "Where's Frank?" I asked, noticing that he wasn't in the room.

"I dunno Mommy, but I saw two coyotes this morning."

"You did."

"I heard them barking outside and scratching at the door. I opened the door but I didn't go outside cause you told me not to. But they let me pet them and then they ran away."

"Those were dogs, Tasha."

"No they weren't Mommy!"

"How do you know?"

"Cause Frank told what they look like before he left."

"You didn't tell me he talked to you?" I said more loudly than I intended.

"You didn't say you wanted me to tell you that."

She started crying again.

"That's all right. I didn't mean to yell at you."

None of what Tasha said made any sense. And I didn't want to wait around to figure it out. I gathered our things together. And with Tasha's keen sense of direction, we found our way back to the car. When we were about a mile outside of the pueblo, Tasha started pointing things out to me along the road.

"Look Mommy! Coyotes!"

I looked out the window on the driver's side and saw two coyotes that had actually stopped to stare at us as we passed by. Tasha made a jingling sound; and when I looked at her, I was surprised to see her playing with a pair of dog tags on a chain.

"Where did you get those?"

"They fell off the coyote when it ran away."

"Let me see them!"

She handed them to me and it was all I could do to keep from driving off the road when I read Frank's name. I wondered if all of this were really happening. And then I remembered the chamomile tea Coyote offered me, and his admission that he was not to be trusted. Was I hallucinating from something he'd put in the tea? Or maybe it was part of the *great mystery* that Coyote said accounted for occurrences which had no logical explanations?

"Are you telling me the truth, Tasha? Did you really get these dog tags from a coyote?"

"Yes, Mommy!" she said, in a voice, unwavering in its conviction.

And knowing something of strongly held beliefs myself, I knew Tasha wasn't going to take any more challenges from me.

When we arrived at the airport in Albuquerque, I'd made up my mind that we would get the next flight to San Francisco to see what great mystery Crystal might have found up in a tree.

•••••

As soon as we arrived in San Francisco, I looked up the phone numbers of local environmental organizations. It didn't take long to find the group involved in saving the redwood trees in Northern California from slaughter by lumber companies. Crystal was one of several people who had taken up residence in a number of redwoods designated to be cut down. The lumber company had a court order that gave the protesters a deadline to leave the trees before the police would arrest them.

I rented a car and we headed up Highway 1 along the Pacific Ocean. As I drove around the hairpin curves high above the ocean, it filled me with more wonder and fear than I ever felt in the presence of the Atlantic. The coastal waters along the Pacific seemed to have been seasoned with the turbulence that people brought with them as the country headed west. Maybe that's why the Pacific reared up so defensively as its tides tasted land.

I stopped for gas at a service station in Point Arena and got into a conversation with the attendant who looked like a refugee from some bad acid trip. When I mentioned that we were on our way to the nearby redwoods, where demonstrators were tree-sitting, he came to life.

"The police won't let you get close enough to join up with them," he said.

"I'm not here to do that. I'm a journalist and I know one of the protesters. I want to do a story about her."

"There's another story you should do."

"What's that?"

"I live not too far from here, right on the San Andreas Fault. If any serious tremors ever happen, part of California would end up separated from the rest of the mainland. That's the reason why people like me moved there. We feel like we're not part of this country anyway, so we want to live on the crack that one day might separate us from America—same way our minds already are."

"Why would you want to wait for an earthquake to take you away from America? Why not just leave?"

"We've already left in our heads. Now we're waiting for nature to run its course. But until that happens we're content to live in what we call *headven*."

I was so intrigued by the guy's idea of *headven* that I drove a few miles out of our way to get a glimpse of the place near Manchester that sat right on the San Andreas Fault. On a road off the main highway and not far from the ocean, the landscape looked like it had been tossed in the air and hit the ground so many times that it was broken beyond repair. It seemed like a fitting home for exhausted Sixties refugees, weaned on the belief that disaster was only a shout away, who didn't want to live anywhere else.

After spending some time walking along the beach with Tasha, we headed further inland toward the redwoods. It wasn't long before the forests, with their gigantic trunks and torso-thick branches, closed in around us. I turned off the road at the sign for the entrance to the North Pacific Redwoods. I pulled the car up to the beginning of a footpath. There was a jeep parked several feet away. Tasha and I got out of the car and were immediately confronted by a state trooper, his face partially concealed by a wide brim Stetson hat.

"This area is off limits, ma'am," he said.

"I'm a journalist." I waved my press pass. "I'm doing a story on the tree occupation. My paper called ahead to let the authorities know I was coming."

He walked over to us without speaking and held out his hand. I gave him my pass and other identification. He looked at the documents and glanced at Tasha.

"They said the other day that they wouldn't talk to the press anymore before the evacuation deadline."

"I know one of the protesters. She'll talk to me."

"Who's this?" he asked, gesturing toward Tasha.

"I'm Tasha," she said, looking directly at him.

"She's my daughter."

The cop opened his mouth to speak but for some reason decided against it. He stared at Tasha from underneath the wide brim of his hat. She didn't blink or avert her eyes. Finally, a smile appeared beneath the hat brim.

"How long is this going to take?" he asked, returning to his deadpan speaking voice.

"Two hours at the most."

"I'm going to have to pat you down."

I extended my arms out, horizontally and endured it without grimacing or looking at Tasha.

"The trees that they're in are marked," he said, as we headed into the mouth of the forest.

I watched Tasha tip her head upward in amazement at these bunched together evergreen skyscrapers. It was eerie, listening to voices and music from transistor radios floating hundreds of feet above us. I cupped my hands around my mouth and yelled up into one of the trees, clearly marked with a number in white paint. The sound of my name, Crystal's and why I was there reverberated high up in the branches. There were other voices in the trees that I couldn't make out.

"Number five!" said a clear voice.

I walked hand in hand with Tasha and found the tree not too far away.

"Crystal!"

There was no response but soon the tree moaned from the weight of someone climbing down. I heard chimes shimmering and then caught sight of Crystal's head and arms, hanging upside down with her legs wrapped around a branch about ten feet above us. Using enormous upper body strength, she pulled her torso up, grabbed hold of the branch and straddled it upright.

"Hey! How are you, Muriel?"

"I'm all right. Why don't you come down and talk? The state trooper didn't follow us."

"I like it better up here."

"That's what Frank told me."

"Hi Tasha!"

"Hi. Can you show me where you live?"

"I wish I could but it's too far up."

"What's going to happen when the police arrive to make you come down?" I asked.

"All of us agreed to make our own decision but not talk about it among ourselves."

"So what are you going to do?"

"I don't know yet but I intend to keep my promise never to set foot on earth again."

"Don't you think that's unrealistic?"

"Maybe. But more than anyone else, you should understand why I can't help overdoing whatever I'm deeply involved in."

"But what would be accomplished if you could live in this tree and never touch the ground again?"

"This tree would live and so could I."

"When I was in New Mexico, Coyote said he was teaching Frank how to be a coyote. What do you want to be?"

"Everywhere."

"And how will you do that?"

"By releasing my physical sensations, so they're no longer confined to my body."

Crystal leaned over to the right as far as she could go, letting her torso turn upside down while her legs remained wrapped around the tree branch. The wind chimes tied around each ankle tinkled. She removed the elastic band from her hair and it hung down to almost the length of her arms.

"Have you lost faith in human beings?"

"No. Just in being one. I want to become just another life form."

"What's so bad about being human?" I asked.

"The earth, air and water could answer that much better than I can."

"Crystal, no matter how much you bend your head out of shape to convince yourself that you can be a mind without a body, you're still a human being. You and Frank believe people have to become something other than human so they won't have contempt for life. I used to believe it was possible to be a superior person who could do horrible things in the name of justice and not have ones humanity suffer. But you know, Crystal, I think we're stuck inside the body and mind we came here with. And if we do the best we can, that's all we can hope for...God, I can't stand it. I'm starting to sound like Raymond."

Crystal pulled herself back to an upright position on the branch and began retracing her climb up into the fullness of the redwood.

"I can't stand the way I used to be," she said, as one of the wind chimes fell from her ankle to the ground. "Living up here is how I can be better than I ever was and begin to sound more like the way I want to."

I picked up the wind chime.

"Crystal! You dropped one of your chimes."

"You can have it."

"I'd like to talk some more."

"We can do it another time."

"When?" I asked.

"Whenever."

"But where?"

"Everywhere."

•••••

While Tasha slept on the drive back to San Francisco, I thought about where the six of us, who spent the last night of the 1960s together, had ended up five years later. Raymond lived almost entirely among the dead and buried of history, with some exceptions for Tasha and baseball players. Naomi had become a wanderer, wondering if there was any place she could ever again call home. Gerald had gone back home to Baltimore, hoping to discard the messy recent past for the more distant, smooth and baby-assed past of his childhood. Frank was lost in the New Mexico desert on his way to becoming a coyote and unnecessary. And Crystal was living in a tree, two hundred feet above the ground, refusing to desecrate the earth any further by touching it, and willing herself to be everywhere.

Two days later when the state police, local firefighters and forest rangers began their climb up the trees to evict or arrest the protesters. A tinkling sound from the tree marked Number 5 was all they heard until they reached the wind chime tied to Crystal's foot and the rest of her hanging from a branch by a length of rope around her neck. She had kept her promise to separate her mind from her body and never come back down to earth.

1975-1977

The end of the Vietnam War left America without an enemy that could be readily identified. Many Americans were shamed by the less than triumphant withdrawal from Southeast Asia and were anxious to find a worthy adversary who would give the nation another opportunity for victory with honor. But the threat did not come from another country or (as it had in movies from the 1950's) another planet. It came from within.

The Watergate break-in, investigation, cover-up and President Nixon's resignation came at the same time as the war was ending—these events only added fuel to the public distrust of government.

While there were those who positioned themselves on either side of the argument over the health of America and others who floated somewhere in between, the disco frenzy caught many up in a desire to simply party. Deejays worked turntables, segueing seamlessly from one record to the next. Heat and sweat mixed with the pounding bass line and dancers were hip-boned together into one churning rhythm express that was making no stops. And as everyone sang along with Donna Summer's disco anthem, "Last Dance," in celebration of this momentary boundaryless community, it seemed all of a piece with the desire of Americans to exorcise their collective demons in a quick fix. They wanted a "Star Wars" escape into a galaxy far, far away, during a time in the future, long, long ago.

RAYMOND

1975-1977

MURIEL RETURNED FROM HER TRIP OUT WEST more haunted by ghosts than ever. Frank's disappearance into the desert and Crystal's suicide seemed to have deepened her belief that the wound she'd been trying to close ever since the night the police murdered Walter, would remain open as the losses of people continued to mount. On the rare occasions when we actually had a conversation, Muriel never failed to bring me up to date on Naomi and Khadijah, including her unsuccessful efforts to find Gerald after he left Baltimore. She was obsessed with keeping them within reach for fear they'd be lost to her forever. Much of what she wrote for *Out In Left Field* involved lost people: children whose pictures were on milk cartons, Americans who were still listed as missing in action in Vietnam, and the *desaparecidos* (the disappeareds) of Argentina. Of course, the one loss Muriel neither wrote about nor expressed to me, directly, was our loss of each other. I'd disappointed her that afternoon in the street, but we could've gotten beyond it, if I hadn't allowed that moment to thicken with grievances against her for not living up to the promise she made that what happened between Frank and me didn't have to happen to us. And I couldn't pass up the opportunity to blame her the way I'd been blaming myself. It was the one way to be together without bringing either of us any further disappointment.

MURIEL

1977

ONE AFTERNOON, I got off the subway at the 72nd Street stop that runs along Central Park. The platform was deserted except for a child, who looked to be three or four, approaching me from the opposite direction. He stopped when he saw me and pressed himself into the wall. I bent down in front of him.

"Where's your Mommy and Daddy?" I asked.

He didn't speak and was obviously terrified that he was lost and alone.

"I'll help you find them. Okay?"

He nodded his head and taking my hand, we walked to the token booth. The attendant called ahead to the departed train, telling the conductor to announce to the passengers that a child had been found and would stay there until his parent returned to get him. I thought about the terror of abandonment in that little boy's eyes for weeks.

I've carried inside me the same fear and anger over the possibility of losing people all my life—the death of my parents, Walter's murder, the deaths of Lucius, the Grunt Collective, Theo, Maggie's Farmers and my break up with Raymond.

It was around this time that I began to experience what I can only describe as homesickness. But what I longed for was not a place but people, the dead as well as the living. I started reading the obituary page of *The New York Times* every day. I would clip and file away all the ones of people whose lives interested me. It didn't matter whether they were well known or not. The only criteria I used was that some current of feeling had to flow from a particular life into mine. I hoped that by populating my life with the lives of people I'd never met, I would quell my longing for people who were nearer and dearer to me that I'd lost on both sides of life.

•••••

After I'd gone to the *Out In Left Field* office to turn in an article, I stopped at a bookstore in the Village. There was a man leaning against a bookshelf near the entrance. He had a beard and long dreadlocks and eyeballed me long enough to give me pause. I didn't dwell on it and went to the biography section. While browsing through a book, I looked up and saw the guy with the dreadlocks, staring at me a few feet away.

"I don't know what your problem is," I said.

"Muriel?" he asked, tentatively.

"Who are you?"

"Gerald."

I looked past all the hair and the baggy clothes and saw the person I remembered.

"It is you! I wouldn't have recognized you if you hadn't said something. I'd heard that you left Baltimore."

"Yeah, about a year ago."

"Are you living in New York now?"

"I'm here. That's about all I can say."

"So what've you been doing?" I asked.

"I spent three years in Baltimore trying to be what I was *doing*. Now I'm taking a rest from trying to be anything."

"What happened to make you feel that way?"

"You sound like you're working on your next piece for *Out In Left Field*."

"I can't help it. It's what I do."

"That's my goal. To be able to say that about doing nothing."

"Would you mind if we went somewhere and sat down and talked for a while?"

We found a coffee shop nearby and Gerald's waist-length dreadlocks drew stares.

"Are you painting?" I asked.

"Not since I left New York."

"Why not?"

"I went back to Baltimore, hoping I could regain my sense of myself by going back to a place I knew. But nothing was like I remembered it, except the same people who never understood my art and thought I left Baltimore as an escape from being black. Now they said I had come back out of guilt, and was too white to be of much help to the black community.

"Of course, I tried to prove them wrong. I joined a group called GO! that was all about keeping the community moving. I volunteered to teach art classes for kids. But the group said my speech and body language were too white and intellectual. GO! was heavily into Mao Tse Tung's *Little Red Book* and I began attending mandatory ideological cultivation classes. I consciously tried to talk and walk in a way that was more rhythmically appropriate to being black."

"Did they actually say you had to do that?" I asked in disbelief.

"They didn't have to. I had my own internal Richter scale that registered my racial authenticity on a daily basis. I failed my own test for black speech proficiency. So I stopped talking for almost two years."

"But your paintings were never an escape from your blackness. They acknowledged it," I said.

"They acknowledged what was obvious. Not what I was hiding."

"And what was that?"

Gerald's mouth shifted within the mass of hair around it. It took me a few seconds to realize he was smiling.

"I was attracted to art because it allowed me to express my fascination with and pleasure in the human body. I loved my anatomy drawing classes. And I enjoyed posing for other artists almost as much. In Western art, the human body is idealized. It took me a while to get over this narcissistic preoccupation and move on to more abstract ways of representing the body. But I never completely abandoned my emotional attachment to idealizing life. That's why I was willing to be so self-punishing in the face of the charges by blacks that I glorified whiteness. They were probably right. But I would never have subjected myself to their abuse, if they hadn't provided me with the opportunity to atone for my sins by idealizing blackness."

"Then why did you leave the group?"

"Once I stopped speaking, I was able to really listen to myself." Gerald stared at me without saying anything. "And I realized," he said finally, "that since I've been inclined to idealize people in art and in life, I don't want to be limited in my selection of who that will be."

"So you're gay!"

"You say that like you've put me in my place. There is no such place. I say, If the shoe fits, I want to wear the wig too!"

"Let me ask you this," I said, after I stopped laughing. "How do you know who you're looking for?"

"You know when you meet the person who convinces you that their eyes are in the back of your head."

"Suppose it's not a person?" I asked.

"What do you mean?"

"The last time I saw Frank, he thought his other half was a coyote."

"I guess we all have to accept whatever we are. Or make other plans."

"The way Crystal did?"

"What about Crystal?"

"Naomi didn't tell you?"

"Naomi couldn't tell me anything because we're not in touch."

"Crystal committed suicide three years ago."

"You mean she took her life."

"That's what I just said."

"I think Crystal would've said that she took her life away from here rather than making it sound like she destroyed herself."

"I see what you mean."

He got up from his chair to leave and reached into his pocket.

"The coffee's on me," I said.

"Thanks."

"So what do you think you'll do now?"

"Anything that leads me to those eyes that can see in the back of my head. If I find them, that would be something to paint."

"Maybe the eyes you're looking for are the ones that were staring at me in the bookstore."

His eyes narrowed, peering at me like points of light in a dense forest.

"You better be careful, Muriel. You may be coming down with a bad case of idealizing life yourself."

Once outside, Gerald waved at me through the glass. It occurred to me that I didn't know where he lived. I began to mouth the words, asking for his phone number. Pretending he couldn't hear me, Gerald put a hand over his ear and walked away.

•••••

In the two years Naomi spent in Tanzania and Jamaica, we rarely wrote. I wanted to be in touch more often, but she preferred that I write only after getting a letter from her. The two letters she wrote came at the end of her stay in each country. I was glad to hear from her, so I didn't complain. And there were parts of both letters that I read over and over.

September, 1975

Muriel:

I don't want to hear a word from you about the tardiness of this letter. And don't expect any descriptions of eye-catching vistas. After a year, I'm just beginning to make some sense of everything I've seen and felt since I arrived in Dar Es Salaam. Thinking back to the days before I left the States, two memories kept reverberating in my mind. The first is a speech I read by Robert McNamara, president of the World Bank (remember him?) who said that two-thirds of the so called developing world (numbering a billion, three million people) live off the land and almost a billion of them make less than one hundred dollars a year. I didn't know how to make real human beings out of numbers like that. But over the last year, I've been able to glimpse the meaning of those mind-numbing figures. Staggering numbers of Tanzanians live in grinding poverty—which has been called the world's least exclusive club.

One of the best people Tanzania has produced is President Julius Nyerere. There was a reception for our group when we arrived and Nyerere attended. He was modest and unassuming; I remember he wore a gray safari shirt and matching trousers. He made a point of greeting us individually and asked each of us to say a little about ourselves. When I told him I was a lawyer, he joked with me about whether there was a difference between the practice of law and the performance of it.

After a few days getting acclimated, our group began visiting the villages that have been the focus of the government's most important economic policy initiative. In 1967, six years after independence, Nyerere issued the Arusha Declaration, which called for farmers, who were scattered around the country, to voluntarily relocate to lands where they would pool their labor and harvest collectively. The thinking was that these farming clusters would increase production and give more people access to schools and clinics. That was the idea. But in practice, these experimental farms drew only two million of Tanzania's fourteen million people.

Our group arrived at a time when the voluntary relocation plan was replaced by one that was mandatory. We were driven regularly by lorry truck to new villages in different regions of the country. There were also reports of homes being pulled down or burned and peasants beaten (and in a few instances killed) who refused to obey the police order to vacate their homes. Wherever we went, I asked people, what they thought of the government's relocation plan. Rashidi, our translator, was from Dodoma, which is very close to Nyerere's home village of Butiama. He was also studying to be a Mwalimu (teacher) as Nyerere had been before him. I liked him a lot, particularly his humor. To his credit, Rashidi didn't try to keep us from hearing about the widespread discontent many felt when forced to abandon their traditional lands.

I made a conscious effort not to rush to judgment (like some people I could name). I tried to listen and frame much of what I said into questions rather than statements. This amused Rashidi who started calling me 'madame questioner.' Occasionally, I would slip and let something uninformed fly out of my mouth. On one occasion, the sight of hungry children everywhere caused me to blurt out why a woman would allow herself to bring so many children into the world, knowing they wouldn't get proper nourishment. It was the only time Rashidi got angry at me. He explained that the large numbers of children brought into the world were acts of resistance by poor people against the equally large numbers of children who depart from the world in their infancy. Rashidi then told me that he was the youngest in a family of ten, of which only five survived.

After being here for several months, it was apparent that collective farms had alienated large segments of the population and, as a result, they weren't producing as expected. When I asked Rashidi why he thought a plan with so many virtues had not gone over well with people, he said that the answer went back to a time before independence. Tanzania had been a region of Africa with more than one hundred twenty tribes and no common language between them. Even with the tradition of building consensus between and among tribes, Nyerere's vision of a Tanzania as one family (Ujamma) would be difficult to achieve. Add to this, British colonialism, which imposed its will through coercion, and one begins to get a better understanding of the inevitable resistance to Nyerere's plan and the unavoidable excesses on the part of government officials who at their worst behaved as the colonizers had: explaining why things were being done but taking little interest in HOW to explain what was being done or WHAT PEOPLE THOUGHT who were directly affected by what was being done. Rashidi ended by saying, with a smile, that as an American, he knew I understood what he was talking about, since we had grappled with similar problems, involving questions of why and how during the war in Vietnam.

What can I say? He was priceless! Here was this kid, barely twenty years old, becoming a Mwalimu to me: a mature, politically savvy, world traveled, thirty-five year old white woman. Everything else I saw during my year in Tanzania goes back to what I learned from Rashidi in that half-hour conversation. And what I've learned is the utter futility in ever resolving questions concerning why and how. I'd like to think it's possible for people, who start out with very little to better their circumstances without violating their humanity. Maybe that's the naive sentiment of a privileged white radical with a return ticket home who has the luxury of expensive convictions she hasn't had to pay for. In a few days I'm off to Jamaica to spread more of my self-righteous humanist folly in the Caribbean. And I will try to be in touch more often.

Love you,
Naomi
Dar Es Salaam, Tanzania

November, 1976

Muriel:

Hey! What can I say? I know I promised to do better as a letter writer. But I didn't promise to succeed. You have to admit—what I lack in frequency, I make up in consistency. It's just a little over a year since I wrote you from Tanzania.

Before we arrived in Jamaica, there was a stop in Mexico for a conference on economic change and the assumptions professional experts make about the people they're trying to help. I met a Mexican doctor who told me that, like many so called specialists, he used to think that women in Latin America and the Caribbean fed their babies gruel instead of milk because they didn't know any better. So there was a drink more milk campaign, emphasizing the nutritional value of protein in milk and eggs. But the effort failed miserably. What the doctor and his colleagues missed entirely was that eggs and milk were much more susceptible to bacteria than low protein gruel. So these women preferred that their babies suffer from malnutrition than die from the effects of diarrhea.

One of my first impressions of Jamaica was the graffiti scrawled on just about every flat surface in Kingston. It expressed the sharp divisions and mixed emotions in the country around Prime Minister, Michael Manley's efforts to bring a form of socialism to Jamaica, which was similar, in theory, to what Nyerere wanted for Tanzania. Like Tanzania, Jamaica is still in traction to its colonial past. I remember going to a reception for us, soon after we arrived, and noticed that the Brits and other Europeans were drinking Jamaican rum while the Jamaicans seemed to all be drinking scotch. I asked a Jamaican woman about this and she laughed out loud.

"Many of us still measure what is of value by how far away it is from Jamaica," she said. "We tend to dismiss what is homegrown, in favor of things coming from somewhere else. You might say we're selling our independence for much less than it's worth and forced to buy it back at a price we cannot afford."

I didn't quite understand what she was saying, but I began to figure it out. When countries like the U.S. decided to lend a helping hand to nations like Jamaica, the trade-off was that the host country agrees to increase what an American dollar could buy, which meant the value of the local currency was reduced. This undermined the formation of land cooperatives, sharply reduced the purchasing power of Jamaicans and lowered production of basic staples, such as sugar, since the fertilizer and pesticides, needed to enhance the yield of the crop, were no longer affordable. Once sugar cane production declined, there were massive layoffs and the cities and towns were flooded with idle and volatile unemployed workers. And the increase in violence has cut deeply into another important source of revenue in Jamaica: tourism.

I heard Manley speak on several occasions. He was a much more physically imposing figure than Nyerere, looking like an aging, rugged version of Lawrence Olivier with swirls of chest hair visible from his open collared shirt. Chants of "Joshua!" would rise up out of the crowds as he urged people to "listen to history and you will hear the footsteps of the world." However, many people I spoke to were worried that those footsteps might be coming from Cuba because of Manley's very public friendship with Fidel Castro. The fear of communism has led large numbers of the middle class to leave the country, taking their skills and money with them.

The effects of American dollars leaving the country and Jamaican currency on the short end of the exchange rate were felt everywhere. Money didn't go very far and there were fewer things to spend it on. The only items that didn't seem to be scarce were guns. Disputes over the hoarding of food by storekeepers sometimes led to shootings. New housing units remained unoccupied because of the frequency of gunshots fired into the aluminum roofs. But the sight that truly shocked me was an entire block of telephone poles that were hacked down with cutlasses! I thought about the rage that must have fueled such an act! Obviously, Manley's efforts to lead Jamaica in its first steps out of Babylon through free public school education, national minimum wage, equal pay for women, establishing farm cooperatives, opening health centers, construction of highways and over 40,000 new housing units were not sufficient to calm the fury that severed those telephone poles.

I thought about this again a few nights ago in Kingston while having dinner with some Jamaican friends. One of them was a writer who angrily pointed out the disparity between the flickering lights from the homes of the affluent in the hills above Kingston and the people crowded into Trench Town only a few miles away. As we ate, the wind carried the smoke and ash from a nearby bonfire to where we sat in the outdoor café. My throat burned and I wondered if this was a reminder of the bonfires that are always brewing, not just in Jamaica, but wherever violence is seen as the most effective method of getting people to change their ways. And I worry about what we've become by growing so accustomed to a world that is perpetually on fire. My time is up here in a few more days. And I'll be returning to the country I've always called home. But who knows? That could change.

Love you,
Naomi
Kingston, Jamaica

RAYMOND

1979-1984

DURING A COURSE I TAUGHT on the Civil War and its aftermath, the class discussion turned to how a nation at war with itself could begin to heal. Webster's Dictionary defined the word *heal* as *the closing of a wound that leaves a scar.* How the nation's wounds would be healed was the focus of Abraham Lincoln's Second Inaugural Address. Given the ferocious convictions that were fuel to the Union and the Confederacy, would the warring factions be capable of reconstituting themselves into a nation again? Many of my students felt that Lincoln believed reconciliation could only begin through a release of the poisonous malice that infected everyone, no matter which side of the war they were on.

Not surprisingly, someone made a connection between the Civil War and the Vietnam War. We discussed the meaning of freedom and democracy, issues which divided the country just as profoundly in the 1960s as they did in the 1850s. And although it had been six years since the withdrawal of U.S. combat troops from Vietnam, we were far from healing the scar left by war.

Not long after that a group of Vietnam Vets proposed a memorial on a site near the Lincoln Memorial, listing the names of all the dead and unaccounted for in the Vietnam war. One of the vets said, "The memorial will make no political statement regarding the war or its conduct. It will transcend those issues. The hope is that the memorial will begin a healing process." It seemed to me that this was what Lincoln's inaugural address had aimed for. And as eloquent as his speech was, the unadorned listing of the individual names of all who were lost would probably exceed the power of Lincoln's words.

I followed the progress of the memorial with great interest. I told Muriel about it and this began the first real conversations we'd had in years. The design for the memorial would be chosen in an open competition. Out of the more than fourteen hundred entries, the selection committee chose a submission from a twenty-one year old undergraduate. The winning design was described as a polished black, granite wall which would rise from a few centimeters to ten feet in height and emerge out of a boomerang shaped cut in the earth. The names of the over 58,000 men and women killed or missing in Vietnam would be engraved on the wall.

What followed was a firestorm of protest over whether such a memorial would honor or denigrate the memory of the men and women killed in the war. Critics questioned the winner's youth and inexperience and the fact that she was Asian. I wasn't surprised that the effort to create a memorial would open up the wound it was trying to close.

All parties finally agreed to a compromise, which satisfied no one completely. The memorial would be designed according to the original plan. But an American flag and a bronze statue of three men, representing the ethnic mix and camaraderie of the combat soldiers in Vietnam, would be at the entrance to the site. The dedication of the memorial was to take place in November, 1982. I expected Muriel would want to visit the memorial immediately. But uncharacteristically, she wanted to wait until the initial surge of visitors subsided. She surprised me again when she asked me to go with her and that we take Tasha.

MURIEL

1984

OUR VISIT TO THE VIETNAM VETERANS MEMORIAL turned out to
be delayed longer than I thought. I wanted Naomi and Khadijah to
go with us but they were very hard to reach. After Naomi returned
from Jamaica, she went to work for an international human rights
group and was out of the country much of the time. I had lost touch
with Khadijah over the years. When I tried to reach her at the commune in Boston, I was told that she had left about a year before. I
asked about Imani and found out that she still lived there but was
not available. I left my number but she never called back.

It took a few days before I found Khadijah working in a hospital
in the Bronx. I got there just before she was due to arrive. When
Khadijah approached the nurses station, her gaze settled on me,
registering more resignation than surprise.

"You sure know how to find people, don't you?" she said.

"You didn't make it easy."

"Just because you like to go looking for people doesn't mean I
have to leave a trail for you to follow." She shook her head like I was
one pitiful person and gave me a big hug.

"So what happened with you and Imani and the commune?"

"I got tired of people being all up over and around me."

"Since Imani's still there, I guess she didn't feel the same way?"

"She didn't mind submitting to group authority but had serious
problems submitting to me."

"I've never thought of you as being a dominating or possessive
person."

"The Movement used to possess me. And after a year or two, it
felt like the commune was doing the same thing. I guess, at some
point, I wanted to see how it felt to be the one doing the possessing."

"How did it feel?"

"Whatever thrill I got didn't last very long. I realized I didn't
want to possess anyone but myself."

"Couldn't you do that and still be with somebody?"

"Maybe. But it didn't happen."

"Are you still in touch with Imani?"

"No. We ran out of reasons for staying in each others lives."

"I hope we never get to that point," I said.

"You're still trying to hold on to people. I wouldn't be surprised if you held seances to commune with Walter, Lucius, Theo, Crystal and whoever else you can't let go of."

"What can I tell you, Khadijah? I have to do what I have to do, which is another reason why I wanted to find you."

She cut me a look, raising a skeptical eyebrow.

"Raymond, Tasha and I are going to visit the Vietnam Veterans Memorial. People can leave mementos and there are some things belonging to Lucius, Frank and Crystal that we want to leave at the wall. I was hoping you'd come with us."

"Why?" she asked.

"Because you're part of everything that's happened to me, to all of us."

"I'm sorry, Muriel. I can't."

I opened my mouth but she raised her hand to silence me.

"Every time I deliver a baby, I'm faced with the possibility that the life coming into the world will end before it begins. This rarely happens but there's always a chance that it might. The most serious threats to a child come after its birth. For me, this is where that wall in D.C. with all those names on it comes in. There's not much I can do about the ways human beings get taken out of the world, but I do know something about how to bring them in. That's the only end of the street I know how to work. Any other part, I can't handle."

I couldn't argue with Khadijah. She had worked her end of the street well enough to help make Tasha's arrival into the world possible.

When Naomi wasn't out of the country, she was based in Washington. I had written her about the visit to the Memorial and asked if she would go with us. Typically, there was no response for a few months. But a week before we left, I received an onionskin envelope postmarked from the Soviet Union.

November, 1984

Muriel:

As you can see from my address, I won't be able to go with you to the Memorial. I understand why it's important for you to go. You're always looking for refuge in the very place that hasn't given you much reason to feel at home. In some ways you're like many of the dissidents I've met here who prefer exile in their own country to the spiritual undernourishment they would suffer by leaving. I wish I had your sense of wanting to belong somewhere. Tomorrow I travel to Odessa, the city my grandparents fled during the pogrom in 1905. They were bound as much to that old world of *yiddishkeit,* danger and persecution, as my parents were to an optimistic America with unlimited possibilities. I was caught somewhere in between. And it seems as though that's where I've remained. As a lawyer, I was between a system I detested and clients I didn't always respect. Married to Gerald, I found myself between a white world I rejected and a black world that wasn't completely accepting of me. But I've gotten used to living in that kind of limbo. And if I belong anywhere, it's there.

Love to you,
Naomi
Moscow, U.S.S.R.

The Vietnam Veterans Memorial stands like an open book between a monument named for the President who represented the official beginning of the united nation and a memorial named for another President who presided over a war that tore the country apart in order to finally remake it into one nation. And it is to that memorial that people go, not merely to gaze at the statue of Lincoln but to drink in his words. Lincoln spoke of the lives lost on the very spot where he stood, and of the inadequacy of any words to convey the human cost to the living and the dead who fought at Gettysburg. And in Lincoln's concluding words, each person reading them, 120 years later, is charged once again with the task of ensuring that the continuing sacrifices of so many will not have been made in vain.

A breeze lifts Lincoln's words from the breath of visitors reciting them

out loud and carries the sentiments toward the Vietnam Veterans Me-
morial where they brush against the over 58,000 names engraved on a
polished black granite wall and all who have come to acknowledge the
lives of each individual on it.

RAYMOND

November, 1984

WE ARRIVED AT THE MEMORIAL SITE at around eight in the morning. I was hoping there wouldn't be many people around at that
hour. And fortunately, there weren't. Tasha hadn't been that interested in coming and was in a typical thirteen-year-old funk. She
kept her distance from Muriel and myself. I stopped briefly to look
at the statue of three bronze combat soldiers at the entrance to the
park. Their eyes showed fatigue and pain and seemed directed
toward something far away. I kept walking, tracking the direction of
their stare and suddenly saw the wall, partially obscured by tree
branches, rising in front of me.

I was pleased that I'd come upon it without realizing how close it
was. I hung back and let Muriel and Tasha walk ahead of me. I
turned around and went to one of the stands, holding the phone-
book thick directories listing the men and women alphabetically,
according to the dates they were killed or missing and the location
of their names on the wall. I found the panel numbers for the years,
1966 and 1967 that covered Frank's tour of duty. Muriel had given
me his dog tags, so I could leave them (if I chose to) at the section of
the wall, which marked the time he served in Vietnam. I didn't want
to go the spot right away. Instead, I walked close to the chainlink
fence separating the grass from the stone walkway. I turned and
looked back at the statues of the soldiers; and it seemed that they
were staring right at the wall.

The names of the first casualties of the war, beginning in 1959,
looked as though they had come right out of the earth, rising along
with the black granite to a height nearly twice my own. At the
bottom and top of the two panels, which met at the wall's highest

point, the years 1975 and 1959 were engraved. It wasn't until I reached the lowest point at the other end of the wall that I realized that the names on the wall appeared to have taken a circular path under the earth, resurfacing at the other end and coming full circle where the first and last casualties met in 1959 and 1975.

The listing of each individual on the wall in the arc of a circle seemed to place them closer to the connection they actually had to one another in life—side by side and face to face. That had been the longstanding shape of my bond with Frank until we rearranged ourselves into a single file and stopped facing each other altogether. I put my hand in my pants pocket and jiggled Frank's dogtags and chain. I walked toward the panels, listing those killed during years 1966 and 1967. I took Frank's dogtags out of my pocket and knelt down to place them near the base of the wall. A shiver went through me over the loss of a person, not among the names on the wall, but one who was part of their circle, making me part of it as well.

MURIEL

November, 1984

THE DAY BEFORE WE TOOK THE TRAIN to Washington, I received a call that Miss Mattie had passed away. I was surprised that my first reaction to the news was anger over something she'd told me the last time I saw her at Mister Percy's wake. She accused me of preferring obstacles to my will to living in harmony with people who were in agreement with me. I had to admit there was some truth to what she said. I told the friend of Miss Mattie's that I would come up to Yorktown in a few days to make arrangements for her funeral. Raymond suggested that we put off the trip but I told him the loss of people in my life was precisely why I had to visit the Vietnam Veterans Memorial.

When we arrived at the entrance to the Memorial site, I went immediately to the directories and found the number of the wall panel for 1970, which coincided with the year that Lucius and the other men in the Grunt Collective were killed. It was a windy day and the hovering trees leaned in closer as though eavesdropping on this meeting between the living and dead. Tasha stopped just as I began making my way along the slowly rising black granite. The further I moved into the cut in the earth made by the lives of all those named on the wall, the more I felt myself entering those places where I'd been cut open as well.

I bent down to place the dogtags at the bottom of the wall and was startled to see myself and my immediate surroundings become one with the names in front of me. I stood up and saw other people join me inside the unlimited space of the wall, bringing with them their own portion of loss as they fingered the names and traced them onto sheets of paper. No matter what any of us felt about the human cost of the War, so starkly engraved on the wall and unseen by most of us throughout Southeast Asia, maybe this was the one place where we could all welcome each other back home.

For years I'd lived inside a wound with so many who were near and dear to me, and some who were near and not so dear. And as I walked along the length of the wall, my stone-hard resistance crumbled. I wept for my parents, Mister Percy, Miss Mattie, Walter, the Grunt Collective, Charles Sinclair, Theo, Detective Garrett, Maggie's Farmers, Frank and Crystal.

When I reached the highest point of the wall where the names of the first and the last casualties of the war met, I reached into my bag for the wind chimes that had fallen from Crystal's ankle. I held the chain, linking the chimes between my fingers, and listened to the sound they made in the breeze. I placed the chimes between the two panels containing the beginning and end of the list. I knew Crystal had said she no longer wanted her physical presence felt on an already overburdened earth. But I didn't think she would mind me leaving her wind chimes on the ground as a memento of her having lived so gently in this world.

TASHA

November, 1984

SOME OF MY FRIENDS think my Mom and Dad are weird. That used to bother me because I wanted normal parents like everybody else had. I tried to make them change but they couldn't do it. I was mad at them for a long time, but more with my Mom than my Dad. My Dad is into baseball, and when I was little, he would get angry at me if I tried to change the rules. He feels the same way about what happens in the world. He always tells me people don't change that much. So I wasn't that upset when he didn't either.

But my Mom was into this thing called *the Sixties*. She made it sound like being at Coney Island, where you went on all these fun rides, especially the ones that scared you. She also talked about how people had to change to make things better for everybody. But she couldn't change so things would be better for me!

I was still a little kid when Mom and Dad stopped living to-gether. After a while I didn't mind because they paid more attention to me and took me a lot of places. Now that I'm almost fourteen, it gets on my nerves when they're in my face about everything I do. And I'm not that interested in going places with them, like I used to. When they told me about coming to the Vietnam Memorial, I didn't want to. But they said I had to. I asked my Dad why and he said it was important for me to see the names of the people who died, so I'd understand what war meant.

"I already know that people die in war," I said.

"There're some other things you should know about war."

"Like what?"

"Whether it could've been stopped before it started, and if it was worth it after it's over."

"Dad, I'm not old enough to know that."

"A lot of grown-ups should've been old enough to know that but they didn't."

"Did you know?" I asked.

"Yes. But a lot of people did. There just weren't enough of us."

"But if I'm not old enough to understand all this, why do I have to go?"

"If kids your age see the Vietnam Memorial now, maybe, when you get to be my age there won't need to be more walls with the names of people on it who were killed in a war."

I always know when my Dad is being a teacher. He says things that make me feel like I'm in one of his classes. This is really messed up because I'm around teachers all day at school. And when I leave, there's another one waiting for me at home. I don't mind my Dad being a teacher, but sometimes I get tired of listening to him trying to figure out how *this* happened and why *that* happened.

Whatever my Dad tries to figure out, my Mom wants to fix. When she takes me places, she always finds something wrong that needs to be fixed. When I was younger, I felt left out and asked what I could do wrong, so she could fix me too.

"You don't need to be fixed, honey."

"Why not?" I asked.

"Because the only people who need fixing are stuck in one spot and can't move. And you're moving all the time."

"But suppose I'm moving in the wrong direction?"

"If you keep moving, you won't be wrong for very long."

That didn't make sense to me, because even when I did something wrong while I was moving, My Mom told me I needed to learn how to do the right thing a lot quicker. And there're plenty other things my Mom's done that didn't make sense. She walked around most of the time like nothing was right. And I'd ask her what was wrong.

"I'm homesick," she said.

"But Mom, we haven't gone anywhere. We're home."

"It doesn't feel that way to me."

"Why not?"

"Because there's something missing."

"What's that?"

"I'm not sure. But I'll know when I find it."

My Mom used to read me these Edward Gorey stories and my favorite was "The Willowdale Handcar." There were these two men and a woman who were friends. And they lived in a place called Willowdale. One summer afternoon, they went for a walk to the railroad station. There was a handcar on the tracks and they decided to take a ride on it. They see all these strange things. Like a little girl splashing around in the mud and a house burning down. A train passes them and a woman, who looks freaked out, has her face up against the window. The woman lives in their town and later they see the woman's boyfriend who's upset because he can't find her. The three people keep riding on the handcar for many months. One night there's a storm, and when lightning strikes, they see a man crawling around on the ground. They find a baby hanging from a hook where mailbags are put. After taking the baby to an orphanage, they pass by a train wreck. They keep going and see the woman who was on the train tied to the tracks. They untie her and she gets on a bicycle and rides away. One day, the handcar goes into a tunnel and never comes out the other side.

I never talked to my parents about this story. If I did, my Dad would want to explain it and my Mom would want to fix what was wrong with the people in it. I like the story the way it is. Every time I read it, I think about what I see when I look at the world. I didn't want to look at the wall. But when I finally started walking past the names of all the people who died, I thought about "The Willowdale Handcar," and how the people on the handcar saw these strange and terrible things happen before they disappeared into a tunnel. Maybe the wall with the names on it is a way for us to find the people who went to Vietnam and never came back.

I see myself, my Mom and Dad and some other people reflected in the wall; it looks like we're all wearing the names on our bodies. I walk over to my Mom and touch her on the arm. When she turns around, I can tell she's been crying.

"Mom? Are you still homesick?"

"Yes, but it doesn't hurt as much anymore."

Push Comes to Shove is an experiment
in publishing and community.
And you're part of it.

Be sure to tell us where you donated money. When you're done
reading, pass along your book to another reader—for free.
Chart this book's progress and donations at www.concordfreepress.com.

ACKNOWLEDGMENTS

There have been many people whose support has sustained me during the long gestation period of this novel. Charles Touhey, Alice Green and Lila Touhey of the Paden Institute for Minority Writers in Essex, New York provided the pastoral environment and generosity of spirit that allowed me to discover the story I was trying to tell. Julie Schumacher, Ann Markusen, Phebe Hanson, Patricia Hampl and other faculty and students in the Graduate Creative Writing Program and the English Department at the University of Minnesota were unfailing in their friendship and intellectual stimulation during my semester as a visiting writer-in-residence.

Of the many readers and writers whose insight helped me to keep me going, I want to thank Jerry Berger, Kera Bolonik, Karen Braziller, Julie Brickman, Sesame Campbell, Faith Childs, Cheryl Clarke, Jaimee Wriston Colbert, Judith Diamondstone, Beverly Gologorsky, Jan Heller-Levi, Herb Kohl, Robin Lippincott, Mary Morris, Dawn Renee Jones and Sharon Olds (whose stories of the labor of childbirth were invaluable), Steve Schrader, Nancy Larsen Shapiro, Shawn Shiflett, Ted Solotaroff (who believed I could reach for something more before I did), Patricia Strachan and Jose Torres.

In many ways too numerous to mention, my friends, former colleagues and students at Rutgers University were a constant and steadying presence during my twenty-six years of teaching. For validating my efforts as a writer, especially at moments when I needed it the most, I want to thank Deborah Allen, Abby Arias, Barbara Balliet, Louise Barnett, Emily Bartels, Delilah Battle, Matthew Buckley, Abena Busia, Leandra Cain, Pat Cain, Cris Chism (my jogging partner who introduced me to Edward Gorey), Ann Cotteril (my other jogging partner), Ann Coiro, Harriet Davidson, Marianne DeKoven, Elin Diamond, Richard Dienst, Ana Douglass, Brent Edwards, Kate Ellis, Rita Finstein, Sandy Flitterman-Lewis, Peggy Friedman, William Galparin, Donald Gibson, Jeremy Glick, Martin Gliserman, Carol Hartman, Allen Howard, Marcia Ian, Cora Kaplan, George & Cleo Kearns, Stacy Klein, Daphne Lamothe, Rick Lee, Jim Livingston, Marc Manganaro, John McClure, Howard McGary, Meredith McGill, Rosalind McInerney, Michael McKeon, Jacqueline Miller, Richard Miller, Rosalind McInerney, Julian Moynahan, Alicia Ostriker, Tzarina Prater, Barry Qualls, Bruce Robbins, Cheryl Robinson, Shifra Rubin, Lise Salim, Larry Scanlon, Anne Sherber, Mary Sheridan-Rabideau, Carol Smith, Sarah Tames, Cheryl Wall (my sister, my sister), Deborah Gray White, Carolyn Williams and Edlie Wong.

I want to express my heartfelt appreciation to Russell Banks, Mary Gordon and Toni Morrison; to Stona Fitch and Concord Free Press for their belief in my work; and to Declan & Sheila Brown, Jamil Blackwell, Betsy McTiernan, Morton Makler, Gay Semel and my son Anthony, just because.

CONCORD
FREE
PRESS